Prophecy

—————

LAURY FALTER

First Edition: February 2013

The characters and events portrayed in this book are fictitious. Any similarity to real persons, living or dead, is coincidental and not intended by the author.

ISBN 13: 978-0-9890362-0-7

For my fans. I keep a special place in my heart for you.
Thank you for reading my stories.

CONTENTS

ψ

1. RALLY

The first hit I felt, the ones that followed…not so much.

That's the brilliance of the human body. It protects you by limiting your senses. By the time I lost count of the barrage of fists slamming into my face, they registered only as nudges with enough power to shift my body from side to side. I didn't notice the blood trickling from my nose or the ringing in my ears. Not yet, anyways.

Through the thick burlap sack that had been thrown over my head just prior to the beating, one that had evidently been used to carry feces at some point, I could see some movement. The slivers of bodies visible through the stretched fabric moved too quickly for any true identification, but I knew there were more than just a handful surrounding me. Maybe if some of them broke from their established dress protocol and wore something other than their damned black uniform and moldavite stone I'd be able to distinguish them.

It didn't matter, though. A fist was a fist.

Another one landed against my cheek, snapping my head to the side and causing the opposite cheek to fly outward like a deflated balloon.

That was a good one. It had enough depth to knock me off balance.

Bring it on, because when it's my turn, you're going to wish you'd killed me.

I rotated back just as my head absorbed another shot.

The only sound in the room was the irregular but consistent grunts, which I surmised came from me alone. When Vires attacked, they did it quietly, devoid of reaction, so I wasn't going to be able to identify them by sound.

Even if I could ID one, it wouldn't matter. There wouldn't be any justice for them, no retaliation by me. But I didn't hold any personal affront about it. Their robotic nature, their fixed movements told me that I was nothing more than an object to them, a target which only needed to be sufficiently suppressed. These men and women had gone through hell and any trace of their personalities had been broken down and erased in order for them to be rebuilt in the manner The Sevens had directed, one that left them absent of emotion or personality. They didn't care because they were taught not to. And that's where we were even. I couldn't care less what they did to me. Every bruise, every cut gave me power, resilience, resolve, because I knew – we all did – that the true attackers were The Sevens. So long as they were hitting me, I was of value to them, and they'd keep me around. And if I was kept around long enough, I could get who I came here for.

The thought of her above all others, stopped me from returning their blunt force with my own. That realization plagued me during every altercation, an ever-present reminder that somewhere, hidden inside these walls, was Jocelyn. That understanding alone reinforced in me that I would bring the fight to them, but not now, not yet. First, I needed to find her.

As another well-placed fist jolted my head to the side, her image slipped across my consciousness, her dark hair

2

flowing, her intoxicating eyes locked on me. They were innocently seductive, pleading with me, having no understanding of what they did to my insides. What she didn't know, what I couldn't tell her because she had been ripped from my arms and stolen from me by The Sevens' Vires was that she tore me up more than any fist ever could.

The pummeling slowed to an end. This assault, I noted, lasted only three minutes; an indication that it wasn't intended to make me submit, only to bang me up a bit, leave me a little bruised and bloody. That meant we would be heading for another "rally" today, where my body would serve as the message, the key talking point.

The bag was pulled from my head then, taking a good section of my hair with it, and the room returned to order, Vires roaming around like nothing had occurred, as if I wasn't standing here with blood streaming from my nose and ears.

I picked up the black shirt I'd been putting on before the assault and slipped it over my shoulders. My head began to throb, with a persistent, and loud, pulsing that jostled my view with each pounding. Blinking in an effort to correct my vision, I finished buttoning the shirt and went in search of the moldavite stone I'd been assigned, wiping the blood from my nose with the back of my hand. It left a smear across my skin, and I smiled.

This was my sick, private joke against them, because what The Sevens didn't understand was that I had been preparing for this fight since birth; not the little nudges I get from this squad but the bigger one, the one that's coming. I'd been trained for this, coached in martial arts, disciplined in pain resistance, and pushed to the breaking point and beyond. That was their weakness, The Sevens. They had no idea what they were up against.

I found the stone, laying at the foot of the bed I'd been issued, as if it were waiting there for me. Someone had

3

placed it safely out of harm's way, a good enough distance from the attack that it wouldn't be damaged.

I almost laughed.

My new "family" stone was given more respect than actual flesh and blood.

I put it on my collar, rubbed away the blood streaming from my ears, and turned for a final inspection in the mirror mounted on the inside of my open locker.

At that moment, I suffered my first physical reaction of the morning. Staring at my reflection in the mirror, like I did at the start of every day, my stomach churned, as it always did. I gave myself a cursory inspection, focusing on ensuring everything was in the right place before that familiar disgust could set in. My lapel was straight, the tail of my shirt was tucked in evenly behind my belt, and both shoes were laced. Then, just before my eyes could narrow in vehemence, I turned to face the room.

A sweeping evaluation of the men and women around me confirmed that no one paid me any attention. I had again become a speck in the sea of black. This didn't surprise me, though. I knew when making the decision to turn myself in to The Sevens that I would essentially become a number, an outcast definitely, but nothing more than number. Anyone who set foot through the door and into these barracks was taught from an early age to eliminate any sign of individualism. But I wasn't here for the same reasons as the rest of my bunkmates. In the eyes of The Sevens, and likely in the eyes of my bunkmates, I was here to serve as a message to the provinces, those people who would, or had, dared to attempt to overthrow The Sevens. I didn't need to know how to handle various mystical weapons or learn their code of conduct or acquire their mannerisms in order to fulfill my purpose here. I only needed to appear before the Dissidents with bruises, a few scrapes, some dried blood, and their objective would be met: Exhibit the Nobilis banged up a bit and it would create fear in the hearts of those who The Sevens control. And this would prevent any future notion the populace might have of opposing The Sevens.

Right on schedule, the Vires in the room began filtering out single-file, with only their footsteps and the rustle of their clothes giving any indication they were moving. I fell in line at the end, equally as alert as the rest but for a very different reason. As we marched toward the mess hall, a course that took us through the dark, winding maze of corridors and into the bowels of the Ministry, I mentally marked every door, every turn, every archway, because eventually one of them might lead me to Jocelyn. There had been no sign of her, and it had been agonizing, but I'd find her. One day, The Sevens, or the Vires guarding her, would slip up, let down their defenses, and leave a clue as to her whereabouts. That was the thin thread of hope from which I hung.

The mess hall was a clattering of dishes and muted conversations. I sat alone, in the back, swallowing dried eggs and undercooked bacon, ignoring the pain in my jaw, and watching. This was my routine. I went unnoticed here, a ghost among the robots, and I took advantage of it. Here, I noted the Vire routines, who was stationed with who, the size of their groups, who dominated them, all of which would be incredibly important when I was able to free Jocelyn.

There were essentially two levels, the beginners and those who had "come of age", which meant they had learned the appropriate skills to be a killer. I was housed with those who had come of age. The youngest appeared to be eleven years old, and he was extremely lethal. Most of all, however, I was interested in detecting if any of them would be following in Theleo's footsteps, the legendary Vire who had defected to our side to assist the Dissidents, and who had since disappeared into oblivion on my final command before committing myself to the Ministry. One group was proving to be of particular interest to me, with their hushed, private conversations and frequent sideways glances in my direction. They were led by a man the size of a tank with pale skin and a massive chest. I knew him only by his aptly-given nickname, Stalwart, and he seemed to know me too. I'd place a bet that he'd told his small two-man contingent to be acutely aware of me and my whereabouts since I first came to the Ministry. Today though, it was me doing the stalking. I was actively listening in on his comments about two Dissidents being interrogated when a voice boomed across the room.

"Jameson Caldwell."

I heard it, although it had to find its way through the ringing in my ears.

When I didn't stand immediately, the Vire at the main entrance to the mess hall shouted it again, firm, brisk. He didn't bother to scan the crowd for me, keeping his eyes front and center, knowing I would be required to respond if I were somewhere within.

Gradually, I rose to my feet and joined him at the door.

"You have been summoned," he said with barely a look at me before spinning on his heel and beginning his "Vire march", a strange hard right-foot plant, down the hall.

He didn't bother relaying details to me. I was a peon, of less significance than a pebble he stepped on. Regardless, I already knew where he was leading me. I had taken this walk countless times over the nine weeks since I arrived. We reached a fairly wide balcony jutting from the side of the Ministry's first floor and as I was surrounded by black uniforms before being levitated into the air, I was no more surprised than when the bag had been dropped over my head earlier this morning.

This was routine.

We were in the air no longer than a few minutes before the sky darkened. It was morning back in Italy, where the Ministry was located, but almost midnight here in Mexico

6

City. Being the largest city in the country, and with the greatest population, it was easy to identify from above. The lights sprawled beneath us blinking back, growing larger as we dropped toward them.

We landed, our feet touching the flat roof of a building inside the city perimeter. Taller structures rose overhead around us with windows lit, so I was shoved through the roof access door before anyone looked out one of those windows and sighted us. We descended the flight of stairs to the first floor, stepping into an enormous area with rigging overhead and a curtain that stretched from one side of the room to the other. Sartorius stood directly in front of it, as if he expected it to part and he would be revealed in reverie.

I had to keep my eyes from rolling.

When he saw us arrive, he beckoned me to him, his cane's moldavite stone glinting in the beams of light that crisscrossed from the casting lights above. As the Vires who had led me here dispersed to take their places with the others in their squad at the various exits, Sartorius returned his gaze to the velvet red folds a foot from him as if they held more interest than me. I had stopped outside arm's reach, facing him, just as he gave his command.

"Bow."

Fighting the urge to resist, I bent at the waist, but did not lower my eyes, words rambling through my mind: *Enjoy it while it lasts. Watch your back you piece of sh-*

"You are standing in the Auditorio Nacional," he referenced casually with an accent. "It is said to be one of the greatest auditoriums in the world, and is a landmark, here, in Mexico City. We own this building, my associates and I. Whilst this declaration is not on paper, it is proven through our use of it now and the many times in the past. I secure it for us on occasions in which an audience is required. It is a trophy, one of many," he said, remaining rigidly immobile except for turning his head in my

7

direction. "You, Jameson, are the most recent in my collection." Without pausing or any hint at how offensive his statement was, Sartorius continued. "Celebrated artists have performed on this very stage where you now stand. And, tonight, you will join them in giving us yet another extraordinary performance." He watched his insult burn through me, and once sufficiently entertained, he questioned, "Do you regret turning yourself in, Jameson?"

I regret having to wait to slit your throat.

"Regret, Jameson," he uttered again, his voice hissing with impatience. "Do you feel it for having handed yourself to us without reason?"

"There was a reason, Sartorius." And her name is Jocelyn.

"Which you must have known would not be honored." Sartorius' snide manner drew me back to him. "We would never give up such a precious asset," he admonished.

"An asset to you," I muttered. "A danger to the rest of The Sevens."

Sartorius chuckled to himself. "And that is precisely why it took so much political capital to keep the two of you alive. You have created a problem for us, Jameson, you and me. My associates want you dead. They don't see the potential in you…the power that can be harnessed."

They know enough to be fearful of it.

Sartorius' attention returned to the curtain. He spoke wistfully, openly enamored, seemingly intoxicated by the future he foresaw in using us.

"She is powerful…," he whispered, "…and you recharge her."

Intentionally, I broke through his ludicrous whimsical musing and reminded him, "She isn't a battery, Sartorius."

He blinked, returning from his daze, and ignored my statement as if it had been nothing more than a breeze passing his ears. "The Dissidents, however, are not so precious to me."

8

I stiffened at the sudden change of subject, and at the acknowledgement of the people who had joined me to openly oppose The Sevens. They had risked their lives in hopes of a life free from the fear and control of their subjugators, and not only had their dreams been shattered, but they now lived in constant fear and far greater jeopardy than before.

"They do serve a purpose," Sartorius deliberated. "But you already knew this, didn't you, Jameson? It's the reason you disbanded them, before coming to us, in a final attempt to keep them safe."

My memory called up an image of the swamp in which the Dissidents had made a home. Beneath the cypress trees, swallowed by thousands of tree trunks, were the shacks and planks running between them; the dwellings where people once baked bread, played music, and shared their catch of the day. There was no music in my memory, no joy or leisurely happiness that the Dissidents had come to thrive on while hiding from The Sevens. Instead, people hauled suitcases or personal belongings stuffed into canvas bags, rowing them in canoes down the village waterways. Boats rammed each other out of haste, the planks shook with the weight of hurried feet. My memory was of the mass exodus brought on by my orders. As if reading my thoughts, Sartorius put them into words.

"You told them to seek shelter elsewhere, to go into hiding, because you knew we would come for them. You knew you couldn't attack as planned," Sartorius surmised. "You didn't have the resources. All heart and no way to use it...such are the notions of a juvenile, Jameson, in believing you could oppose us...." He clucked his tongue quietly at me. "So you told them to scatter, didn't you, young Jameson? Don't be so harsh on yourself, however. In reflection, releasing them was the only correct course of action you took."

I glanced at him, because Sartorius didn't delve out compliments. I was skeptical, and his follow up statement justified my suspicions.

To drive home the point he was making, he added, "Because we are coming for them, Jameson. And one by one they will be found."

I clenched my teeth before my instinctive response could come out. *I'm going to kill you. I'm going to gut you, pull out your entrails, and make you watch. You stupid sack of shhh...*

He knew I cared for them, and he was using it against me. And the fury he imparted from his warning only strengthened with his final utterance.

"Under no circumstances will what you see tonight provoke you. You will not move. You will not speak. You will show no emotion. Am I understood?" My silence caused him to repeat it. "Do you understand me, Jameson?"

My level of alertness peaked then as I tensed for whatever it was he had planned.

"Jameson," he said, demanding I answer.

My lips opened just enough to quietly hiss my answer. "Yes, Sartorius, I heard you."

Since handing myself to The Sevens, I had been to so many rallies that I'd lost count. They had been fairly consistent in process and purpose, with only the location and audience changing. Held in either warehouses throughout Germany, coffee shops closed for the night throughout South America, open fields in Madagascar, it didn't matter. Sartorius followed the same agenda. But not once had he made that kind of threat.

Leaving my side, he motioned with a snap of his hand to start the rally. As was typical, once again, I found Vires on all sides of me, strategically placed there before the curtain could part and slide to the end of the stage.

Before us, sitting in the upwardly sloping red velvet seats, were thousands of witches, some with pointed hats, some with the handles of their broom laid across their laps, some appearing as typical as an average businessman. Most wore the traditional black cloak so common in our world. But there was no unifying characteristic other than the family stone they wore somewhere on their bodies.

Besides this, what stood out to me was the multitude of them. Mexico City was one of the most populated urban areas in the world, with easy transportation to and from the metropolis. Of course there would be a great number of us here, and they would all have been required participants tonight.

By design, a rally evokes...even demands jubilation from its audience, and is bolstered by food, drink, dancing, social engagements. Those are the very purposes for which people gather. But that was not the goal here tonight, and they knew it. There was no excited chatter, no mingling across the aisles, no sense of joy at all from this crowd. Those who knew each other gave a simple, quiet nod before returning their attention to the stage. A woman in the back row grunted as she shifted in her seat, which could be heard with distinct clarity from my position on the stage.

We were in a different city, in a different forum, and yet the result was the same. I had seen it at every rally. These people had been summoned here not by their own free will or for their enjoyment of the arts. The Sevens required their attendance to ensure that what would be shown on the stage tonight would not be misconstrued, or easily dismissed. It would be remembered, scorched into their consciousness, and serve as a message of what happens when one disobeys The Sevens.

Sartorius stepped up to the edge of the stage and raised his hands in the air in a grandiose gesture, using the moldavite stone on the tip of his cane to enhance his image of false supremacy.

Using their native language, he bellowed in Spanish, "Channelers, Elementalists, Levitators, Healers. Witches...Friends. Tonight, I am not a Seven. I am an inquisitor, and eyewitness to atrocious crimes, the result of which has left us, our world, in a state of vulnerability. This is something we cannot risk.

"It is wrong, I suggest, to reject the rules we agree to live by. It is wrong because they have been established for your safety. To challenge them puts all lives in danger...mine...the person sitting beside you...your own...."

Sartorius delivered his concealed threats with magnificent impact. His speech had been repeated nearly every evening for weeks now, time enough to perfect each pitch, tremble, and pause. The eyes that stared back at the stage confirmed it. For the most part, they had been empty, as they always were, and grew tenser until fear seemed to have become a palpable entity which had crept its way out of their gazes to settle in their terrified, downturned grimaces. He was an extremely effective orator, innately suited for these rallies.

"Dear Friends, you have been called here tonight to bear witness to punishment for treason, barbarianism, and conspiracy, the likes of which we have never seen in our world. If left unchecked, these crimes flourish, corroding our way of life, gutting us from the inside out. And as you bear witness, I implore you to keep in mind...extraordinary dangers such as these call for extraordinary measures."

I stood straighter at this point; readying myself for what usually came next. At this point in the rally, a fist would hit me somewhere in the back, I would fall to my knees, and the pummeling would start. There would be no bag shoved over my head this time, giving the audience an unobstructed view of the pain being inflicted on my body. My facial contortions served to further influence the audience against breaking the crimes Sartorius was accusing me of.

But nothing followed now other than Sartorius' voice, as he roared a command that I hadn't expected.

"Bring out the Dissidents!"

Once my mind registered this change in the agenda, my head snapped to the side in search of what he was insinuating. From the wing opposite me, through the darkness, figures began to emerge. Dressed in torn, faded garments, a group of Vires led them to the front and center of the stage, neatly lining them up in a row behind Sartorius.

As they came into view, my fingers curled into fists, tightening with each new Dissident who took the stage. Sartorius watched me closely because he was privy to knowledge that no one else here was aware of.

I knew every single one of them.

Sartorius strolled to the beginning of the line and shouted their names as he passed by. "Daniel Aymes...Teresa Mill...Bartholomew Pierce...Kathryn Davidson...Joseph White...Arthur McMillan...Cornelia Sullentrop. You have been convicted of treason, barbarianism, and conspiracy to harm others. For this, you will pay the ultimate price. However, in an effort to show greater kindness than what you have shown us, we have graciously allowed you to determine the method of your own death."

The last word emitted from Sartorius' mouth spurred me into action.

My arms rose to encircle the Vire closest to me. With his head lodged between my muscles, I used his body weight to send a sidekick into the hips of the first Vire to respond. He stumbled backwards until he lost his footing, collapsed to the floor, and slid across the stage.

One down.

I cranked the neck of the Vire I held enough to hear the split of bone, a sound that confirmed he was no longer a threat.

Two down.

I threw his lifeless body at the Vire lurching toward me. They both fell into a pile, tripping two more as they approached.

The attacks started coming from all angles, which I fended off using the techniques I'd learned from Theleo and improvised defense moves. My arms and feet found their targets easily as more Vires advanced, sending a steady stream of contact my way. My motions were smooth, effortless, a mastery of precision and strength. I felt in control of them and of those around me. "Come on!" I heard myself roar. "Come on!"

Then came the blow from above.

It was swift, silent, and effective. A damn good shot.

I fell to my knees a second after the strike landed on my head, directly from overhead, the one area I hadn't kept in my sights. Whoever had levitated, had done it well.

My head spun.

My eyes refused to settle on any particular point.

My mind screamed at me to stand, knowing I had only seconds before…

And that was when my time ran out.

The kick to my face launched the first round of attacks on me, and I welcomed them.

My head whipped back and my body spun off kilter. Then I was on the floor, the cold, grey concrete slab that made up the stage where I was told to perform tonight.

And if ever there was a performance that combined blood and pain, I delivered it.

This was the hardest beating yet. Blood ran from every opening on my face and from several gashes across my skull. I determined this by the warmth that now covered my hair and skin. My right eye swelled shut and my left incisor rocked loosely from its place. But it was the sharp pain radiating from the side of my ribcage that made it obvious I had suffered a fracture. It intensified each time someone's foot or fist struck my body.

I had been warned not to move, and Sartorius seemed intent on reminding me. He foresaw this happening. I now understood his keen focus on me as the Dissidents were escorted to the stage and for the cause behind his little pep talk before the rally began.

From my one good eye still able to open, I found him in the middle of the stage, just beyond the line of Dissidents who remained in place, and noted his smug expression. My beating wasn't just for submission; it was also a tool to drive home his message about what happens when one of us stepped out of line. I had done this, literally, and paid the price.

When they were finished, Sartorius strolled to me, bent down, and clapped. The sound reverberated across the silent theater. "Excellent performance, Jameson. *Excellent* performance."

I opened my mouth to curse back but my body was lifted by two Vires using my arms to hoist me up, and I was dragged to the side of the stage. I readied myself for the release and the certain fall to the concrete floor, where my body would suffer more extensive damage. But despite my props being out of breath, a fact I took an enormous amount of pride in, they didn't drop me. Sartorius, apparently, had ordered them to keep me upright...and visible for all to see.

Sartorius turned back to the audience and proclaimed loudly a warning that was most commonly heard from Peregrine. "Rebellion will not be tolerated. To reinforce this point, we will begin the punishments."

In immediate response, three Vires took their positions behind the row of Dissidents, and their purpose was clear:

15

A Levitator, a Channeler, and an Elementalist would offer a range of lethal blows to choose from.

The Vires restraining me tightened their hold, knowing my opposition would come quickly. Being prepared for it this time, they kept me pretty well locked down.

Not considering me much of a threat any more, Sartorius pinned his attention on the first Dissident in line. "Daniel Aymes, for your role in breaking the laws established for the sanctity of our world, by what means do you wish to die?"

With his back to me, I couldn't see his expression, but the quiver in his shoulders told me everything I needed to know. He was terrified. Still, despite the fear swallowing him, Daniel remained silent. I remembered him clearly from the village. He was skilled in accounting and had formed a complex, but fair, bartering system. He knew nothing about fighting, or dying. This was his first experience with both.

Sartorius gave him no extension of time. Almost immediately, he replied casually, "Very well then." After a quick nod from Sartorius toward the three Vires readied behind the Dissidents, Daniel's body was flung upward, slamming into the auditorium's overhanging ceiling, a force that sent a shower of concrete back to the stage. When Daniel's body returned, it landed with an explosion that rocked the auditorium.

Groans and shrieks from those unable to stifle their reaction rose above the crowd. Heads turned away, a few vomited in the aisles.

I processed these reactions only slightly because my own had taken over. A roar resounded off the walls, coming from me, my vision blurring from its intensity.

Fighting against those restraining me, I weakened them enough to free myself. But I didn't get far. Sartorius sent additional Vires to subdue me, plenty to immobilize every limb and form a supplementary circle for increased protection.

"Teresa Mill," Sartorius said, wasting no time in starting again. "By what means do you wish to die?"

After a glance at Daniel's body, she followed his conduct and refused to answer. When Sartorius recognized these responses for what they were – final acts of rebellion – he moved more rapidly. After another brief nod by Sartorius, a Vire took hold of Teresa's arm and proceeded to channel his vehemence directly into her. She was dead in seconds. The next four Dissidents suffered fatal injuries that ranged from becoming encased in fire to being pressed against the ceiling until they were asphyxiated. With each victim, I fought harder, and was suppressed with growing hostility.

Sartorius didn't care that these were the people who The Sevens had promised to keep safe so many generations ago, and who now were being punished simply for seeking a life of freedom. What mattered now to Sartorius and his associates was that they served a purpose; they were minions, pawns in The Sevens' goal to dominate. This rally was meant to drive home this very point.

The last Dissident standing was Cornelia. I had met her once, after an invitation for dinner at her cottage in Salem, Massachusetts. She had housed a defected Vire, one who had stolen a record of the first channelers' prophecy of the future; although I couldn't be certain that was the crime that had led her to the stage tonight. Sartorius' sneer, and the evident pleasure he took in standing before her, made me think it was.

"Cornelia Sullentrop," he stated, his eyes sparkling at what was to come. "By what means-"

She didn't let him finish. The hunched, squat body of hers held more resilience and contention than the audience before her as a whole, and it wouldn't allow Sartorius the benefit of taking power over her. It was, I knew by the straightening of her back and the lift of her head, what drove her to whisper her defiant last words.

Her lips lifted in a bold smile and she hissed, "Something prophetic this way comes."

Sartorius' face twisted in offense as rage followed closely behind, because he understood exactly what she meant: He hadn't won. He could take her life, and all of those on the stage, but it wouldn't deter the end. The future…the prophecy…was still coming, and when it arrived it would be The Sevens who lost.

My broken ribs sent pulsating sparks of pain through me and my swollen eye throbbed, but I welcomed the distractions. Physical pain made me alert. My energy high, I could unravel her riddle too. And it gave me hope. Ignoring the odd sensation of my loosened tooth, a grin spread across my lips.

Sartorius' own lip curled in unmistakable insult as he brushed aside his suit jacket and withdrew a dagger. No sooner had it appeared did it disappear, thrust deep inside Cornelia's chest.

I didn't have time to feel remorse, or pity, or fury. Sartorius pulled the blade from her body, motioned for the Dissidents to be removed, and spoke again before Cornelia collapsed to the stage. His next command brought on a feeling I hadn't expected, and an intensity I wasn't prepared to handle. He spat the words, "Bring out Jocelyn Weatherford," and all I sensed while searching the wings for movement was agonizing desire.

2. REUNITED

I had just witnessed the death of seven innocent individuals, and their murderers were now escorting the woman I love into the execution frenzy.

Committing the faces of those leaving the stage to memory, I would make sure they would die for it. The fact they were acting on Sartorius' command didn't mean a damn thing to me, not when it came to Jocelyn.

She was here to serve a purpose, that much I knew. There was no other rationale for Sartorius to risk his prized possession in this way. There were too many variables he couldn't control...a revolt from the audience, Dissidents following them here, a rescue attempt which only a handful of Vires would be present to stop. So, whatever the reason was to bring her, it was worth the risk of losing her.

Then all my rambling thoughts came to a halt, because Jocelyn appeared from the dark.

Wearing a white dress, her arms and shoulders bare, she was entrancing. Every person in attendance had their eyes pinned on her. But their reasons were different from mine. They saw her as a symbol, while I knew her to be a person. They had dressed her in a way that looked delicate, but I knew her true hardiness.

She had lost weight, which told me that she wasn't eating enough. Her movements were languid, which meant she was fatigued. Her eyes were hollow, empty of emotion, either a reaction to the environment or as a result of the wall she must have built to preserve herself from what she was enduring.

I wanted to hold her, carry her away from here where she couldn't be used as a tool any longer. I wanted to lay her down, kiss her, feel her body against mine. I wanted her to be safe. I wanted her happy. I wanted the hollowness in her eyes to be filled with life again.

She didn't recognize me, at first. A scan of the stage told her only that a Vire had been beaten and was now being restrained. I could see this in her expression when her innate need to heal others kept her eyes on me a bit longer than they should have.

I'm here, sweetheart, I said, trying to channel across the depth of the stage to her. *I'm right here with you.*

She hadn't lost her yearning to help others. I could see that, but it was during that lingering gaze on me when she saw who was hidden beneath the blood and pus and swollen skin. Her face contorted, not much, just enough to be picked up by an observant eye. And her body instinctively shifted in my direction.

Yes, it's me. I'm right here.

The Vires escorting her corrected her path and she ended up in front of Sartorius. If he had been observing us, as I suspected he was, then he knew that placing us in the close proximity could cause upheaval. Still, as if he had all the power and influence in the world, he casually extended a hand to her, silently insisting that she take it. She responded hesitantly, taking his fingers cautiously.

You haven't turned her, have you, Sartorius? You failed to recondition her to willingly do your bidding, didn't you? I thought, my excitement returning, energy surging through me. *You told me once that was your ultimate wish, and even though she's now within your power, in the flesh, without anyone to help her, she resisted you. You are a failure of a man.*

But my excitement turned to alarm and my entire being contracted because he led her across the stage to me. Sartorius did nothing unless it was to his advantage. If he brought her here tonight, and he now wanted to bring us together, there was a depraved reason behind it.

Having seen my reaction, Sartorius warned, "Steady yourself, Jameson."

Nevertheless, he stopped several feet from me.

Only after the flare in my nostrils subsided and the clench of my jaw abated did he continue. Then he made a demand so quietly, so blunt without emotion that I questioned whether I heard him correctly. "Touch her," he said.

As I processed his words, his eyes narrowed at me.

"Touch...her."

"No," I replied flatly.

I wanted nothing more than to touch her, to feel her skin beneath my fingers, and to make sure she was not an illusion conjured by brain injuries from the beatings or from my desperate need to see her again. But Sartorius' insistence raised questions, and triggered an automatic refusal from me.

"TOUCH HER!" Sartorius bellowed, causing many in the audience to stir.

"No."

His jaw jutted out in fury at being denied before a crowd which my presence here was meant to subdue, Sartorius refused to yield. Instead, he proved to what extent he would go to rebuild his reputation as one to be feared by jeopardizing the life of his most prized possession. Raising the dagger he had used to impale

Cornelia, still coated with her blood, he placed it against Jocelyn's neck and then leveled his eyes at me.

You son of a...

I glared steadily at him but I didn't hesitate, immediately advancing the three paces it took to reach them, lifting my hand to her face and placing my palm against her cheek. It was easier than I thought, or than I wanted, drawn there by her eyes, the edge of Sartorius' blade, and my desperate need to remove the space between us. At the very same time, her hands rose and settled against my face, and her touch sent a rush of exhilaration through me.

She felt the same because at the moment our skin met she whispered my name... "Jameson...," she breathed and her melodic voice riveted me.

It was hushed, filled with sympathy, and it echoed through me, reminding me of my own ability.

It had been so long since I had channeled with anyone that it felt...surreal. But I was glad this reminder was with Jocelyn and no one else. It was intimate, and something I wouldn't want to share with anyone but her.

"Jocelyn..." I whispered, making sure my lips did not move. Still, I sounded hoarse in my own mind.

She smiled, such a beautiful smile.

It had been nine weeks since we saw each other and the urge to be with her rapidly became uncontrollable. There was no stopping the flood of emotion pent up for so long, and it broke through with overwhelming force. Nothing, not The Sevens, nor the distance, could ever diminish the feelings I have for her. And this became obvious when the simple touch of our hands wasn't enough. Not for me.

"Damn it all," I said out loud, giving in, moving forward so eagerly our bodies stopped my motion.

She gave me a perplexed look.

"I'm tired of being reserved," I heard myself grumble before my lips came down on hers.

I suddenly became acutely aware of her hips against mine and the smell of flowers in her hair, the feel of her dress as it brushed across my forearm, but nothing dominated my senses more than the feel of her lips. They were soft and trembling with emotion until they grew impatient, wanting.

"You feel so good," I thought.

"Jameson…," she sighed, her voice thick with emotion in my head.

The audience faded away; there was no longer any murmur from the crowd as they observed us, no theater walls forming a temporary prison, no Vires on hand to control us, and no Sartorius watching with intent curiosity. There was only the feel of her touching me, her movement, her desire for me. Nothing else in the world mattered at that moment.

All the worry over her safety, the loneliness that had settled in the pit of my stomach and the fears that invaded my nightmares over what she was enduring…all of it was gone. In its place was Jocelyn, my sweet Jocelyn…

Suddenly, a lone voice brought a punctuated end to my reverie, one that had no business being here.

"Sartorius," she called out, the distinctive curtness of Lacinda, our province's Surveyor, carrying the point, while carefully keeping her tone submissive.

A second passed before his cane knocked against the floor, and Vires abruptly pulled us apart.

"Enough," Sartorius instructed. "We will allow them contact." He narrowed his eyes at us in warning. "*Decent* contact."

After returning my concentration to Jocelyn, I noticed blood, mine, smeared across her chin. She was immune to it. I wiped it away as gently as I could, leaving my hand on her cheek, because I wasn't done touching her yet…but then, I couldn't imagine a time when I would be.

23

Her eyes softened, and a shallow pool of tears swelled behind her lower eyelid.

Her hand rose to my face, again pressing against my cheek.

"I knew it," she said, channeling to keep our conversation private. And for the first time I realized that she might be having the same worries about my wellbeing as I had about hers.

"Stop," I told her.

But she sobbed anyways, attempting to stifle it so that it became lodged in her throat. "What did they do to you?"

"Made me an example."

"No...," she sighed, her eyebrows crossing deeper in despair. The tears threatened to spill, something I didn't want to see.

"I'm fine."

"You don't look it," she countered, her willful side emerging. I liked seeing it, even if she was using it to oppose me.

"We're together," I stated. "I'm fine."

She understood my meaning immediately, which caused a staggered exhale.

"I've...," she began but didn't seem to be able to find the words to follow.

"Missed me," I finished for her, owning the arrogance of that statement.

"No, missed is too shallow...I've ached for you, Jameson."

My lips rose in a grin as much as the swelling would allow. "I know how that feels," I said, my voice soft.

She met my smile with her own, that gorgeous lift of her hips that always takes my breath away, and I knew something with absolute clarity...

It was worth the beatings to see it again.

Sartorius shifted enough to redirect my attention, but only briefly. Weeks had passed since Jocelyn was ripped from my arms. I didn't know what she had endured, how she was coping, or how to convey that I was looking for her, and I had little time to say it. So, I summed it up into one question.

"Where are they keeping you?" I asked, continuing to channel, attempting to call up her memories of her holding cell.

"Underground, surrounded by rock," she said, and an image of bars made of stone formed in my mind. Just beyond that were jagged rock walls, which appeared to be damp. My initial reaction to this image was not a good one. To subdue me, she added, "They haven't hurt me. I'm blindfolded whenever I leave, so I can't be more specific."

"Blindfolded?" I said, not making any effort to conceal my fury.

Her eyes softened once again, and she changed the subject. "You look…like this is the first time you've seen me." She tipped her head into my hand, pressing against me, stirring my need for her again.

"In Olivia's store?"

"You remember?"

"How could I forget? It was the day I fell in love."

She nuzzled her cheek closer to my hand.

"Screw decent contact," I growled, and reached for her.

Sartorius' cane came up between us, pointing at me, threatening me.

Go ahead, I thought, and Jocelyn picked up on it.

"Jameson, no," she urged and laid her hand delicately on my forearm. "Please don't. I don't think I could live through seeing you hurt again." She stopped and shuddered as the image of my face materialized in my mind. It was fairly gruesome.

"It looks worse than it feels."

Still, her eyes pleaded with me.

"I'm going to get you out of here," I blurted, and had to check myself to ensure I had channeled it. My lips hadn't moved, and neither did Sartorius, so I deduced that I had.

"Not yet," she replied hastily.

"Tonight, Jocelyn. Right now."

"No," she insisted, and I couldn't understand her resistance. Then she added, "There are others with me, and I won't leave them."

"I'll get them out. I promise."

As if she hadn't heard me, she replied, "Kalisha is there. She knows the future, Jameson. She's read the records."

"That's good news. We'll get to her. I promise."

Again, she flatly ignored me. "Maggie Tanner is there, too."

I paused, stunned by her words. "Maggie Tanner from the academy?" I couldn't digest that news right now, both because it wasn't immediately important to getting Jocelyn to safety and because it seemed improbable. "Why would The Sevens imprison her?"

A movement came into view from my left, rapidly approaching us. Jocelyn saw it coming too and braced against the motion, but it didn't deter her. "I love you-" she said quickly as she was yanked away and our channel was broken. Still, in Jocelyn's ever defiant manner, she finished her thought verbally, unwilling to be deterred. It came out in the same compassionate tone and haste that she had been using. "Incantatio Sana."

"That's quite enough, I should say." The same sharp voice that unfairly ended my intimacy with Jocelyn earlier interrupted us again, as its owner began edging between Jocelyn and me.

Jocelyn's eyes tore from mine as she was jerked roughly to the side, and I stepped forward angling my strike at the person who now held her. That single, fluid motion did two things. It was effortless enough to make

26

me realize that while I was attempting to seek answers from Jocelyn, she had given me back my health. The searing heat from my broken rib was gone, the blood no longer seeped from my wounds, I could see clearly through my eye again, and the loosened tooth was no longer dangling. In short, I felt strong again. Unfortunately, my lunge toward Jocelyn's captor also sent a squad of Vires down on me. I was thrust downward before being slammed hard against the floor, and soon I was looking up from the cool concrete slab flattened against my stomach. Ignoring the sensation left by a foot digging into my back, I found the one I had been attacking stooping down, her almond-shaped eyes watching me with intrigue.

"Such virility, Nobilissss," she said with a smirk.

"Surveyor," I grunted.

"You remember," she murmured, openly flattered.

"I remember you being restrained against a wall the last time I saw you," I said stiffly, craning my neck upward to catch her expression.

Her smirk wavered. "Well, we'll need to replace that last image with something more pleasurable."

She had her hand still wrapped around Jocelyn's forearm and I noticed her fingers beginning to squeeze tighter, forcing the color to drain from Jocelyn's tender skin.

"Release her, Lacinda," I commanded flatly, and to my surprise she lessened her grip, although I judged that it was more likely due to Sartorius.

The entertainment boring him now, he told her, "Retreat to the wings, Lacinda."

She hesitated, her gaze finding its way back to me briefly. But she was a smart woman with years of experience under the suppression of The Sevens, while still rising through the ranks to become one of their most trusted confidantes. She knew her place, and how to keep from losing it. Snapping her hand aggressively away from Jocelyn's arm, she did as she was told, wearing a snubbed expression as she found a spot to the side.

Now it was my turn to smirk.

Sartorius turned to the audience then and his voice rose until it echoed off the walls, ensuring all could hear. "Those needing to be healed may now come forward. You will form a single line directly in front of the stage. Those who do not need care may leave. My Vires will show you how. You will do so quietly, without drawing attention, and you will leave in groups of no more than four."

As the audience dispersed, some falling into line at the stage's front edge, Sartorius gestured Jocelyn forward, as if he had done it many times before. That stoked the anger simmering in me and I felt my lips curl back. Only Jocelyn calmed me as I watched her gracefully take a seat in front of the line. There was no hurry to her pace, she seemed almost complacent, and it dawned on me why. Even though it was being commanded of her, she wanted to do this, to heal these people, because it was who she was. It was very likely the only peace she found while in the grip of Sartorius and his associates.

Throughout the process, Sartorius evaluated her closely. It was obvious that he was using her as a tool, showing the audience that no one was above him, not even the Relicuum. It was also clear that he was guaranteeing that her ability to heal had returned after she and I made contact.

But why now? I wondered while watching from where Sartorius left me, underneath someone's boot. She was in his charge for nine weeks. What prompted him to need her abilities now?

Something's coming. But what?

These thoughts lingered with me until the last person was healed, and I was unceremoniously yanked to my feet.

Lacinda immediately returned to Jocelyn's side, and wrapped her fingers tightly around her arm.

"Come," she commanded, and spun around to haul Jocelyn away. Evidently, Lacinda knew this drill well.

Halfway across the stage, she gave me a look and her expression flashed from a frown to lust, but her scowl had returned by the time she was facing forward again.

Once Jocelyn turned toward the back of the stage where I was being restrained, her eyes didn't leave mine for a second. I was relieved to see there was no fear in hers, but there was sadness, and it pissed me off. Because of it I tried to send her a message, to soothe her, to prepare her.

I'm coming for you...

Tonight...

And then she was gone.

3. ERAN

Typical military barracks enforce a lights-out period when troops are required to get some shut-eye to recuperate from the hard day of readying themselves and the base for war. This wasn't the case with the Ministry. Men, women, and children trained at all hours, Vire officers held meetings even in the dead of night, and the base was always on full alert, with all units not actively doing something order to standby. This made my one-man, midnight missions a little challenging.

Every night I waited until my unit was asleep before getting out of bed and leaving the barracks. After nine weeks I knew the sleeping habits of every one of them, and could mentally check them off as they went comatose for the night. I followed the same routine tonight. The difference was, this time I had something concrete to look for.

If Jocelyn was locked inside a rock cell, there was a good chance she was underground. So that's where I headed.

The corridors were busier tonight than usual; there was almost a palpable feeling of nervousness from those I evaded while hiding in deep doorways or circumventing down adjacent hallways. Some carried canvas bags similar to the ones used at Ms. Veilleux's school, which obviously contained weapons used more commonly in our world. Others carried stacks of traditional weapons, choosing swords and daggers as their preferred method of offense.

I had no delusions that this was what the stockpiling was all about…an offensive move. I had watched The Sevens accumulate weapons for the last nine weeks, readying themselves for the invasion of our world and, subsequently, the rest of humanity.

And they were getting closer to the date of attack; the tension in the air forecasted it.

I made my way around several corners, descending at least five sets of stairs before finally reaching the bottom of the Ministry. Progressively, I noticed the walls turn from aged plaster to brick and finally to stone, the pressure in my head increasing with the steady decline. Finally, I reached the substructure that made up the Ministry. Here, a hallway, pockmarked with doors, stretched a hundred yards before coming to an end. I pulled out the tool I had formed from mess hall utensils and systematically worked my way down the hall, picking the lock of each door. Inside every one, I found a small armory, but no Jocelyn.

It wasn't until I reached the second to last one that I finally got a clue.

That was when I heard the scream. It was blood-curdling and I could not discern whether it came from a man or a woman. It got me moving again, fast.

The noise was coming from the floor above, which I reasoned once I heard it again, this time intense enough to reverberate through the ministry walls.

Whatever was happening to her, it was…

My mind wouldn't allow me to finish that thought. Instead, the clear, distinct words of revenge came to me.

I'll kill them. Every last one of them.

31

The methods were already filtering through my mind.

A third scream led me to a door on the floor above. Without hesitating, I breached the room, where I saw a knife poised over the bloodied body of a person strapped to a table. This I saw the instant I breached the room. I also caught sight of the Vire behind the door, preoccupied with another battered body. My left hand found the wrist of the Vire holding the knife at the same time as I thrust my right leg toward the other Vire now coming at me. My foot sent the one flailing backwards where he hit the wall with a thud. At the same time, I twisted the wrist I held and it cracked, releasing the knife from its grip. I caught it in midair and sent the blade into the gut of the Vire who had been holding it. The other Vire came at me again. The scuff of his feet behind me told me from which direction and at what pace. I swung around and swiped the blade across his throat just as his hand reached my neck. His fingers gave a slight squeeze and then fell away as the blood from his mortal wound spilled down his chest. The man clutched his neck, but the damage was done. He knew it, locking his eyes with mine as he dropped to his knees and tipped backwards while the life drained out of him.

I swung around and bent over the table, searching for the face beneath the layer of caked blood. Eyes stared back at me with a mixture of anticipation and recognition, blue in color, and, thankfully, not Jocelyn's. Relief washed over me, but only for as long as it took me to become remorseful for feeling it while taking in this person's injuries.

The nose and one ear had been removed. The Vire had evidently begun working on the right eye judging from the loss of its eyelid. The person's skin was charred, remnants of an incantation that seared the outside of a person's organs.

I could think of no other time in which the desire to be a healer had been stronger than this very moment.

"What's your name?" I asked.

"Th-Th-Thib…"

"Take your time," I said, although he didn't seem to have much of it left.

He must have sensed it too because he forced the name from his lips, blood sputtering as he said it.

"Thibodeaux."

The result of his effort sent him into a coughing fit, spraying more blood, which I didn't fully register because my awareness was on his name.

"Thibodeaux?" I repeated quietly.

There was a reason this man had recognized me. He was the same one I went to every year for school supplies, the one whose prominent family owned warehouses worldwide of rare and distinguished artifacts, the one who had given Jocelyn The Rope of The Sevens.

I had known him my entire life, and yet I couldn't recognize him.

The Sevens used various methods to accomplish what they needed, but they had their favorites. La Terreur, an extreme type of sickness that set in just before death, had been used on the penal colonies in the past; hanging was common in the Ministry's main courtyard; and the traditional home invasion wasn't rare throughout the provinces. But this…I had never seen this…. The Vires who had done this to him weren't interested in making him an example, as was their usual purpose. No, Mr. Thibodeaux was a Dissident, and he had been tortured for information.

"I'm getting you out of here," I stated, and instantly started freeing him from the ropes strapping him to the table.

But his head rolled back and forth. He was limited to that one method to tell me to stop.

I opened my mouth to argue with him when our eyes met, and I saw the life behind his ebb away.

33

I didn't hesitate, turning toward the other body slumped against the wall behind the door, searching the face for any sign of Jocelyn. When I realized it was a woman, my heart stopped. The long black hair matted with blood across her face, covering it almost entirely, sickened me and sent me into a rage as I crossed the room.

A single word escaped, although in my haze I didn't process right away that it came from me.

"No…NO!"

I reached her and fell to my knees, my hand sweeping the strands from her face as I descended, my eyes franticly searching for any sign of life, any at all.

"No." My throat closed off, a sob constricting it. The rest of my breath was released in a moan that seemed to echo its way through my chest.

My fingers still held back the hair that clung to her skin, thought it was parted just enough to expose her features. My hand was shaking, but it was removed enough to allow me to see her clearly. I knew every fine detail of Jocelyn's features, the curve of her cheekbones, the subtle indentations at the sides of her lips, the delicate slope of her nose. I memorized her from the second she turned to face me in Olivia's store on the day we met, and it was this memory that was conjured as I inspected the face of the woman before me.

Only the long, narrow nose of Mrs. Thibodeaux made me breath again. It emerged from behind her hair, crusted with pus and dirt.

I withdrew my hand while settling back on my heels.

The two of them had died together, tortured in a small room for information they probably never had in the first place.

Damn it, I thought wearily.

The grief I felt washed away by what I could only describe as hatred, directed solely at the seven individuals safely in their living quarters elsewhere in this fortress while the Thibodeauxes were tortured to their last breath. I had seen enough blood spilled for several lifetimes now, but still I coveted the blood of seven more. Rising to my feet, I fought the incredibly strong urge to leave the room with vengeance as my goal.

Not yet, I told myself.

Jocelyn...

Placing my hand against the wall, I appreciated the feel of the cool rocky surface. My palm flattened as much as possible to take advantage of its chill, which I used to distract me from my emotions.

I can't allow my anger too much influence over me. That's how people die. And if I die, Jocelyn dies.

Whether it was the severity of that concept or the cut of the rock against my skin, I'll never be sure. But I do know it was the flattening of my hand, that simple act that told me what I needed to know.

With my head down, I didn't see it at first. My fingertips registered it before my mind.

The rock wall is dry, I realized, *bone dry.*

Jocelyn was being kept in a cell surrounded by dewy rock, moist enough to glisten, to reflect back. I knew this because I had seen her memory of it. What hadn't registered at the time was that only one element leaves a reflection...

My head snapped up.

Water.

As if fighting its way in, the memory of Lacinda dragging Jocelyn on and off the stage in Mexico City hit me with the force of a sledgehammer.

Lacinda...water...

Lacinda lives on the cliff of the Oregon coastline...

That cliff borders the ocean...

Yes, I muttered to myself, finally reaching the conclusion my mind was leading me to.

Jocelyn was being held at Lacinda's...

I paused, my muscles tensing.

Beneath Lacinda's house.

Bastards.

If The Sevens hadn't led us to her home under the false pretense of agreeing to a truce weeks ago I wouldn't have put it all together. But they had…and I now knew exactly where to find her.

Rapidly straightening to a standing position, I headed for the door, plans I'd designed to escape the Ministry returning to me, the desire to get to Jocelyn overpowering. But as I stepped in front of it, a movement on the opposite side brought me to a halt. Ironically, I processed the shape of the person coming through the door at exactly the same time as he did with me.

There was no hesitation from either of us.

Our fists crossed in the air, making contact with each other's jaws. Our heads simultaneously whipped to the side. Just as I was pushed back into the room, I hurled him to the side, against the wall to the left. From there, the struggle to gain ground over the other sent us over chairs, to the ground, and finally slamming into the wall opposite the door.

Our fists pulled back with equal speed, aiming at the other's face. And that was when we came to a stop.

"Eran Talor?" I muttered, sucking in a deep breath, refilling my lungs.

He blinked, seeming to be just as surprised as me. "Jameson?" He said this in an accent, which I always assumed to be English.

"What are you doing here?" I asked in a rush.

Laughing through a scoff, as if we hadn't been about to inflict serious bodily damage on each other, he said casually, "I was going to ask you the same thing." We released our grips and stepped back, each of us taking a quick glance at the door to ensure no one else was coming through. "I came for Magdalene. The damn…" His face hardened, and I sensed the frustration he was going through. "They've got her pretty well hidden."

"Yeah, they have a talent for that...," I mentioned, noting that we'd come to the mutual conclusion without much data that 'they' were The Sevens. "What kind of business do they have with Maggie?"

He ran his fingers through his hair, a clear sign of agitation. "She can harm them, and they know it."

I interpreted that to mean..."So they want her dead."

"They want her out of the way," he clarified.

"In order to do what?" While I had my own beliefs about their end goal, I wanted to hear his version. Right now, there was overwhelming evidence that he knew more about them than I initially thought.

He stared back at me, unflinching, as he answered. "The Sevens aren't who they seem to be. They aren't like one of us." Pausing, he reconsidered that concept and corrected himself. "They aren't like one of you."

My eyebrows furrowed in confusion. "You know about our world?"

He stared at me, inquiring, and again I got the feeling he knew more than he was letting on. "Your world?"

I admitted to myself that it was an odd way for me to put it, and then shoved the thought aside. A strong part of me wanted to tell him. While knowing the jeopardy of admitting the truth, I reasoned that Eran was locked inside the headquarters of our world's most vicious enemy. He had a right to know what he was up against. "The witch world," I added, leaving him to figure it out from there.

"Right....," he muttered. "That's what you call yourselves."

"Yes." To be clear, I said, "We don't advertise it."

"No, I haven't seen anyone wearing pointy, black hats or carrying wands."

This time I did laugh, at the irony.

The fury beneath his expression remained unchanged. "Regardless, I haven't been fooled into thinking those in your world aren't lethal."

"We can be," I said, and immediately became reserved. "How do you know so much about us, Eran?"

Diverting his attention briefly to the ceiling where footsteps loosened pebbles of rock down over us, he hesitated. When they faded, he confessed, "Magdalene and I are well aware of what you all are capable of. We studied your Vires, this place you call the Ministry, those who you call The Sevens. And what I said still stands. The Sevens aren't one of you."

"Yeah," I replied, my voice thick with sarcasm, "that I know. What I can't figure out…is who you are. Why are you stalking The Sevens, and what does Maggie have to do with them?"

He opened his mouth to speak when the rumbling of footsteps below us drew his attention.

"They're getting closer," he determined.

"Did you come alone?"

He nodded. "You?"

I gave him the same response.

"So it's pretty much the two of us," he deduced.

"Against an army of Vires," I concluded. "Excellent."

He didn't seem alarmed, which struck me as a bit insane. Instead, he looked pointedly at me. "You still haven't told me what you are doing here."

"Was just getting to that," I said, and then paused, noting the paradox of our situation…

We'd both come to find the woman we love.

"I'm here for Jocelyn."

His eyes narrowed. "So they have her, too," he muttered and shook his head. "What do they want with her?"

"To use her."

Eran didn't show any sign of surprise hearing this, but my follow up statement caught his attention.

"The two of them are together."

His eyes widened. "Magdalene and Jocelyn? How do you know?"

We paused to listen as the rhythmic pounding of a unit's footsteps passed. They now came from the floor above, but I had a feeling they would be at our door soon. Getting back to the conversation, I lowered my voice. "They're not here."

"Where then?" His voice came out as a demand, harsh and tense, in a manner I identified with.

It would have been too difficult to explain. So my reply was short, and came out as a command. "Follow me."

We made it halfway across the room before we were stopped.

The faces of three Vires appeared in the hallway, Stalwart, the meaty one from the mess hall, being the first. He stepped inside the room as the remaining two followed. My muscles stiffened, readying for the brawl while Eran came around my side and settled into a fighting stance, just as the last Vire to enter turned and closed the door.

Before we could be locked in, though, the room broke into chaos.

I still held the dagger used against the Thibodeauxes, and brought it up to Stalwart's neck, shoving him against the wall. Eran somehow found a sword and placed the tip of it into the second Vire with the blade running along the neck of the final Vire in Stalwart's contingent.

Their eyes were alert but there was no fury in them. And I didn't expect there to be. Vire's were trained from an early age to suppress their emotions.

"Sheath your weapons," Stalwart commanded in a low, deep rumble.

"That's not going to happen," I said, keeping my blade against his neck.

"Men, sheath your weapons," he repeated in a way that didn't seem to be directed at me or Eran. The grating sound of metal against metal filled the room and ended suddenly, leaving a void of uncomfortable silence.

"Eran," I said. "Keep your weapon where it is."

"I have no intention of doing otherwise," he muttered.

Stalwart ignored our stances, and the threat to their necks, and began to speak. "Your weapons threaten yourselves more than us."

"Cast," I solicited, "and I will cast against you."

This didn't seem to concern him.

As if I hadn't heard him, he dared, "Use your weapons and you will find escaping from the Ministry to be impossible. Your efforts to reclaim your women will fail. They will exist separate from you for the remainder of your lives. That, gentlemen, will be more devastating to you than a quick death for us."

He made a good point. As I calculated the situation we were in, I realized that Eran and I were ready for battle, but, ironically, we seemed to be the only ones.

"Who sent you?" I asked, knowing their excursion to the depths of the Ministry wasn't because they were simply on a midnight stroll.

"Sartorius knows your plan." My grip tightened around the blade's handle. Stalwart, evidently, had seen combat because this didn't seem to intimidate him. "And you picked a fine time to implement it," he sneered. "Security has been added tonight, something having to do with the interrogation of two Dissidents." In a motion that brought his skin tighter against my blade's edge, Stalwart tipped his head toward the table behind us, at the one where Mr. Thibodeaux lay, and added derisively, "Looks like that's been accomplished."

What struck me while listening to Stalwart was the same trait that made me notice him in the mess hall. He was human, a part that seemed absent from the rest of the Vires.

"If you don't want the same happening to your women, you'll need to trust us."

"And why should we do that?" asked Eran, rightly suspicious.

"Because we were given orders to kill you, and you're still breathing."

"Which means you have an agenda," I countered.

Stalwart smiled. "Doesn't everyone?"

Another valid point.

His smile fell away. "If I wanted you dead, I would have taken the opportunity given me long ago."

"And how would you have done that?" I tested, more curious than alarmed.

"By ensuring my weapon landed where I was instructed."

"Which was?"

"Where yours is now," he replied, again tipping his neck against my blade.

"And where did it land instead?" I asked slowly, because I was beginning to understand what he was inferring.

"Just above your upper lip, Jameson Caldwell." After making this declaration, he studied me, waiting for my reaction.

I didn't reply immediately, my initial response being the involuntary tensing of my muscles as a single string of words began repeating in my mind, which I eventually vocalized.

"You were the Vire sent to kill me at birth."

His reply bordered on humor. "Pleased to finally meet you."

Only then did I lower my weapon.

"What are you doing?" Eran muttered.

"He missed on purpose," I replied. "Which means-"

"You have an ally," said Stalwart.

I glanced at Eran and then at his sword. He seemed opposed to the idea of dropping our guard but, hesitantly, he unpinned Stalwart's men. I noted, however, he didn't sheath his sword.

"They will be coming for the bodies," Stalwart warned, "and that means we'll need to get moving. Incantatio alligaveritis." The last two words rolled off his tongue as if they were a part of his message. They weren't. I instantly knew what he had done, well before Eran.

The sword Eran held dropped to the ground, the clang vibrating off the rock walls, spurring me into action. My blade returned to Stalwart's throat.

"Remove the binding cast."

"No," Stalwart retorted. "I know you...I don't know your friend. Until I trust him, he won't be relieved of his restraints."

"Remove-"

Eran cut me off. "Let it go, Jameson." He inclined his head toward Stalwart and demanded in a way that didn't leave room for disagreement, despite the fact his hands were now bound by an invisible force behind his back, "You can use me as a prisoner."

"We intend to," replied Stalwart, decisively.

As if he hadn't heard Stalwart, Eran continued. "Under one condition...you'll be taking me with you."

I figured out Eran right there. His abrupt demand said it all. He had no intention of challenging Stalwart. He had one concern, only one, and it had nothing to do with his own wellbeing. His sole purpose was getting to Maggie, and he would do whatever it took.

His resolve was impressive, but then I had the same feelings about Jocelyn.

Stalwart showed his agreement by seizing Eran's arm and leading him through the door. I trailed his men, observing as they marched with an air of authority through

42

the Ministry. We crossed the path of four Vire contingents, all without any opposition. Not a single curious glance was made in our direction.

Apparently, Eran noticed this too. "What do you do here Stalwart?" he asked, once we were in a vacant hallway.

"I ensure the safe transport of prisoners."

That stunned me. "But you were sent to apprehend me?" I asked, muddling my way through understanding. "Why didn't Sartorius send someone whose job is to arrest and detain?"

Stalwart paused, and the stiffening of his shoulders told me that he didn't want to answer.

His gruff reply reinforced my theory. "You'll need to ask him that."

I didn't speak again because, at that point, I got the distinct feeling we were being led into a trap.

4. LACINDA

We chased nightfall to the opposite side of the world, reaching the Oregon coastline just as darkness fell. The last hint of light peering between the jagged tops of pine trees on the horizon slipped away as our feet touched down on the soggy earth, and we stared up at Lacinda Pierce's two-story Victorian home. It was just as I remembered it, dismal, lonely, and reminding me of an animal studying us from the shadows. In the distance waves crashed against the rocks down the cliff face below us, bringing back to me the memory of Jocelyn's damp prison walls. It got my legs moving the second I found my balance.

"What's your name?" Stalwart's gruff voice asked from behind me, even though Eran's brisk pace was rapidly reaching mine.

"Eran...Talor."

"You took that well, Eran," Stalwart noted.

"Air transport doesn't bother me," he stated impassively. "What does is that I don't know the layout of this house. Anyone want to fill me in?" He came into view at my side then, so I figured it was up to me to answer.

"There is a parlor off to the right, a set of stairs to the second floor in the entryway, and a basement below the structure. Wish I had more details, but I haven't been past the parlor."

Eran gave me a fleeting look. "If that's as far as you've gone, how do you know there's a basement?"

My response was flat, wanting to end the questioning so I could focus entirely on the house, and any potential risk that might suddenly emerge from it. "Because that's where Jocelyn and Maggie are being held."

On that assertion, neither of us bothered to slow our pace. At the door, my foot landed just to the left of the handle, and its accompanying thrust opened it, spraying wood splinters into the house. I expected there to be at least one Vire waiting on the opposite side. There wasn't. Instead, we were met only with a dark, vacant foyer.

Eran entered first, stopping just inside for a look around. The lights were off, and it was silent. Even the grandfather clock in the parlor had ceased its ticking. "Is this house unoccupied?"

"No," Stalwart and I answered, both of us grumbling at the realization that we should have met some resistance by now.

Again, I got the feeling we were being led into a trap. This scenario brought me back to the first time I visited Lacinda's house. We hadn't faced any opposition then either, not until the end, when it suited The Sevens best.

Eran sensed something was wrong too because his arm flew backward, fingers extended. "My sword," he said in reference to the weapon one of Stalwart's men had picked up after Eran's wrists were bound. "Now."

The man waited for Stalwart's approval, and handed the sword to Eran. This spooked the other one who muttered something that sounded like the beginning of a cast, "Eye of bat, tongue of cat..."

Eran and I didn't wait for him to finish.

"Stairs," he said.

"I was thinking the same thing," I replied.

We went in search of them, any flight that would take us down, not up. The rooms of Lacinda's first floor were empty of furniture and lacked any sign of descending stairs. They were also silent, each consecutive one unsettling me more as the lack of Vires caused me to wonder what in the hell was going on here.

A possession as priceless as Jocelyn wouldn't be left unguarded.

Having now come full circle, we ended our search back in the entryway.

"Maybe they moved them," suggested one of Stalwart's men.

"Yeah," said the other one, "yeah, maybe they learned you escaped and, for caution's sake, transferred them to another location."

"That's possible," I said, "but it doesn't *feel* right."

Eran shook his head, perplexed. "No, it doesn't. I feel... Magdalene is close by."

The first one who spoke snickered. "You say you *feel-*"

"Shh," Eran snapped.

This was good because if Eran hadn't quieted him I would have done it. What Eran honed in on was the same thing I'd picked up on right before Eran shut him up. It was faint, but distinguishable.

"You talking about the whistle?" asked Stalwart.

"Yes," stated Eran, both of us approaching it simultaneously. "I am."

I held out my hand in search of the breeze squeezing through the opening in the wall, while Eran began pushing against the panel. As he moved farther left, the wall gradually swung open, making a quiet scraping noise and revealing the hidden staircase behind it. More importantly, the walls were made of chiseled rock and glistened with water.

The staircase spiraled downward for a good fifty feet until reaching a dark hallway where yellow light flickered from the sliver below the door at the end. We opened it to find three cages lining the back wall, the cell bars made of rock.

I didn't recognize the woman in the first cage. A passing evaluation of her told me only that she was dark-skinned and elderly. She stayed directly in the center, unmoving, ready and suspicious. The next cage held Maggie Tanner, who immediately leapt toward us, her hands wrapping around the bars that held her in. Her eyes were eager, harboring the same intensity Eran had when it was clear he was thinking of her. The last person who came into my view was Jocelyn.

I crossed the room before my mind knew what my body was doing. She reached out to me, her arms coming through the bars that kept her trapped. Then I felt her chilled body against me, and her struggle to hold on through the cool bars separating us. The dress she still wore from earlier left her arms bare, leaving her exposed to the cold, which made infuriated me. That feeling only grew as she trembled against me.

I tore the black shirt – a standard issuance of the Vire uniform – off me and pulled it around her. The cavern air hit me, and only made me more vengeful toward Lacinda for leaving Jocelyn under-dressed. Jocelyn didn't seem to mind any longer, though, as her eyes settled on my chest.

She cleared her thoughts with a few blinks and then said, "How…" She paused, seeming to struggle with the fact that I was standing here. "How did you find us?"

"The water," I said, my gaze flickering to the shiny walls behind her. "Seepage from the ocean waves…."

One side of her lips rose in a half-smile. "On the stage…in Mexico…" She laughed through her charming little nose. "I should have known what you were doing."

"Yes," I chastised, teasing. "You should have."

She smiled to herself and muttered, "Memories can be potent."

"Especially when they concern a prison cell," I added. "It's time to get you out of here."

I kissed her, delicately, intending it to be swift, but my need for her brought on an abrupt surge, pressing my lips momentarily harder against hers. But it seemed to leave her happily stunned.

I pulled away with a deep sigh, partly because I didn't want to let her go and partly because this was where my plan ended. I knew she would be enclosed in a cage, but I didn't know where to find the key.

"How dense are these bars?" I asked out loud, taking hold of one to feel the stiffness against my grip.

"Dense," the firm voice of a woman answered. It came from the first cell, closest to the door, the one holding the woman I'd never seen before.

She pointed to a bar that she had dented while chipping away at it. "This took me five years, and I don't think we have that much time."

I stopped to evaluate her, which she openly acknowledged by standing her ground and doing the same back. Her confidence was admirable. It couldn't be easy living as a spectacle in the confines of a cage. And I was certain that was how Lacinda treated them. Pets to be toyed with, manipulated for entertainment.

"So you're Kalisha?"

Her eyes widened, slightly, but she didn't shift from her rigid pose. "If you know who I am, then you know what I was?"

"Yes, I'm aware you were a Vire."

Stalwart and the two men behind him darted their eyes in her direction.

"Then you'll be leaving me here," she said as if this were a foregone conclusion.

"No, Kalisha," I replied, and summed up the offensiveness of her assumption by adding, "We aren't The Sevens." I took a step back to assess the cells further. "But you're right about one thing...we don't have five years to chisel you out. We'll need to think of something else."

Eran followed my footsteps, doing his own review of the cells. "Damn stone," he muttered with a shake of his head. "If they had left just one piece metal...."

One of Stalwart's men snickered. "And that would have made it any easier?"

"Yes," replied Eran, flatly, irritated at having to answer.

Maggie, in support of her boyfriend, mentioned, "Eran has a way with metal."

Expressions of curiosity rose around the room, but we didn't address the oddity of her statement. There was a more important issue at hand. Unfortunately, with my back to the door, I didn't see it coming.

"You can stop your pondering," Lacinda suggested, her tone thick with sarcasm. "You'll find no way in."

My immediate reaction was to groan in annoyance.

Turning, I found her entering the room with an air of authority, dressed in some kind of gown, the usual kind...flimsy, and nearly translucent. She had on earrings that dangled to her shoulders, blue to match her dress. It was obvious to anyone with eyes that she had put some thought into her appearance tonight.

Her eyes scanned the room, narrowing slightly at Jocelyn, before landing on me. "Nobilisss...," she said with her traditional hiss at the end. "You've come to save your woman in a daring escape? How very...noble...of you."

I wondered if she knew how ridiculous she sounded.

"You two know each other?" Eran interrupted, casually.

49

Lacinda's head snapped in his direction, her face stiffening as she barked. "Silence him."

The command initially made no sense. She had entered the room alone. And there was no one but her interested in shutting Eran up. Then the feeling that we were entering a trap returned full force, as Stalwart's men moved to seize Eran's arms.

Stalwart did his part also, by bringing a blade to Eran's throat.

"NO!" Maggie screamed and launched herself at them only to be stopped by her cage.

Disturbingly, the bars remained steady. Maggie's frame was small, but her lurch didn't result in even a slight quiver through the bars.

Eran, to his credit, didn't seem concerned about the knife at his neck. He kept his gaze on Lacinda, and I sensed it was because he believed, as I did, that she was the key to opening the cage doors.

Regardless, the distance between Stalwart and me was too far. He'd slit Eran's throat before I made it two steps in his direction.

"Traitor," I muttered, although my depiction of him had no effect. Stalwart kept his attention on Lacinda.

She noted our interaction and drew in a sharp breath before giggling. "Oh, you mean, you thought he would assist you? Oh, Nobilisss.... Now that *must* be upsetting."

She leisurely strolled to me and placed one of her hands on my chest. Her head tilted upward, attempting to meet my eyes, which were positioned on the wall behind her.

"Such rampant testosterone in this room," she whispered. "Each of you men expels it with such vigor." She leaned in to purr a sigh, even as I turned my head away. "Mmmmmmmm, I can almost feel it coming from you."

Something touched my throat below my chin and I jerked back, taking a step to add distance. Only after I searched for what it was, and saw the fury in Jocelyn's expression, did I know Lacinda had placed her lips on me.

And I understood the purpose of it instantly. We were in her den, this was her game, and she was going to use it to her advantage.

She clucked her tongue at me. "Nobilisss, so sensitive…. Such a virile man can't have issues when a woman gives him a kissssss."

"He can when you are the woman," I claimed, which sent her confident expression plummeting.

"You honestly don't see how good we can be for each other, do you? No vision of how the two of us can reign over our world, together, the Surveyor and the Nobilisss."

"The Sevens reign over our world, Lacinda, or has the weight of your earrings somehow blocked the blood flow to your brain?"

Her fingers rose to toy with them, their sparkle catching in the reflected light from the flickering torch above Jocelyn's cell. "You like them? They're made of my family stone." Before I could deny her a compliment, she continued. "I saw you coming…tried to veer you away, make you second guess your conclusions on where Jocelyn might be hidden. But you had to find her, didn't you, Nobilisss? Because you are that good. Oh, give in to me…," she pleaded, tilting her lips at me. "We are so strong together. Give in to me…."

I groaned in disgust, my upper lip lifting before I had any control over it.

Those were the very words I had once used to convince Jocelyn of my love for her. It sickened me to hear this woman apply them to the two of us.

"Jocelyn and I were meant to be together."

"Oh," she said and exhaled loudly in apparent disgust. "Who says? Some ridiculous, old piece of parchment paper? You know better than to believe in a destiny that isn't driven by your desires."

I swiveled my head to lock eyes with Jocelyn. "*She* is what drives my destiny, Lacinda, because *she* is all I desire."

The tension in the room rose several degrees, entirely caused by Lacinda. Her fingers came to my cheek, only to be blocked by my hand. She used what leverage remained, her fingertips being the only part able to move, and pressed my head back in her direction.

"Lacinda," I said carefully. "You believe in the records as much as I do. I'm tired of playing your game. You'll need to open the cells now."

"No," she sighed, wistfully. "That's not going to happen. I'll tell you what will. You'll release me, we'll go upstairs, and we'll plan our rise to power."

"You are delusional."

Disregarding me, she continued, her tone darkening with each word. "Your friend here, the one with the blade to his neck, will find it slit across his throat, and Stalwart will return with his men to the Ministry where he will inform Sartorius that your precious Jocelyn has died in the midst of the conflict to apprehend him."

"Which would be false. And you, being the Surveyor, are fully aware of the consequences you'll face for lying to The Sevens."

She paid no attention to my warning, instead uttering her own threat in response. "No, Jameson. That part of the message, the one about Jocelyn's life, will be entirely true."

Impulsively, my hand flew to Lacinda's neck, squeezing, making indentations deep enough that she was forced to lift her chin. My fingers tightened, and I felt something shift beneath her skin.

Bones.

Yanking her toward me in a motion that sent her hair flying forward, my demand came out as a snarl, "Release her or you die."

Stalwart made a move toward me, but I stopped him.

"Any closer and Lacinda's neck gets crushed. And I doubt Jocelyn will be much in the mood for healing the one who imprisoned her."

The truth in my words being starkly evident, he remained in place.

"Now your men will step away from Eran, and you will follow them to the wall, where you will turn and face it."

Stalwart motioned for his men to listen to my order and each of them retreated to the door.

"That's far enough."

As this took place, Lacinda became increasingly agitated. I thought, at first, it was because she was losing her grip on the situation. Her prisoners were about to be freed. It was her attempt to scream at me that cleared up that belief.

Her voice emerged hoarsely; fighting its way past the pressure of my fingers. "She's going to kill you! That is her destiny! Let me end her and prevent it from happening!" she pleaded. "Let me take her life to save yours!"

I responded with a roar, which left my hand around her neck precariously shaking her head. It wasn't intentional, but it did shut her up. I then laid out the reality of her situation clearly so there could be no confusion left. "Listen closely, Lacinda, because *your* life depends on it. If Jocelyn is harmed by you or by your orders, I will stalk you, biding my time until you least expect it. When your guard is down and no one is around to protect you, I will take you away from all that you know to be safe and true, and I will, with slow, agonizing precision, take your life. The methods I will use won't be pretty. I won't spare you, not for a second, no matter the length or depth of your screams. Are you hearing me, Lacinda? Do you understand the warning I am giving you? Because if you don't I will use on you the skills I learned at the hands of

53

Theleo Alesius." I suspended my threat long enough for her to recognize the name of our world's most notorious Vire. "I love Jocelyn. She is the air I breathe, the force that causes my heart to beat, the incentive for the blood to flow through my veins. She is the reason I exist at all. Regardless of your political aspirations, disturbed sense of lust, or for whatever reason you have used to convince yourself that you and I were meant for each other, you will abide me, or you will find yourself dead."

The silence blanketing the room was deafening. I could actually hear Lacinda's pulse quickening as my warning sunk in.

Sensing the truth in what I was telling her, she nodded, her wide eyes never leaving mine until they closed and she began to concentrate.

"Lapis terrae vis hominum aperit portam, ita ut iusserit."

My years of Latin instantly translated her words into what she meant: Stone of earth, power of men, open this gate, as I so command.

Instantly, one side of each cell slowly swung open, and Lacinda's prisoners slipped through the opening before the bars had time to stop.

Jocelyn rushed to my side but stopped short of touching me. Instead, she stared, waiting for my next move. It came swiftly, completely unanticipated by me...or the recipient of it.

The rage in me surfaced like a tidal wave, suffocating all logic, blinding me. My reaction was impulsive, driven by a maddening desire to inflict insufferable pain on Lacinda for hurting the one I love. And so I flung her in the opposite direction of the cells, sending her as far from Jocelyn as possible, where she ended up with a slap against the wall, and collapsed at Stalwart's feet.

Lacinda released a whimper but didn't move.

Instantly, my hands were on Jocelyn's cheeks, evaluating her, inspecting her for any sign of injury or retaliation she might have incurred since the few minutes we had on the stage, anything that might overpower her ability to heal herself.

"I'm not hurt. Not physically," she confirmed.

Only then did I release the breath pent up in me. It came in a rush as I shook my head in amazement. "I was so sure…"

She knew what I was thinking, what had consumed me since we'd been separated, not only weeks ago but also tonight. "You were sure Lacinda would hurt me in retaliation? For being the one you love?" She smiled tenderly at me, a move that made me want to pull her close. The only reason that kept me from doing it was Stalwart and his men. We weren't safe yet. "I think," Jocelyn went on, "that she believed she could win you over."

Jocelyn's eyes shifted to the topic of our conversation, beyond my shoulder.

"She clearly had no idea what she was up against," I said, a grin surfacing freely for the first time in weeks. "She has nothing on you."

The smile that brightened her eyes sharpened my need to hold her, but I didn't get the chance. A rustling sound told me that someone was moving, and that the noise was coming from the direction of doorway.

By the time I spun around, I caught only a glimpse of Stalwart carrying Lacinda in his arms, her feet dangling loosely, his arms cradling her as they disappeared into the dark hallway. Stalwart's men swiftly stepped in to block the door. Eran, reached them first, demanding, "Step aside."

The men stood firm.

"MOVE!"

They didn't.

I stopped next to Eran, and warned, "Move or you will be hurt."

When they didn't budge, and with all of us knowing Stalwart and Lacinda were probably on the first level by now, I took the guard in front of me as Eran took on the other. Our fists landed at nearly the same time, sending Stalwart's men backwards against the doorjamb in near unison.

What struck me was that they didn't put up a fight; they made no effort to defend themselves, taking the full brunt of our force without any detectable cringe. I think even Eran tuned in to it because he paused uncomfortably before stepping over their bodies and taking off down the hall.

By the time we reached the first floor there was no sign of Stalwart or Lacinda, but there were footsteps behind us. I turned, ready to tell Jocelyn she needed to stay back when Maggie appeared in the concealed doorway.

Instead, it was Eran who delivered a warning. "Magdalene…," he said cautiously.

Ignoring him, she moved past us, into the foyer, her head swiveling from side to side in search of Stalwart or Lacinda. Jocelyn rushed by me, surveying the room the same was as Maggie.

"Jocelyn, you need to stay back."

"Both of you need to stay back," Eran demanded, pinning Maggie with a stare.

Evidently, he didn't like his girl involved in danger any more than I did.

Just as Maggie had done, Jocelyn disregarded our demands and moved to Maggie's side. "They're gone?" she asked, scanning the area as Maggie was doing.

The level of frustration at her placing herself in the line of conflict was apparent, but there wasn't time to discuss it.

Only a brief moment passed before Maggie ducked her head while staring through the foyer windows, "No, they're not." And then she disappeared, moving faster than I'd ever seen a girl manage, leaving the front door open behind her.

Eran pursued her, out the door and down the steps before Jocelyn or I even had time to respond. Then I was on the porch, with Jocelyn at my back. My arm immediately rose to block her from pursuing them because I saw something that made me question the legitimacy of my eyesight.

Stalwart and Lacinda had vanished, Eran and Maggie too. But just above the tree-tops, fading into the night sky, was a pair of massive birds, their wings flapping furiously in the same direction Stalwart and Lacinda had been going.

5. DISSENSION

"Jameson...Jameson."

It was Jocelyn's voice pulling me out of my concentration, coaxing me back. I knew this because only she could rouse me back to life.

I turned to face her. This time, though, it was the urgency in her tone that did it. "Right, I know...," I assured her. Despite the threat I'd left with Lacinda, The Sevens' next step was an obvious one. "They'll be coming back."

"Quickly, and with a larger force," Kalisha declared, coming up behind us.

"Then we'd better get going." I stopped, though briefly, to level my focus on Kalisha. "All of us."

Her reaction was a slight drop of her jaw, a clear sign that she felt some relief at being included, and from the looks of it she hadn't experienced that sensation in a very long time.

Less than a minute later, we were in flight, Jocelyn using her ability to levitate us upward.

Once we were out of unaided sight from the ground, she asked in a rush, "Where's my family?"

When I was done listing their safe houses, she wanted to know about mine, and I told her. Sedated by this news, she finally asked for our destination, one I'd purposefully kept from her until it was necessary because I knew how she would take it. "The village?" she repeated, confused.

I nodded. "Remember the platform built on stilts just outside the village boundary? The one where we...where we almost..." I paused realizing she might not want me to bring up the first time we attempted to make love, not with Kalisha right next to us. "The one where we..."

"Celebrated our birthday?" she finished for me.

"That's the one."

Cluing in, as she always seemed to do, she pressed, "Why not the village?"

I opened my mouth to answer and then didn't.

"What, Jameson? What aren't you telling me?"

Every effort I ever made since meeting her was to ensure Jocelyn felt only pleasure, no pain. And now I was about to fail in that undertaking.

She had been locked away for weeks, without any news from the outside world, from our world. And she had no idea that it was in shambles.

"What, Jameson?" she persisted.

I sighed, a sign, I was sure, that made her think I was refusing to concede to her. She began to insist again when I finally answered her. "The village is gone."

Processing my disclosure, we dropped slightly in the air before she contained herself.

"Gone as in destroyed?"

"In a way. It might as well be."

"What happened?"

"I disbanded it."

She looked at me in shock.

"It was the only way to ensure their safety."

"But we were strong, Jameson," she argued, as she tended to do.

"Not strong enough."

She fell silent, evaluating me. "What happened after I was abducted from the bayou? After we were separated?"

I looked away, knowing she wanted to hear, believing wholeheartedly that she shouldn't. But she would learn about it eventually, and it would be better coming from me.

"We fought them, Jocelyn. Hard. The number of Vire uniforms on the ground when it ended was…It was like the night sky had turned on its head, covering the earth in black. But it wasn't enough. We didn't get enough of them. A few got away, went back to the Ministry to acquire more forces, more units, more contingents…more Vires. The thing was…I knew it was happening, because if I were those Vires it's exactly what I would have done. So I ordered everyone to pack up, to leave, hide before the Vires returned with a force we couldn't handle." I then confessed the other part of my motivation for forcing the village to scatter. "It was the only way to make sure they didn't kill you right off. You would still be useful to them if you could serve a purpose. Sartorius found one, and you lived."

"Jameson," she said, her voice just above a whisper, her hand reaching out for me. But I couldn't bring myself to meet her halfway, not after having failed her in so many ways. That wasn't what she was thinking, though. She only had my welfare in mind, always. "Everything you've been through…It's not fair. We should be worrying about classes, tests, where the best house party is on Friday nights." Her voice hardened as she went on, the wind speed noticeably picking up along with it. "We shouldn't be consumed with surviving day to day. We shouldn't have enemies so devoted to killing us that every move we make needs to be strategic by design." As she finished, her voice became bitter. "We shouldn't have to hide."

I knew what she meant. We deserved our freedom. She had just been released from a prison encased in rock, and she was no closer to it than if she were still huddled inside those bars.

I wanted to hurt someone...preferably a Seven. But also I wanted to tell her that it wouldn't be long now, that the fight would be brought to us if we didn't bring it to them. Instead, I held back, knowing it would serve no purpose. In the end, all I could do was place my hand over hers, trying to comfort her with touch as best I could. We stayed that way until the bayou came into view, when the sight of two figures standing on the platform caused her fingers to slip away.

"I thought you said the village is unoccupied."

"It is," I assured her. "We aren't in the village."

As we landed, I noticed that the bayou had a mystique about it tonight, as if the moldering cypress tree stumps, the glassy, black water, and the silent insects who inhabited this part of the world knew that a secret meeting was about to take place.

Jocelyn continued to squint through the darkness until we were close enough for her to distinguish the women. Being that one was squat with a robust belly and her companion was thin, frail, and stood like a drill sergeant, I knew Jocelyn would figure it out quickly.

Then she laughed, a sound filled with relief, and the second her feet touched the ground, she ran for Miss Mabelle to throw her arms around the stocky woman's shoulders.

Jocelyn sighed into her meaty shoulder. "I never thought I'd see you again."

And finally...*finally*...I saw the first unrestrained sign of happiness in Jocelyn since she had been ripped from my arms and imprisoned. Since then she had slept on a rock floor in an empty five by five cell, used as a tool by Sartorius and as a game piece by Lacinda. And still, here she was ignoring all that, ignoring those memories in favor of making this new one. She amazed me.

Despite the old woman's frown clearly visible over Jocelyn's shoulder, there was contentment in her eyes, too. Unfortunately, it never made its way into her response. "N' what a loss that woulda been fer ya," she replied without any hint of humility.

When they separated, Jocelyn hugged Miss Celia as Miss Mabelle pinned her eyes on me, like a cobra preparing to lurch at its prey. "'bout time, Jameson," she spat. "Been here so long now, I got moss growin' up my arms."

"Nice to see you too."

Miss Mabelle scoffed and rolled her eyes at me.

By that point, Jocelyn pulled away from Miss Celia with a perplexed look on her face, her eyes darting back and forth between the two women. "You've-you've been here the entire time?"

"Sho' have, afta' helpin' all dem otha' witches find a place ta hide."

"Wadn't easy," added Miss Celia, shaking her petite head. "Wadn't easy no way."

These women always seemed to acquiesce to a compliment, so I said, "But I knew you could do it, and do it well."

"Shish," Miss Mabelle sniffed, and turned her head away.

"Why here?" Jocelyn interjected. "I thought it wasn't safe to be here."

"It weren't, not until all you witches left. Now it's nothin' more than swamp with a few stilt houses, least that what The Sevens seem ta think."

"They want the people, not the place," added Miss Celia. "By the time we got everyone placed, Sevens decided not to come 'round hea no mo'. They mo' interested in otha' things...." She turned pointedly to address the quiet woman standing behind us. "Like people who cause trouble fer 'em."

Miss Mabelle took her ever-present cane and dramatically ambled around me, giving me a disdainful glare in route before stopping purposefully in front of Kalisha.

With a firm slam of her cane against the platform, she stated, "It's an hona' to meet ya. You done good, girl. Took a lot to keep all that ya know to yerself."

Kalisha blinked in apparent surprise. "You know me?"

Miss Celia smirked shrewdly. "'int much we don't know."

"Kalisha," I interjected, "these women have been made privy to the records that forecasted our future, the same ones that you and your contingent stole from The Sevens...which landed you in prison all those years."

"Are you Vires?" she asked, coming to the only conclusion she could.

Miss Celia chuckled.

"No, we ain't," said Miss Mabelle spinning around to return to Miss Celia's side, peering over her shoulder mischievously on her way there. "But we jus' as dangerous."

Kalisha, who remained in a state of cautious amazement, overcame it, and a smile rose up as her eyes trailed Miss Mabelle back to the edge of the platform. As if she finally came to the realization that she was in like-minded company, she asked a seemingly banal question that did a good job at stirring the rest of us. "So you know that our future rests in the hands of these two, then?" She gestured toward Jocelyn and me.

I noticed the faint clever grin rise on Miss Mabelle and Miss Celia's faces, and was just about to question them on what they knew that we didn't when Jocelyn launched into answering Kalisha's question. "They've heard the highlights, but not the details. We need to fill them in."

Kalisha gave her a deliberate stare, which seemed like she was asking if we were ready for that part of the story.

"They can handle it," Jocelyn reassured her.

Kalisha nodded and opened her mouth to speak only to have Miss Mabelle stop her. "Not yet. They's some otha's who'll wanna hear dis, too."

"Oth-" I began before filling in the blank. "We aren't alone out here in the bayou, are we?"

Without answering, Miss Mabelle tapped her cane impatiently against the wood plank. "Come on now, chil', don't have all night." That was Miss Mabelle's courteous way of asking Jocelyn to use her levitation abilities, to which Jocelyn responded with a smirk in my direction.

"Some things just don't change," said Jocelyn, a message meant solely for me.

"N' ya kin be thankful fer that!" said Miss Mabelle with a sharp nod. "Back ta the village, Miss Jocelyn…n' ya kin hurry it up."

Stifling a smirk at her sharp tone, Jocelyn lifted us all into the air and deposited us, by Miss Mabelle's instruction, on the dock outside the shack my parent's had resided in while here. It was dark, silent, and seemingly barren. Regardless, when Miss Celia cleared her throat to insinuate it was time for Jocelyn to return the black shirt I'd given her, she did it quietly. It wasn't until we were all inside, the door closed behind us, that I heard any sign of life. It came from the corner of the room, a rustling that immediately made my muscles tense. After so many weeks in Vire territory, my nature was to prepare for a coming threat. But when the dim light of the lantern gradually flooded the room, it was familiar faces staring back at us.

And I openly laughed at myself.

The rustling instantly grew louder as Jocelyn and I became engulfed by our families. No one spoke, the threat of being overheard was still a concern, but they showed their distress for each of us in their expressions. Jocelyn's mother, Isabella, gave me a deep nod of appreciation for bringing her daughter back while hugging her tightly. I wondered if she'd ever let her go, literally or emotionally. Being notorious for her strong sense of protecting others, it actually surprised me when she agreed to allow me to infiltrate the Ministry on my own. But then, she probably knew there was no other way.

When the room settled, my smile faded, and I launched into the news I'd been keeping to myself, knowing it would tear at them. "I'm happy to see you, all of you. I truly am, but this is not a safe time for any of us. You are exposed here, whether you believe it or not. Being inside the Ministry gave me firsthand knowledge of the dangers we're facing, and they are not...," my expression grew sullen, "...they won't be easy to overcome. The Sevens have weapons, stockpiles that would fill every shack in this village from floor to ceiling. Their forces are almost ready for attack, and they're working around the clock to get to that point. They're organized, prepared, and they have a plan in place. My guess is that it's a pretty solid one because they've been torturing Dissidents."

I saw heads nodding, and Isabella spoke up. "We're getting word of disappearances every night, from every province." She paused before adding, "Isadora is gone. Braith. Cornelia. The Thibodeauxes."

My jaw tightened as the last two names evoked painful memories. I kept their deaths to myself seeing no reason to drag our families through their last minutes. Instead, I summarized my assessment for them. "They've targeted those who pose the most danger first."

And The Sevens will pay for that, I said to myself.

While taking a second to draw in a deep breath and recalibrate my emotions, Jocelyn surprised me with news of her own.

"That's not all," she mentioned, and then struggled with how to phrase the words. "There's really no appropriate way to say this so I'm going to just...say it. Sartorius isn't like us."

That instantly made me curious. It was the same warning Eran had given me back at the Ministry.

Then she dropped the bomb she'd been withholding. "Sartorius...he has wings."

Everyone, myself included, reacted with astonishment, some more disbelieving than others.

"Wings...?" Alison repeated skeptically.

Knowing she was facing an uphill battle to convince her audience, Jocelyn reminded us that this wasn't so far-fetched.

"When the Ministry was attacked there were sightings of large birds swarming overhead, and a feather was left behind."

"So you're saying...Sartorius attacked his own Ministry?" Charlotte asserted sarcastically, and I gave her a stern look.

"Maybe," she said plainly, emotionless, even though they were staring at her like she'd lost her mind. "But I'm also saying that Sartorius, and very likely the other Sevens, are not human."

Kalisha, who had been obscured by the dark corner where the lantern's light didn't extend, stepped forward, sending nearly everyone in the room to their feet.

"She's right," said Kalisha. "I've seen the wings myself."

Having no idea who this woman was, they gawked at her, trying to determine her reason for being here, and, more importantly, her trustworthiness. They had a lot to lose by coming here, their lives included.

Jocelyn saw their alarm and stepped in. "Kalisha was in prison with me for the last nine weeks, although she was incarcerated a lot longer than I was." They assessed her even closer then, a reaction that I figured stemmed from empathy. "She has information that The Sevens want to keep to themselves, so they locked her up for...," She turned to Kalisha. "How many years?"

"Over twenty," she mumbled, maintaining a vigilant eye on the room. "I lost count."

"The information is about our future, all of us," said Jocelyn before delivering the most impactful part. "Because it's the contents of the last record."

There was no need to mention which record. They guessed it immediately, and everyone in the room leaned forward.

Jocelyn ushered Kalisha farther into the room, a move the defected Vire clearly hesitated over making. Standing awkwardly before the rest of our families, she delivered the information we all wanted – but were apprehensive – about hearing.

"When my contingent agreed to separate and move in opposite directions, I had nowhere to go. Before...before defecting," she paused to assess what impact this might have on her audience. Seeing none, she continued with some small measure of relief. "I was stationed in countries throughout Africa. I knew there was a risk I'd be found there if I returned, but it was the best place to blend in, become part of the populace. I found a village, small, on the outskirts of Jima, in southwestern Ethiopia. I married a nice man, gave birth to a beautiful child, and raised many goats. No one knew of the record, not my husband, not my child. This was to keep my family - and my village - safe. But one day I fell ill, very ill," she enunciated as her gaze sank and she shuddered at the memory of it. "The illness was difficult, nearly taking my life, but that wasn't...it wasn't what took my life. It was what took my soul." Her lips briefly pinched closed in anger. "I truly believed I would die. I have never been so close to death. They called the preacher to make sure he would be ready for my passing. But before I did, I had to give someone the Great Secret. It could not be left to The Sevens alone. Someone *had* to be told. So I asked my husband to find someone who could read Latin. This was the language the records were written in. I speak many languages, and I can extrapolate from the Latin word, but I am not fluent. And this was too important a message to leave to hearsay and assumptions. He brought me an old man, an elder in the village who had been trained in the city. I told them where the record was buried, and they brought it to me. As he put to voice the words I had so carefully hidden, I saw the terror come to his eyes. He was reading ahead, you understand. Having figured out quickly what the record was, he couldn't stop himself. When it became too much, he refused, trying to hand it to my husband. They argued. It was their voices, the level at which they spoke to each other that kept us from hearing what was coming." She halted, her eyes glassing over, and it was clear she began reliving that potent memory.

"Kalisha?" I prompted.

She blinked several times, raised her head again, and continued in quiet anguish. "They came through our village like flaming ghosts, lighting our homes on fire. These were Vires who I knew, trained with. I saved some of them from a sure death in past conflicts. They took my husband, my son, and they...." She stopped, this time swallowing back the tears. "They found me. They found me and then took everything from me. And I will give anything to see my vengeance done," she seethed, "because what they left, all they left were words on a page. Words that told of the future...It said that forces would unite, a movement that would begin quietly and gain momentum as The Sevens fell. It said that a noble lass – a term converted over the years to Nobilis – would lead them. It said the Relicuum would acquire the elements by death of a Vire. This would be pivotal, the completion of her cycle of rebirth. It said she and the Nobilis would bring to an end a conquest by six winged beings. The six would die one by one in varying ways. The seventh would live to witness an act of altruism, an act in which the Relicuum takes the life of the Nobilis. This act leads to the end of the war."

When Kalisha finished, the entire room sat quietly staring back at her, dazed, as if they hadn't picked up a word of what she had said. It was Charlotte who reacted first.

Bolting to her feet, she demanded, "You are going to kill my brother?"

"Quiet down, Charlotte," I warned. Always so dramatic....

"I will not," she snapped, although the level of her voice was lower when she spoke again. "Is that correct?" she persisted, her fury directed at Kalisha. "It said that she," she pointed a finger toward Jocelyn, "would murder my brother?"

Kalisha appeared very uncertain at the moment.

I was about to step in again when my mother reacted to the news.

"That's...," she shook her head, clearing her thoughts. "That's never been written in the archives...no history books mentioned it...and it's not an insignificant detail." It was clear to me, even before she asked her next question that she didn't want to believe Kalisha. "How can...how can you be certain?"

"It's the records that tell us the future," said Kalisha, her meaning clear. She was doing nothing other than conveying their contents.

"I knew you couldn't be trusted." Charlotte was still at it, seething like a rabid dog.

"Knock it off, Charlotte," I warned.

"We're talking about your life, Jameson, but you're taking a cavalier approach about this whole thing," she pointed out, and then she stopped and her eyes narrowed. "How long have you known?"

She could see right through me. She always could. Even as kids, she knew when I was the one who snuck the last brownie off the plate. That was one of her gifts. And one of her faults was pigheadedness. Charlotte wasn't one to back down until she was answered, so I gave her what she wanted, sort of. "A while. That's the best answer you'll get from me."

She shot me an exasperated look, and then I saw the face I knew so well, an expression that meant she was now on the war path. "Am I the only one in this family who cares?"

"No," said Burke, standing. "You're not.'"

This was heading in the wrong direction.

"I'm with you, too," Alison stated, pushing herself off the wall and folding her arms across her chest.

Dillon was quiet about his support, showing it by standing with an uncomfortable, downward gaze.

My parents remained seated, although they didn't need to make an exhibition of their support.

Then, in almost perfect synch, every sibling in the Weatherford family stood.

This was getting out of control.

Frustrated, I walked into the middle of the room. "Drawing a line in the sand won't solve anything. We need to stay *together*, united. There are far stronger forces preparing to kill us. *They* are the ones we need to focus on, and *they-*"

"Aren't here in this room," Charlotte pointed out. "She's the threat, Jameson. Don't you see that?"

As much as I didn't want it to, that perspective, that unproven viewpoint, incensed me, and I had to consciously subdue the words of retaliation from coming out. After a long pause to steady myself, I tried to reason with her while influencing the rest of those listening. "When Jocelyn and I started to date, none of you spoke to me for weeks. You left me alone at the breakfast table, you walked out of the room when I walked in. You avoided me at school during lunch."

Jocelyn reacted to my admission with a surprised turn of her head.

"And when you finally sat down to talk me out of my feelings for her, you pointed out everything that her family had been blamed for." I allowed that to sink in and then added, "We *assumed* they were guilty without ever looking at the facts. And the facts are, she hasn't made a single move to hurt me...ever. *Everything* she has *ever* done has been for the purpose of keeping me safe. Are you going to see her as guilty before proven innocent? Are you going to make the same mistake again?"

I have them, I thought. *My points are valid. They can't dispute them. This argument is over.*

I even saw the surfacing of apprehension in Burke's face.

And then my mother, my own mother, stood up, and her words made me feel as if I were being gutted. "We all know how you feel about Jocelyn. And sometimes – I'm not saying this is one of those times – but sometimes, those feelings can cloud our judgment. Yes, we were wrong about the past, but the records were written to tell us the future, and they have been accurate thus far."

"Which doesn't prove a damn thing."

"Now, that's enough," she retorted sternly.

I couldn't believe she was scolding me. That tone hadn't been used on me since I was ten and I told her that I wanted nothing at all to do with being the Nobilis.

The tension in the room was so thick I felt if someone didn't open the door, I was going to open the window, by breaking it with my fist.

"There's something you've forgotten," I said, hearing the fury in my voice and allowing it. "You like her, too."

Without hesitating, Alison commented snidely, "That was before we knew she was going to kill you."

I instantly turned my head in her direction. When she noticed the look in my eyes, she took a step back. "She is the woman I love. You're going to need to accept that."

"Enough, Jameson," Charlotte snapped. "Sometimes people need to be saved from themselves."

"So you're willing to condemn someone before they've done what you only believe they *will* do?" I countered.

"Yes," she replied, firmly.

"Careful, Charlotte," I warned, knowing full well that she wouldn't like my next statement, because it was too damn close to the truth. "You sound a lot like The Sevens right now."

Her eyes widened as she sucked in a sharp breath. But the expletive she was preparing to utter never made it out.

From behind me, in a quiet, firm voice, Estelle began, "Incantatio-"

"Go ahead," Charlotte sneered. "Casts don't work here in the village, remember?"

"Stillo," Estelle finished with unabated satisfaction.

"Wait!" Jocelyn shouted, because she remembered what I had – that the cast over the bayou had been lifted. Unfortunately, we were too late.

When Charlotte's mouth began to drool I mentally translated the Latin word 'stillo', although watching the result would have been sufficient.

"Dribble?" asked Dillon, who was still studying the language.

And that's exactly what Charlotte's mouth began to do. Slowly at first, and then flowing to a rapid gush, until she was left bent over, cupping the spit pouring from her mouth.

6. BAD BLOOD

"Recant!" my mother shouted in a way I'd never heard before. "Recant your cast right now!"

But Mrs. Weatherford didn't seem capable of letting that haranguing go by without addressing it. "If your daughter would keep her mouth closed, this sort of thing wouldn't happen."

Her message was twofold, and we all knew it. Charlotte shouldn't have provoked a fight, but because she had, Lizzy was going to mock her for the drool.

Several snickers hissed at that remark, all of which came from the Weatherford side. And that was the spark that lit up the room. A second later it became a maelstrom, a disorganized symphony of casts and chants.

"Sanguis innocentium…"

"Scale of serpent, claw of cat…"

"Copias bonum…"

"…make way for the unrepentant, and pack on the fat."

"Damn it," I muttered rushing in front of Jocelyn, blocking with my arms outstretched, confronting my family in a way I had never done. There was no remorse, not from me, not as the screams around me grated my ears.

They were all in a defensive mode now, but would soon shift to offense, and Jocelyn would be their intended target.

Watching the speed at which their lips moved and the lust for retaliation in their eyes, I knew I didn't have much time.

"Jocelyn," I called over my shoulder. "Back up. Slowly."

Her hand came around my waist, and I felt some measure of relief to know she was there, and functioning. And then we began the gradual, tense trek toward the door.

In our agonizingly slow pace backwards, I kept my focus on the rest of them, cataloguing the effect of every cast. Jocelyn's aunt and uncle, Lester and Lizzy, had their eyelids seared shut, blinding them into powerlessness. Isabella was bleeding from both ears, intermittently shaking her head as if that might clear whatever cast had settled over her. Regardless, she remained undeterred, her lips moving faster than anyone's in the room. Vinnia was a strong force, too. Despite the icy cast set on her, and the shimmer of frost on her skin, she actually leaned toward my family, into the fight, teeth chattering as she sent casts back. Estelle, who had always come across as flighty and impulsive to me, showed none of it now. The drill of her stare at my family was amazingly rigid, even as the boils bubbled up beneath her skin. Oscar, Spencer, and Nolan were each debilitated in their own way, at least one extremity swelling until it looked like it might pop. This had to be painful, but they didn't seem to notice.

My family didn't fare any better. An odd, purplish growth crept up Charlotte and Alison's arms. Burke frantically attempted to wipe something off his skin in between casting, and I knew that someone on the Weatherford side was channeling his worst nightmare, a spider infestation. Dillon kept collapsing to the ground, his limbs sporadically giving way to a cast that seized his ability to control them. My parents became stricken with some sort of stomach ailment, both of them doubling over in pain, their necks stretching upward so that they could continue to cast.

I couldn't believe what I was seeing. Here were people I knew from birth and I didn't recognize them at all. Their heads shook with each word. Spit flew from their mouths. They shouted words like "rot" and "despair" and "disease."

I thought they had lost their minds, until I remembered what all this was about…To protect me from Jocelyn. Here I am trying to keep her from danger against The Sevens, and it's my family trying to hurt her!

They didn't understand. They hadn't realized that she has NO CHOICE! They don't know the pressure she is feeling to know that she has to kill me. They're blaming her and it's not even her fault. She has to kill me. Or else everything we've done – everything we've become – will all be for nothing. The Sevens will win and the world will be a wasteland, a human playground for them. She doesn't want that, and she doesn't want to kill someone she loves. But if she doesn't millions of people will die. There is no other alternative for her. They should be SYMPATHIZING with her.

I was sick and found myself shaking from an uncontrolled surge of emotions. I couldn't imagine what Jocelyn was going through…. I wanted to open my mouth and shout "STOP!" but that would draw the attention to me, and to Jocelyn who was behind me.

No, I decided, get her out of here first.

The only two in the room who appeared unaffected by this bizarre fight were Miss Mabelle and Miss Celia. As I passed by them, I saw their expressions, and they were, of all things, pleased.

It wasn't until Dillon produced a fireball – the same kind Sartorius had used to burn down half the village not so long ago – that everyone came to their senses. I saw it first, his intent gaze directed on the lantern illuminating the room. When the flame grew, and the room brightened, I shouted to him, my hands coming up in warning.

"Dillon, no! No!"

The rage in my voice stopped everyone in the room, as if a switch had been turned off. Their voices settled, hesitant and slow, as reason returned to them.

Jocelyn and I were at the doorway by then, just as they began to blink, to clear away the disturbing feeling of launching unwarranted attacks on people who minutes ago they considered their friends.

The room became silent, still, each observing the opposite side with distrust. They only seemed to be shaken from their stupor when Jocelyn made a declaration. It was unyielding and calm, and seemed delayed after all that had just taken place.

"I won't do it. I can't. I will die at the hands of The Sevens before I end Jameson's life."

And that statement brought on a wave of consideration that had been thrown to the side in favor of violence. I could see the understanding creep across their faces, the disturbed realization that they weren't the ones who had the most to lose.

Jocelyn is in a much more challenging position over her future than the rest of them. She has to face the horror that it must be her hand to take the life of someone she loves because if she doesn't tens of thousands, possibly millions, of people will die. And she has to do it alone.

Still, resentment was still alive in Estelle. Her glare said it all. But she did the right thing, as hard as it was for her. "Incantatio dimittam," she muttered.

Instantly, Charlotte's mouth began to dry. She was still bent in the corner, almost cowering in embarrassment in a way I'd never seen her act before, allowing her drool to spill freely now. She had given up trying to contain it.

Despite the drying of her mouth, the front of her shirt remained drenched, a good reminder of just how potent the Weatherford casts can be.

Estelle began it but the rest followed suit, rescinding their casts one by one until all cuts, bruises, sores, and incapacities were removed. They then stood staring awkward, and still skeptical, at each other.

In the quiet, an unfazed Miss Celia, started for the door. "Well, best get ya to ya new livin' quarters."

She said this in a manner that made me think she was checking something off a to-do list, without any reference to what had just occurred in the room.

When no one followed, she looked over her shoulder at us and demanded, "Ya comin'?"

The Weatherfords were the first to respond, which meant my family remained behind. Miss Celia and Miss Mabelle took turns taking small, obscure, undetectable groups to their new covert hiding places, with greater security than what the open and exposed bayou could offer. Isabella, however, didn't shift from her position in the corner near the door, keeping a close eye on my family as they filtered out, as Kalisha stood reserved a few inches away.

Steadily, the number of those of us in the room declined. Most of my family left without incident. The exceptions were my mother and Charlotte. On her way out the door, my mother stopped at Jocelyn and, in her subtle way, warned her against taking action.

"I can see how hard it is for you," she said, referring to the dark future between Jocelyn and me. "But there comes a time when you must think of others. If you love Jameson, you will let him go."

"She already has," I informed her. "It's me who's sticking around. So you can stop blaming her. She has no say in the matter."

She gave me a concentrated stare, one I'd seen before. She was telling me that she disagreed with me staying.

"There also comes a time," I said, using her words to drive home my point, "when you need to trust in your son's decisions. You've trained me for this, mother. All those years of midnight lessons, this is what that was all about. It all was leading to this point. You need to trust me now. Let me live my life," I said as a reminder, "because, whether you like it or not, Jocelyn is the path I've chosen."

Although she obviously disagreed, she didn't counter it. Knowing there was no hope of convincing me, and that I had made up my mind, she hesitated, still holding on to hope that my mind could be changed, and then gave me a light kiss on the cheek before leaving.

Charlotte and Alison were the only ones remaining of my family. Their continual glances in Jocelyn's direction didn't leave me any more relieved though. I'd seen those expressions in the past, right before a cast was made to destroy the romance between our classmates or to give someone the flu that left them out of school for weeks. I gave them each a barely discernible shake of my head, warning them against whatever it was they might be planning in the dark recesses of their minds.

As if Charlotte had been waiting for the right moment, when Miss Mabelle returned and called out to them from her boat, her mischievous smile surfaced. And on her way out the door I knew why, as she uttered a phrase in French. "Votre contact sera aussi venimeux à vous comme une veuve noire." It sounded oddly familiar, like something Miss Celia would say in her native language, but the direct translation of it made no sense to anyone else in the room, it seemed.

Charlotte and Alison left with firmly planted glares on Jocelyn, unaltered, even as they made their way out the door.

"Your touch will be as venomous to you as a black widow? That's what they said, isn't it?"

"Yes," I said, apprehensive. "That's correct. I've...that's not a cast I recognize. I think she picked it up from Miss Celia."

"Well, she had the last nine weeks to do it," Jocelyn joked, trying to lighten the mood.

I didn't feel like laughing, though.

Jocelyn, who always proves she has more courage than the rest of us, boldly reached out a finger toward her forearm, the one decorated with the jewelry embedded with her family stone.

"Careful," Jocelyn's mother and I cautioned her simultaneously. It was clear by Isabella's expression that she didn't underestimate Charlotte or the potency of her power any less than I did.

My jaw clamped shut and I began considering what action to take if Charlotte hurt Jocelyn. My thoughts grew more menacing as Jocelyn placed her finger on the top of her arm.

When it settled there, I held my breath, and then she pressed in, showing no affect. An echo of relieved sighs filled the room.

Isabella and Kalisha were taken soon after by Miss Celia, leaving Jocelyn and me entirely alone. The sounds of their departure faded into the night slowly, only to be replaced by the quiet resonance of the bayou. Water almost undetectably slapped the stilts on the planks below our feet, crickets carried a steady tune along the river's edge, and insects hummed throughout the trees, as Miss Celia's motor faded away.

"Jocelyn," I said.

"Jameson," she sighed, her breath intoxicating me.

Then, as a clear sign that neither of us could hold back any longer, I took her in my arms. Her body clung to me, my hands pressed her closer. I wanted her more than I'd ever wanted anything in my life. And then I found her pulling away, grunting, gripping her abdomen, and beginning to tremble.

"Jocelyn," I said just before she collapsed in my arm. "Jocelyn! What's wrong? What's wrong?"

She continued to moan, writhing, twisting, the pain visible in her expression.

"Jocelyn, talk to me," I said, trying to get her to look me in the eye. "Tell me what you're feeling."

"Stomach…pain," she grunted. "Weak…sh-shake…shaky."

"Use me," I urged. "Channel from me."

She loosened her grip on her shoulders, prying apart her solid white fingers to place them on my arm. The pain instantly worsened, and she screamed out.

There was only one thing left to do. I saw no other option.

"Can you heal yourself, Jocelyn? Sweetheart…can you heal yourself?"

She gave me a weak nod, which was the only indication she could muster.

Rolling back into a bending position, she clutched herself and concentrated. It took several minutes of writhing and moaning, but eventually her symptoms subsided.

Then it finally came to me what had just happened.

"Your touch will be as venomous to you as a black widow…," I muttered, recalling the words, my teeth automatically clenching against my growing rage.

"Wha…?"

"Charlotte."

"You mean the cast?"

I nodded, because I needed a second to douse my anger.

Jocelyn blinked, confused. "But we already tri…and you're touching me," she began to counter, and then her eyes widened with understanding. "If *I* touch anyone else," she moaned, "I will feel the venom of a black widow spider." Her head dropped and she stared at the floorboards. Then a quiet laugh shook her delicate shoulders. In it, I detected a sign of respect. "Clever…"

"She was smart enough to do it as she was leaving," I said, my temper flaring again despite my efforts. "She knew that would hurt you," I fumed, marching to the door to look outside, just in case the boat had broken down, just in case they might have returned for some reason, in case fate had somehow given me a chance to confront her and demand that she remove the curse. But the village was quiet, only the soft sound of Jocelyn's footsteps approaching me from behind broke the silence.

"She did it to protect you."

"She's going to remove that curse," I said in a low growl.

Because she couldn't touch me, Jocelyn moved around until she was standing in front of me. "She won't. We both know that. Don't dwell on it, Jameson. I want to appreciate the time we have together."

It took several long breaths and for Jocelyn to shift into my view for it to dispel but eventually my anger dissolved.

Still, I couldn't stop my tone from being despondent when I said, "I've been apart from you for weeks, and now that we're together, we can't touch."

Her eyes filled with sadness as she reached a hand up to my cheek, stopping before it got there. It hovered in midair before dropping to her side.

"I'll find a way," I vowed. "I will find a way, Jocelyn."

She nodded, hopelessly, and shifted her eyes past me, out the door and into the bayou.

The sound of the motorboat Miss Mabelle was using reached us, telling us that we'd be leaving for our new, secret residence.

Damn, I thought. I wanted just a few more minutes with her. Just a few more....

Jocelyn turned to me, oblivious of my need for her.

"So this is why Miss Mabelle and Miss Celia waited here all that time? Nine weeks on the platform? So that we could be led to safety?"

I nodded my confirmation, still trying to work through the need to be with her a little longer.

"Thank you, for coming for me and defending me."

"Jocelyn, I love you. I will always come for you and I'll always defend you."

She smiled softly at me. "Do you know I always feel safe around you?"

"You should. I'd give my life for you."

"And I would do the same," she said, her insinuation clear.

"I know that, and soon my family will too. They'll accept it, they'll need to."

She smiled teasingly. "Because I am the air you breathe?"

"Yes."

"And the force that causes your heart to beat? The incentive for the blood to flow through your veins?"

"Yes," I said, fighting the urge to pull her to me. "You are the reason I exist at all."

An intoxicating grin rose up behind her eyes, stirring me.

Damn you, Charlotte. Just wait until you fall in love.

A thump outside told me that Miss Mabelle had landed.

Jocelyn peered out the door but hesitated.

"You're different now," she said, turning back to me. "Something's changed you. Our time apart, the Ministry, I don't know, but you're...more unyielding."

She was right. I didn't see anything the way I had when we first met. Back then it was simple: make covert deliveries to the prisoners, be an admirable Officer to the village, study hard. Everything had changed. Sacrifices were greater and harder to make. It felt like Death its self was seeking us out. I was more driven...diligent...mindful than I had ever been before.

"Is this a good change? Did I change for the better?"

She considered this for a few seconds and then a subtle smirk crept up and with her provocative voice she whispered back to me, "It's an attractive change."

That simple, sincere response made me feel the best I had in weeks. I didn't think anything could improve on it, until I closed the door behind me. My hand lingered on the doorknob as it dawned on me that Charlotte's cast kept Jocelyn from touching others, but it didn't impose any restrictions on me.

"Come on, now," Miss Mabelle snapped. "Hurry it up. You roomin' tagetha'. If that don't make ya rush, I don't know what will...."

It did, because I had every intention of testing out my new theory tonight.

7. "BEDROOM"

Our new home was cramped, dimly lit, and reeked of mildew. Our hosts weren't all that inviting, and the atmosphere of the place was gloomy. But it appeared adequate enough to do its job, which was solely to keep Jocelyn safe.

Lucky for us, a fog rolled into New Orleans while we were in the air, giving us cover to land just outside the door of Mr. and Mrs. DeVille's store in the heart of the French Quarter.

It was a few hours past midnight but not everyone was asleep. Music from the clubs down on Bourbon Street was still pumping, and a light seeping through the small, dirty window next to the DeVille's door confirmed that our hosts were up.

They shouldn't have been. The place should have been empty, but it seemed that there had been a change of plans.

Miss Mabelle safely delivered us but she didn't wait any longer than was needed. I thanked her, Jocelyn gave her a hug, and she left, walking alertly through the overgrown foliage of the DeVille's courtyard and out the front gate.

We waited in silence and then the door opened. Mr. DeVille cautiously peered out. Recognizing us, he ushered us in and quickly closed the door, missing my heel by an inch in his hurry. It was clear he didn't want to risk being seen, and that was diligent of him. It's the kind of vigilance that kept you alive. He waved us on, guiding us down the narrow hallway and into their storeroom.

Mr. and Mrs. DeVille own a shop in the heart of the French Quarter, filled with various tools of sorcery that some in our world find important or appealing. The front room held a mismatch of statues, candles, gris-gris bags, and other miscellaneous objects placed where they were last left, in no particular order. The back room, which was off-limits to customers, was no different. It held stacks of outdated, dusty, leather-bound books, broken candle holders, and ceremonial furniture with either gutted cushions or broken legs.

Once inside, the dankness makes a person feel like they are in an underground cavern. My mother used to call her shopping trips here "field trips from reality". Unfortunately, we'd come full circle now, where the surreal had become the new reality.

Mrs. DeVille ambled around the corner, where her hunched figure suddenly stopped. At first, I thought it was because she expected an argument from me as to why she wasn't in hiding. But after a tip of her nose to stare over her glasses at me, she gave me a disapproving look from top to bottom. "Nice uniform," she muttered snidely, strolling past me to a ten-foot tall mirror bordered by sterling silver serpents.

I glanced down and realized that I still looked like a Vire.

"Be nice, Love," Mr. DeVille chastised, to which she responded with a look of disgust. "They've both been through a lot."

"While managing to drag us into it all along with them," she said as a glaring reminder before spinning around and dismissively sticking her butt in the air at us, as she began to dig for something in the pile of trash in the corner.

As I watched her there were several notions going through my head. First, her view of the situation was dangerously warped. Second, and more importantly, I wanted to tell her that it wasn't *us* doing the dragging. It was our *enemies*, who were also her enemies, whether she wanted to recognize it or not. Someday they would be the ones knocking on her door, busting it down, and they wouldn't be nearly as apologetic or as thankful as we are for her hospitality.

Bringing all this up wouldn't help any of us. Instead, I directed my comment to another point of contention. "You're supposed to be in hiding, Mrs. DeVille."

"Mmmhmm," she mumbled, deep in the boxes surrounding her head. "And we're not supposed to be harboring known felons. It isn't something I'm proud of, you know."

"Felons?" Jocelyn said.

Mr. DeVille frowned and started for the front room, throwing his hands in the air at the door, and abandoning whatever effort he was going to make. "I'll just tell you," he grumbled. "They're sending out declarations, saying you are the reason behind people disappearing, that you're leading a Vire contingent around to kill or apprehend those who agreed to join you."

"Jameson?" Jocelyn said, offended. While I didn't need it, I appreciated her support. But none of this took me by surprise. I had been counting on it. The counter-propaganda lessons my mother had forced on me at age twelve, while Dillon and Burke were outside playing, were beginning to come in handy.

"So they're trying to make the Dissidents fear me," I assessed. "Does anyone believe it?"

"Some, not many. But every time they find some kind of possession of yours at the site of another abduction, your credibility-"

"Starts to stink," Mrs. DeVille's muffled voice broke in.

"You know whatever was left behind was planted there, don't you?" After our houses were raided?" I ventured.

"We do," he said in a way that told me not everyone else did.

I nodded, deciding I needed time to contemplate this information. Nothing could be done about it now, anyways.

"So we're taking a big risk trying to help you two out," Mrs. DeVille added in a surly tone.

"How is the rest of your coven?" I asked, changing the subject.

"Miserable," she retorted.

"Are they safe?" I was insinuating, without having to point it out, that I had helped secure their secret homes too.

Her slight pause made me realize she'd picked up on my message. "Yes."

"Good," I replied.

"Mr. DeVille," Jocelyn interceded. "Why is it you and Mrs. DeVille aren't hiding like the rest of us?"

Mr. DeVille opened his mouth to speak, but she beat him to it.

"Because we're smart," she snapped. "We left that 'secure location'," she said, stopping her dig long enough to raise her fingers and imply quotation marks. "We were on our way home before the rest of you Dissidents went and killed all those Vires in the swamp. But wouldn't have mattered if you hadn't. Killed 'em, didn't kill 'em. Fight, no fight. There was no way I was going to stay in that hovel."

Jocelyn and I glanced around her home noting they weren't all that different, but neither of us bothered pointing that out.

"So you weren't implicated," Jocelyn clarified.

"How could we be?" she demanded. "We weren't anywhere near that mess when it happened."

That won't make you innocent in the eyes of The Sevens, I thought. *It's only a matter of time before they come for you, too.*

My gut told me to voice that perspective, but I knew she wouldn't listen.

Jocelyn didn't seem to be finished with her questions yet, anyways. And I didn't blame her, either. She'd been out of the loop for nine weeks. "On the way here, we were told that everyone in hiding is strewn across the city, surviving in conditions similar to ours."

"Yes, well, lots of people are displaced right now. All will be back to normal soon. You'll see." Her hand came free, swinging upward, her fingers clutching a brown canvas bag. "Aha! Got it!" Planting her free hand against the wall, she attempted to stand, but the weight of her round torso caused her to shift off balance and lean awkwardly to the side. Seeing her heading for the ground, I ran to help, stopping her fall just before her hip hit the sharp corner of a throne chair. She frowned and brushed me aside, straightened her clothing, and then shoved the bag at me. "Here."

I took it, opened the bag, and made sure that its contents were just as I'd left them. It was odd to think that this one simple canvas bag, literally, held the keys to our defenses against The Sevens.

Without another word, her job here finished, Mrs. DeVille met her husband at the entrance to the hallway, and without a goodbye, they left for their residence in the back of the shop.

"Thank you," Jocelyn called out, receiving no answer in return. When she gave up waiting for it, she looked around aimlessly. "Umm, okay..."

I knew what she was thinking, but she was so intriguing to watch that I didn't break her concentration right away.

"Where...?" she muttered, and then giggled. "Okay...."

Completely amused, I strolled to the large snake mirror Mrs. DeVille had been digging next to and shoved it aside where it exposed a square carving in the wall.

I wedged open the parcel of wall and set it down inside as she came up behind me. Then I flicked a switch and a bare light bulb hanging from the ceiling made the room visible. "So, *this* is where we're sleeping," she stated, appraising it.

In war, luxuries weren't options for those in the trenches. I was hoping she'd be all right with it. And then, without hesitation, she slipped through the wall and sighed, "What an improvement over an underground jail...."

Good, I thought, and then realized my error. *She is so much stronger than I give her credit. Always...*

"Better than the Ministry?" she asked, half teasing.

And I laughed under my breath. "Far better."

The unpainted particle boards that made up the walls and ceiling gave us little space, just enough to stand, to walk three paces to the bed, and to fit a twin-sized mattress adjacent to the back wall.

"Estelle would have a fit if she saw it."

"And that's why Estelle is staying in a furnished room below the Fielding family's main staircase," I said while stepping inside, repositioning the mirror back into place, and securing the wall.

Then I faced the room and found her spinning slowly for a view of our new room. It was obvious she was evaluating the differences between a room beneath a staircase and one behind a wall. "This isn't much better, I know," I said, and she cut me off.

"It's perfect," she blurted, stopping to stare at me. "Perfect," she said again, softer.

When neither of us moved the tension in the room soared.

I hadn't felt her in so long, and I knew what was waiting for me. God, I wanted to hold her so badly.

Prove the theory, my mind shouted. *Reach out and touch her. You won't hurt her!*

But Jocelyn turned and sat on the bed, and I missed my chance. "It's odd that Mrs. DeVille argued with you about the need to hide. She was part of Ms. Veilleux's coven, she knows about the future, she even helped give me the scar that prompted this war into being. But I think…I think she truly believes we'll all be fine."

"Life-altering changes can be hard for some people." That sounded preachy, so I followed it with, "I think she's in denial."

"Hmm," Jocelyn mumbled, contemplating it. "Oh, uh, I think these are for us." She put a hand on the stack of folded clothes at the foot of the bed. "Compliments of our housekeepers," she added with a grin.

I crossed the small room to pick up the shirt.

"It'll be good to get out of these," I said, ripping the Vire shirt off my shoulders.

"Mmmmmhmmm," she mumbled, sounding a little distracted.

I unbuckled the black belt and yanked it off my waist before shoving the pants down to my ankles. Stepping out, I picked them up and threw the whole damn thing in a pile in the corner.

That was when I saw what was preoccupying Jocelyn and came to a stop.

Her eyes seemed to be locked on my chest, maybe a little lower, but when I went silent, they drifted back to my face.

"You're smirking," she pointed out.

"And you're fascinating."

"Not as fascinating as you."

"Oh," I laughed, "You're wrong about that."

Doubting me, she decided to test me on it. "How am I fascinating?"

"Jocelyn," I said, standing over her, staring down at her until our eyes met. "I don't know of a single person who has survived a Vire prison...except for you. I don't know of anyone with more influence over our world...than you. And no one captivates people the way you do when entering a room. No one is like you, Jocelyn. Not a single one."

Neither of us spoke a word, and the tension between us came back. Without inhibition, her eyes coursed over my body, taking it in.

My entire soul screamed at me, telling me to move toward her.

Do it now, you wuss! I actually heard that in my head. *Touch her! This is your chance!*

"So, what's in the bag?" she asked, and again the opportunity passed.

I grunted, angry at myself for letting it.

"What?" she asked, thinking I said something.

"Oh, nothing," I replied concentrating on picking up the canvas bag and carrying it to her. She took it, opened it, and assessed the contents.

"Keys?" she asked, confused.

"To the Thibodeaux warehouses."

Her eyes grew larger. "This was what The Sevens were torturing the Thibodeauxes for, wasn't it?"

"Yes," I said through gritted teeth. I hadn't let the feelings attached to that memory go yet. "Mr. Thibodeaux brought them to me before I left for the Ministry, and asked me to take them. Almost like he knew The Sevens would be coming after them."

She set the bag on the ground and watched me for a second. "You had all this planned, didn't you?"

"What do you mean?"

"The hiding places, our secret bedroom, everything." Without waiting for me to confirm, she added, "And you planned for the two of us to stay together, here, at the DeVille's."

Not sure how she'd take that, I braced myself for the confession. "Yes, I arranged for you to stay with me."

She nodded, slowly. Something was on her mind.

"Are you ready to try it again?" she asked, without warning.

"What?"

"Feeling me," she said, and stammered for a less openly sexual suggestion. "T-Touching me."

And it dawned on me that she had come to the same idea I had.

"Maybe it's me who can't do the touching," she suggested. "Maybe I can't start it or reciprocate it, but I can receive it."

"I wondered the same thing."

"Okay," she said, taking a deep breath, preparing herself. "Let's give it a shot."

It was incredibly bold of her. At the shack, I saw the pain in her face, wracking her body; and here she was ready to try it again.

"Are you nervous?" I asked in a low, hushed voice, trying to put any inhibitions she had about it at ease.

"No, I-I don't think it'll hurt."

A mixture of excitement and relief washed over me. And then the agony she suffered in the shack flashed through my mind.

Don't rush this, I told myself. *This has to be precise.*

Kneeling down in front of her, I positioned my hands over her thighs, hovering there for a second.

My breath became locked in my chest.

And then I settled my fingertips lightly over her dress.

And we waited.

A second passed.

Another second passed.

And then she smiled.

"Nothing," she said simply.

I let go of my breath, and we both laughed.

"Okay," I said, hesitant but hopeful. "Now for the real test…"

Picking myself up, I stayed bent, putting my hands on both sides of her, where her hips lightly brushed the outside of my thumbs. It was an innocent connection and still it stoked my craving.

Slowly, I reminded myself. *Slowly.*

With extreme patience, the kind I didn't know I had in me, I gradually closed the distance between us. And then, finally, my mouth met hers and I stayed there, waiting.

And then she let out a moan.

No!

Damn it!

I jerked away, my hands coming up, ready to hold her, knowing I couldn't.

I searched for her body and found her bent over in pain, her face filled with suffering.

But she was still. Her eyes were closed. Her fingers were curled, gripping the bed sheets, but that was the only sign of tension from her.

She opened her eyes and focused on me, and there was no pain in them, only yearning.

That was my sign.

I pressed my lips to hers again, drinking her in, letting myself satiate the need I had for her since I saw her on that stage. My eagerness pushed her back, onto the bed, and she went with it.

My lips never left hers, and when the bed stopped her movement, I lingered above her, close enough to feel our chests touch with each breath.

It felt like we had been pardoned…but only for a day.

Her lips were motionless, yielding too easily to me. Her arms lay limply at her sides.

I could touch her, taste her, feel her against me, but she couldn't respond. She couldn't release her own pent up craving. She was restricted to an immobile body.

A single word coursed through my mind as my lips fell away from her and I sucked in a frustrated sigh. "Damn it."

Whether Jocelyn picked up on my actions or overheard my thought, it wasn't clear, but she acknowledged it. "I want to, Jameson," she said with uninhibited yearning.

"I know," I said, my voice gruff with frustration. This wasn't fair to either of us, but mostly it was unjust toward her.

"Lay against the pillow for me, Jocelyn," I whispered.

She looked at me curiously and then shifted backwards until she was in line with the bed. And then my breathing stopped because I was seeing a side of her I hadn't before. The swell of her breasts, the fall of her dress between her legs - all of her - is what I dreamt about. And now she was here, giving herself completely to me.

If I took every moment of carnal tension I'd ever encountered in my life, every infatuated thought, every corporeal fantasy and put them together, this moment far surpassed it.

When my breathing started again it was ragged, and I felt completely in awe of her. "Jocelyn…you are the most beautiful woman in the world."

Her hand lifted, less than inch from the bed, moving toward me, but she caught herself and lowered it.

Yes, what I had in mind would be the only way. But she needed to understand something first.

"If I do anything that brings on pain, anywhere or to any degree whatsoever, you need to tell me. And if I think at any point in time that I'm beginning to cause you pain, I'm going to stop."

She nodded, watching me, wondering what I was doing.

And then I settled next to her and laid my hand on her stomach, where the excited beating of her heart made it through the fabric to my hand.

"Is this all right?" I asked her, gauging what she might be feeling.

She smiled contentedly. "It's perfect," she said, her voice coming through my head.

"Close your eyes."

She did, and I watched her for a second, amazed that I was lucky enough to be here with her.

"Tonight, Jocelyn, is entirely about you."

I lifted my palm until only my fingertips were left in contact with her. Taking all the time needed, filling in for the time we lost, I languidly drifted the tips of my fingers to the soft curve of her neck, where I trailed them along the outline of her chin as gently as I could.

And she quivered.

Satisfied, I carried them to her lips where I traced their teasing contours, noticing that her warm breath was beginning to come faster now. My fingers drew an unhurried path from there, down her arms, to her thighs, where she trembled.

I'm not sure how long this took, my journey across her body. Time seemed like a distant concern to me. I only noticed the staggered rise and fall of her chest, the tilt of her lips upward in a preoccupied smile, the wistful sighs released when I touched her in places I'd never been before.

And when her body arched up, and she released a moan, relieving all that had been building in her, she forgot restraint, and she responded to me.

Her moan, filled with so much pleasure, with such satisfying liberation, turned to torment, and she curled into a ball burrowing her face into my side.

I cradled her head in my arms, doing my best to comfort her, until it passed. When, finally, she lifted her head and I saw the exhaustion in her eyes.

"Sleep, Jocelyn."

I could see her fighting it, but her eyes were already beginning to shut.

"Sleep…"

Within seconds, she found the peace she needed. And then, when I was sure she wouldn't wake up, I followed my own advice.

The next thing I knew the DeVille's were under attack.

8. SISERA

The breaking of glass followed by someone's brisk command to "drop to your knees" woke me, and I was out of bed before I heard Mrs. DeVille's ensuing panic-driven voice shouting, "Don't hurt him."

I'd known Mrs. DeVille my entire life. I'd watched her drive children to tears and adults to their breaking point. She cowered to no one...unless they wore a Vire uniform.

I was at the makeshift door by the time the sound of breaking glass reached me.

"Resist," said someone with authority, "and you'll face the full penalty for your actions."

In the words of Vire language, this translated to: death.

In the seconds it took for me to put the cut-out of the wall on the ground, she was already countering with a whimper. "We aren't resisting."

By the time I was leaning out the cut-out, I felt something sweep along my shoulder, diverting my attention.

It was Jocelyn. She was holding out the Vire uniform.

Good idea. Might be of use.

I dressed as quietly as possible and then motioned for her to stay here.

It was almost incomprehensible to me, but she listened and agreed.

Good, I thought, *just hope she stays that way.*

I could focus now on the DeVilles, who were clearly about to see their necks slit.

"Please don't hurt us," Mr. DeVille was saying as I pulled the mirror aside, cautiously so that it wouldn't draw their attention.

I determined by the distance of their voices that they were coming from the next room, the front of the store, but I was still gambling that no other Vires were clearing out the other rooms.

A deep voice with a hint of an Indian accent broke in and what he said wasn't comforting. "You have aided and abetted felons."

Have aided and abetted…in other words, in the past.

They don't know we are here.

"Were you involved, Mrs. DeVille, in the attack on our Vires in the Louisiana bayou?"

"No!" she quibbled. "We weren't! We honestly weren't!"

Following a pause, the Indian said simply, "I do not believe you."

Mr. and Mrs. DeVille exhaled anxiously, loud enough for me to hear.

"We will take all actions necessary to prevent it from reoccurring."

"Please-" Mr. DeVille pleaded.

"However," said the Indian, cutting him off, "leniency for your actions will be considered if you give us information on the whereabouts of Jameson Caldwell and Jocelyn Weatherford."

The mirror was now out of the way and I had a full view of the room. There were no Vires in here, but through the door, directly on the opposite side, were the backs of two men dressed in the same ridiculous uniforms that were now so familiar to me.

I left the bedroom and slid the mirror back into place, keeping Jocelyn safe as best I could.

Safe, I thought, *we should have left the second I knew the DeVilles hadn't gone into hiding.* They should have, should have been on a riverboat. Only Jocelyn and I were supposed to be here right now, and the place was meant to appear vacant. But no, Mrs. DeVille had a stubborn streak, and it was about to get her and her husband killed.

I had no weapon, and the junk collected in the backroom didn't offer anything that wouldn't break on me with the first strike. I'd have to go in without. That was virtually suicide, but I didn't have much choice.

The Indian was waiting on the DeVilles to answer as I entered the room, hoping my Vire uniform would buy me enough time to assess the situation.

I stepped up beside the two Vires in the doorway and took a sweeping glance at those present in the front of the store.

There were about thirty Vires in all and the DeVilles shoved inside this small shop. But no one in the room drew as much interest from me as the one with the turban on his head. He stood, stately, with a moldavite-encrusted robe, hands properly crossed in front of him.

Sisera. One of The Sevens, who was noticeably out of his territory of control.

I didn't wait to find out why, because Sisera's voice had ceased and he was staring across the room at me with a peculiar expression.

I struck the first Vire in the knee and he collapsed.

The Vire beside him turned, but not fast enough. I took out his knee just as efficiently. The two of them squirmed on the ground, clutching their legs, as the next Vire came at me.

He was a big boy with a torso the size of a dump truck, but he went down pretty swiftly when I swept his legs and crushed his windpipe with the edge of my palm.

By then, my presence was known and whoever had the ability to levitate used it before I could take out another one of them. I was slammed against the wall, where something round protruded into my back. Vaguely, I remembered a framed picture being mounted there, but the sight of Jocelyn in the doorway ended all rational thought.

Instantly, she saw me, and I fought the damn Vire whose restraint kept me against the wall. She ran, fast - in my direction - only to be jerked backwards. And that was when I saw the Vire holding her from behind.

I'd never seen a lamb being led to the slaughter but this was what I knew it would look like as she stopped in the doorway.

"NO!" I shouted. "Let her go, Sisera. This isn't your province," I proclaimed.

Sisera strolled leisurely across the room until he was standing directly in front of me. "I'd tell you to bow, Jameson Caldwell, but I am fairly certain you cannot follow my command."

I wouldn't bow anyways.

"Sartorius won't appreciate you overstepping your bounds, Sisera," I said in another appeal to his intellect. My statement was true, and it was the only logical argument I could make.

"Not that it is any of your concern. You will be dead soon enough. But for the rest of you," he called over his shoulder, addressing the Vires accompanying him, "Sartorius no longer controls this province. After the debacle of your escape, his authority has been revoked. I control the province now." Sisera ambled to Jocelyn with a speculative stare fixed on her. "You two have caused enough turmoil. It will end here. Unceremoniously." He tipped his head toward the Vire holding her, a casual, indifferent gesture, as if we were nothing, less than nothing.

"Sartorius is setting you up," I called out. "Kill Jocelyn or myself, and you'll never find out how."

I was wrong. I did have another angle to work.

Sisera came to an abrupt stop, his translucent pasty skin turning whiter, his dark eyes locked on the floor as he considered my warning. It was enough of a sign that the Vire holding Jocelyn didn't follow through with Sisera's first command, and that was what I'd been counting on.

Sisera spun on his heel, his head lifting in interest, as he approached me again.

"Convince me that you speak the truth and I'll consider delaying your death."

The irony was, in that instant, when I was only trying to conjure up enough evidence to preserve Jocelyn's life, the truth actually came to me. I had known Sartorius was setting up the rest of The Sevens, but I hadn't figured out how he would do it, not until now.

With my response formulated in my mind, I opened my mouth to deliver it when I saw the movement. It came from behind Jocelyn. No, from behind the Vire holding Jocelyn, from down the long hallway that led back to the door that we'd come in through last night. They struck with damn good precision, taking out the one holding Jocelyn and yanking her back out of the room before she could fall into the mess they were about to create.

I thought there might be an army coming down that hallway, but I was wrong. Only two entered, and that wasn't enough.

They were going to need me.

I put my hands against the wall, trying to pry myself from it, as the two of them made their way through the room, dropping one Vire after another. They worked in tandem, their swords swinging with impressive accuracy, so that the last Vire fell only a few seconds after they started. He must have been the one holding me back, because when his heart was punctured, I slid down the wall and slammed into the counter below.

The DeVilles sprinted by me, in a frenzy to get to safety.

Launching myself onto my feet, I ran for Jocelyn, who I found plowing through the junk the DeVilles had collected in the backroom.

"Jocelyn," I called out, marching for her.

She paused long enough to recognize that I was in the same room as her. She spun around and we collided in the middle, only for her to crumble to her knees, clutching her stomach, as she had done in the shack and in bed.

"It-it'll...pass...," she fought to say.

I held her, keeping my eyes on the entrance to the other room. Voices were muffled, but they seemed calm. Maybe Sisera was dead by now?

When she took in a breath and began to stand, I knew she was stronger, healthier again.

"Did they hurt you?" I asked, adding for clarification, "The Vires?"

"No," she said with a shake of her head before gesturing me back to the stack of junk. "Come on. We need something to fight with...."

"So that's what you were doing."

She nodded and continued on.

"Jocelyn, there's nothing here that will help us." I glanced at the door. "Besides, I think the fight's over."

She froze, listening, and then straightened up. I could tell there was no way she planned to walk into that room doubled over in pain, even if it still lingered. She was far too proud. Sure enough, she went for the door, and I had to slip around her to make sure I went in first.

Sisera wasn't dead.

He stood where he had been; the two people who had taken down his entourage, swiftly and without injury, stood in front of him, their backs to us.

He seemed to be defiant, but – this shocked me more than anything else, more than anything I'd experienced in my life – Sisera was scared.

Sevens feared no one; they acted immune to it, as if they knew something that the rest of us didn't. But his eyebrows were creased and beads of sweat were saturating the turban at the top of his forehead.

"Do you have any last words?" his attacker asked. This was another surprise, because I recognized his voice. It was English, or at least I'd always assumed it to be.

Even while staring into the face of death, Sisera would not submit. "I do, Eran Talor," he said tauntingly and then grinned. "Incantatio-"

At the very same time Sisera began his cast, Jocelyn spoke up. "Eran?"

As Eran turned, the person beside him, the one who fought next to him, dressed in black leather with cut outs in the back between the shoulder blades and wild brown hair, stuck a sword through Sisera's heart, ending his cast.

And there it was...the death of the very first Seven. It was impossible, unbelievable, surreal. Shockingly, we were the only ones to witness it, this death that would go down in our history books as the day the first one fell. Still, all I could think was...*Damn, I'd like to have been the one.*

And then the person who took the life of Sisera - a Seven, an untouchable, someone who seemed to be impervious to death - turned around, and I found that the one who had done this was our high school clairvoyant...Maggie Tanner.

Eran didn't seem to notice Jocelyn or me marveling at what had just taken place. He made sure Sisera was dead, which from my account a few feet away, the rapidly decomposing body he'd left behind looked to be, and then strolled back to us.

"We keep showing up in the same places, don't we?" Eran remarked casually, his accent only slightly thicker from the exhilaration of the fight.

"Yes, we do," I said, still trying to wrap my head around what was happening.

"We were tracking him."

"Tracking?"

By that point, Maggie had joined us; after wiping the blade off on Sisera's body like a Viking warrior, she sheathed it and came to stand by Eran, smiling as if condemning a Seven to death was a daily occurrence.

"Nicely done." He leaned sideways to whisper this into Maggie's ear, as if they were the only two in the room.

"Thank you," she murmured, gazing up at him, and then turned back to Jocelyn and me. "After we split up at Lacinda's, Eran and I went back to the Ministry, found this one leaving, followed him here, and…well, you see the result."

I laughed, unintentionally. This was all just so damn surreal. And then something came to me, in a flash, like it had been sitting at the back of my mind waiting for this moment to come forward. "So you are the allies," I said more to myself than to them.

"Allies?" Eran remarked, and then appeared to seriously consider it. "Yes, we could be."

"I think they are," Jocelyn mumbled. "Maggie was the ally The Sevens said they had captured when they coerced us into that truce. They said they didn't need a truce because they already had what they needed."

Maggie frowned at the memory, and I was left with the sense that her ego had been damaged for being caught.

"They offered up a truce?" Eran asked, doubtfully.

"A false truce. It was used to manipulate us."

"Of course…," he muttered, and, once again, I got the impression that he knew The Sevens better than most did in our world.

"And," Jocelyn went on, "when we were locked away together, Maggie, you told me that your crime for being there was knowledge…how to kill The Sevens."

"That's right."

"We might have just figured out a part of the prophecy." I grinned at Jocelyn, and she beamed back at me. It was a small victory, but a good one. A damn good one.

Maggie broke in on our silent victory celebration with, "What prophecy?"

Right, I thought. *Of course they wouldn't know yet.*

I wasn't sure how they'd accept the news, but what could it hurt by telling them? I'd just seen Maggie take a Seven's life. Everything else seemed to pale in comparison. "There are records that prophesize about what is coming…in our war against The Sevens."

Oddly, this didn't seem to faze them. Something else did, however, which Eran addressed. "So, you've known about them, the Sevens, for how long?"

"For centuries," I said, interposing.

"And it never occurred to any of you how unusual it was for them to live that long?"

I couldn't stop a smirk from coming up. "Longevity isn't something we lift an eyebrow at in our world."

"So," said Maggie, frowning. "They thought they could dominate your culture, your world, as you call it, while preparing for complete domination over the rest of us."

"That's right," said Jocelyn astounded that Eran had come to that conclusion. "How did you know?"

"Because that's what their kind does."

Hearing this, Jocelyn settled back on her heels, and paid close attention. "How much do you know about The Sevens?"

"Enough," said Eran.

But that wasn't sufficient for Maggie, who grinned slyly. "We know how to kill them."

"Apparently...," I said and tipped my head at Sisera's now badly decomposed body. It was almost as if it was making up for lost time.

"What do you think we should do with it?"

"Well, you're not going to leave it here," said Mrs. DeVille from behind me.

I looked over my shoulder at her. "Nice to see you back, Mrs. DeVille."

I was referring to her physical person as well as her attitude, and she knew it.

Giving me a look of disdain, she turned to leave the room.

"Mrs. DeVille?"

Pausing, she stopped to glare back at me.

"Thank you for not turning us in."

Her mouth turned down further in blatant displeasure over being involved at all. She grabbed her husband and they began to straighten her naturally disorganized store. Neither of them had any idea that they would need to leave soon because they were in more danger now than they'd ever been. So I made a mental note to ask Mrs. DeVille to send a message to Miss Mabelle and Miss Celia about what happened here, so that they could be the lucky ones to explain how staying in the store where Sisera was killed wouldn't bode well for the DeVilles.

Part of me wanted to leave Sisera's body where it lay, as a sign to the rest of The Sevens that he wasn't worth the effort. But something greater needed to be done with it, something that would get the provinces talking about justice again.

We silently assessed our options on what to do with it, but there was only one way I could envision that would actually benefit us.

"Fear is how The Sevens drive us, our society, our world. Showing the provinces that they are vulnerable would give the people genuine proof that they can be defeated."

"So what do you want to do?" Eran asked. "Prop him up in a public place?"

I couldn't decide whether he was joking or not, but he wasn't smiling.

"No, I'd say we drop him where we can be sure he'll be found by The Sevens."

Jocelyn was the first to nod, but Eran and Maggie were close behind.

"The Ministry," we said together, breaking into grins.

As Eran and Maggie bent down to pick up the body, I realized that I'd never thought of them as anything more than classmates who get more than their fair share of gossip. They probably thought the same about us. Now, we were embarking on a war together, against a mutual enemy, and we all had equal stakes in the effort.

"What do you think we should do after we leave Sisera's body at the Ministry?" Jocelyn asked openly to everyone, but it was Maggie who responded.

As she carefully picked up Sisera's now spongy, decomposed shoulder, she laughed under her breath. "We go after the rest."

9. THE PLAN

It was still dark outside when we transported Sisera's body from the DeVille's store. After deciding there was no logic in all four of us carrying it to the Ministry, I stopped Maggie and Eran from trying to lift it from the floor. It didn't look like the thing would make it intact, anyways. Instead, we discussed meeting at noon in the bayou. I gave Eran and Maggie directions to the village and they headed down the hallway discussing whether to stop at Café Du Monde for a bite to eat, casually unaffected by the grim situation we faced.

Jocelyn changed into the clothes Miss Mabelle brought her, black and form-fitting that accentuated her curves. I didn't know whether to thank Miss Mabelle next time I saw her or make it clear that I couldn't be distracted by Jocelyn again. I kept the Vire uniform, thinking it might come of some use again. That was the only time we wasted.

We reached France before sunrise, with Jocelyn levitating the body next to us the entire way. The flight was short, ending with us hovering over the Ministry.

It looked different now. Usually, nights were spent with the grounds dark and a number of sentries on the walls. It was guarded tonight too, but there was activity. Lots of it.

Lights - generated by both flame and electricity - marked the most used paths. Along them, Vires walked with purpose, with objectives in mind, levitating supply crates into the courtyard.

"What are they doing?" Jocelyn whispered, in awe of the process.

"It's called staging. They're preparing for an attack."

"On?"

"Us." I felt myself frowning and corrected it, because we had the upper hand. "Right now, they think they have it all planned out. They see the future and it's in their favor. Everything is executing perfectly for them, in their tightly controlled world. But we're about to throw a wrench in their machine down there that'll send everyone into panic mode."

"Jameson?"

"Yeah?"

"You're smirking."

I laughed, and it actually felt good.

"Are we ready?" Jocelyn asked.

"More than we've ever been."

Jocelyn released Sisera's body, where it began a rapid plummet. But before it had reached ten feet below us, my head was thrown back and my body arched in a way that made me feel like I was tied to a rocket. And what a hell of a launch! The wind howled in my ears and the Vire uniform I still wore sucked to my chest, flapping like crazy behind me. Jocelyn had never levitated me like that before, and in it I felt the rush of her power. It was…exhilarating, intense, and sexy…an enticing, teasing kind of sexy.

It was also smart because within seconds I looked over my shoulder to find Vires coming after us, their bodies pointed like missiles in our direction.

The excitement I felt for Jocelyn was redirected, and turned darker. I had a strong urge, a fixation to take them on. One by one or all at once, didn't matter to me. This was my first chance outside the Ministry to avenge us, all of us, for what they had been helping The Sevens do to us for years, and I could feel the need for the settling of scores surging in me. Only one factor held me back. Jocelyn would have to be present to keep me aloft, and that endangered her.

Instead, I shoved aside my feelings and told her, "Company came."

She nodded as an expression of determination began to etch across her features, again, an incredibly enticing look for her. "Hold on," she said but didn't elaborate.

Then she dropped us, descending so fast I barely had time to take in the horizon. It was lit, but dimly, and there was something protruding from the earth, a slim, sweeping structure built of open trusses.

The Eiffel Tower. We're in Paris, I realized.

She set us down on a side street in a shopping district somewhere within the city. Store windows were lit, showing off clothes and jewelry, but there was no sign of anyone in the darkened shops beyond their displays. The drone of traffic carried to us, but I saw no cars anywhere. A street sweeper hummed by us, sipping coffee from his driver's seat, oblivious to what was about to happen.

In short, we were alone.

Jocelyn exhaled nervously, frantically scanning our surroundings. "There's no one around." She stopped suddenly and looked at me. "We shouldn't have landed."

As if on cue, the contingent of Vires, ten in all, fell to the ground, their landing on the pavement hard enough to vibrate our feet. And my excitement at the prospect of a fight returned.

"Thought you'd hide in the crowd?" the first one mocked, taking a step toward us. "You'll need another fifteen minutes, but you won't last that long."

"You're right," I said. "We'll be out of here in five."

To add a little gravy, I grinned at him. He didn't like that very much, and launched a fist at me. I ducked. Another one followed. I shifted and it skirted me. At that point, I felt like the odds were unfairly stacked against them. Even when they used the elements against me or tried to break into my thoughts with high-pitched chatter to distract me, they failed. When the end came, and I spun around to find Vire bodies littering the street, I actually felt sorry for them.

"Jameson, sweetheart," Jocelyn called out, her voice shaky from the adrenaline I knew was coursing through her.

I swung around to face her and saw the tilt of her head toward a man in a business suit holding a briefcase up in a way that made me think he was trying to block something. His jaw was slack, too, so I was fairly certain he'd just seen too much of what had just happened.

There was really no way around it now. He saw what he saw. It was good for him that no Vires were left with fully functioning capacities or he'd be gone by now, abducted to the Ministry where he'd be murdered to prevent knowledge of our world from being exposed. That, I'm fairly certain, happens more often than most people think.

He was still standing there as I walked by him on my way to Jocelyn, looking like he was trying to appraise the situation and wrap his mind around how a single guy could take out ten men without injury.

I slipped my hand into Jocelyn's, and informed him, "You'll want to leave now. More of them will be coming."

He nodded silently, jaw still dropped, but at least his feet started to move.

Jocelyn and I waited until his back was turned before she lifted us into the air, which made me grin. If he were to look back, he'd really have something to gawk about.

We drifted over New Orleans, where a dense fog blanketed the city, giving everything in sight a grey tint and a shiny coating. The delivery trucks were just now rolling into the French Quarter, newspaper stands were opening their metal doors, and hazy lights lit up cafes and coffee shops ready for the morning rush.

"Beignets sound good, don't they?" she asked, wistfully.

"I'm sorry, Jocelyn, we can't risk it," I said, my heart breaking at having to tell her no.

She nodded, knowing it would be reckless. In fact, it would be suicidal.

But they did sound good. Damn good.

As a substitute, I thought something else might satisfy her need for normalcy.

"Head toward the Garden District," I said, and she gave me a curious stare until I told her which street. Then she understood.

We stopped first at her house. It was still standing, so Miss Mabelle was doing a valiant job of keeping that up. Their cars packed the driveways, like the Weatherfords would walk out the front door at any point in time with their key in hand. The yards were groomed, no mail collected on the porch. In general, it looked like nothing had changed.

I glanced up to study her reaction and found her smiling. Unable to stop myself, I reached out and touched her cheek, with my thumb settling at the edge of her lips. She had a seductive way about her, even when she was so innocently baring her soul.

"Someday, I'm going to pick you up from that house," I said, pointing down at it, "and take you out on a real date."

Her smile widened. "You better."

"Oh, I will."

When we stopped at my house, it looked the same...still standing, cars jammed into the narrow driveway. Alison had pulled in behind everyone else, blocking the exit, even though Burke would harangue her for it, like he'd done so many times before. And then it was my turn to smile, because I realized that it's the little things that make a moment poignant.

We left, carrying with us a sentimental longing for what we had been forced to leave behind. I could guarantee we were both thinking about classes, and homework, fights over whose turn it is to use the bathroom. What had seemed like hassles before were now welcome signs of everyday life.

The village only perpetuated that feeling of despondency over a life left behind and the mass exodus cast a lasting impression that could be felt through the silence. The shacks stood uninhabited, ropes for tying the boats hung dejected off the docks, some having slid from their loops and left submerged in the murky water. The fog had settled here too, and it hovered undisturbed, unaltered by movement.

When we landed at the first shack we came to, neither of us broke the silence for the first few minutes. And then I stepped up and took Jocelyn's hand, just as she remarked, "I used to feel at home here." Her voice was hollow in the vastness of the bayou.

"I was thinking that, too."

The life of the village was gone now, carried away with the last of the dissidents. The truth was it felt like a graveyard, empty, holding nothing more than the imprint of those who had lived there.

I shifted my feet, listening for the creak of the dock as it echoed across the water. "Before the mass exodus, before the village was built out, when it was just 'the village', a Vire prison, I came here on my own to listen to the families. And there was always something, something to tell me that regardless of all that The Sevens took from them, they still lived. Whether it was in the music they played or in their teasing or in a heated debate, there was always life here. The Sevens tried to make this place miserable, but it overcame."

"The prisoners are free now," Jocelyn said, trying to comfort me.

"They will be. Soon."

"And permanently." That voice came out of nowhere and I wasn't prepared for the location of it, which was right behind us.

By the speed of my turn, Eran picked up on it. "Weren't expecting us so soon, were you?"

"I was expecting to hear you approach. Where's your boat?" I asked, because it was noticeably absent.

He brushed off my question and then walked to the edge of the dock. "We have other transportation options. So, this is the village?"

"It's…" Maggie paused, determining an appropriate description. "Quiet."

"It should be," Jocelyn said.

"No one lives here, not anymore," I added. "Nonetheless, we should get out of sight."

"Agreed," Eran said, approaching the shack next to us.

"Not that one," I informed him, just as Jocelyn made a motion to intervene.

Apparently, we had come to the same conclusion. They may be vacant, but they were still a home to some.

"This way," Jocelyn instructed, already walking the plank which lay between the docks.

Seeing their eyebrows raised in confusion, I offered an explanation. "My parents' shack is the undesignated location for all meetings. It's not far."

"Your parents lived here, too?" Eran asked, surprised.

"A lot of people lived here."

He nodded, and then he and Maggie paid close attention to the shacks we passed as we made our way across the village.

"What's with the purple curtains?" Maggie asked after we stopped.

Jocelyn snickered and explained, "My cousin has a flare for fashion."

Maggie nodded thoughtfully for a few seconds before saying, "You guys really made this a home, didn't you?"

I was about to respond, but then I opened the door and the bodies inside made me freeze in place.

When Eran saw me step into a fighting stance, he reacted swiftly, stepping through the door and into the one-room dwelling, vigilant about what he might find. But then I held out my arm and blocked his chest, and he knew to relax.

We faced a roomful of silhouettes in the hazy light streaming through the purple curtains Maggie had just mentioned. It was of some relief that I recognized them but I remained on alert, because the last time we were all in the same room together none of us left truly unscathed.

Isabella came forward first, just as Jocelyn passed by me. She caught her daughter by the shoulders and held her back for inspection, and from that I knew she'd heard what had happened.

"So you know?" I asked and Isabella nodded, focusing entirely on her daughter.

"Know?" Burke chuckled. "Little brother, our whole world knows." He said this as he came forward, leading the rest of our families.

They gave us quiet congratulations, patting Jocelyn and me on the back and grinning. Only then was my tension minimized about both families being here. So long as they weren't focused on each other, I judged us to be in good shape. In fact, the only contention felt was between me and Charlotte, who wisely kept her distance.

Miss Mabelle and Miss Celia held off their congratulations, taking a seat on stools closer to the door, making me think they believed this wasn't even half over. And they were correct. We had six more of the seven to go.

"If anyone hasn't learned of it," Isabella stated, releasing Jocelyn's arms so that she could fold her own across her chest, "they will soon enough."

She then tipped her head at Maggie and Eran. "Who are they?"

I introduced them, although everyone but the adults already knew them from school. The fact we knew them made our parents curious, but they didn't get the chance to inquire further.

Spencer, who was a bit darker than the rest of the Weatherford siblings, seemed more interested in Sisera's demise and didn't give them the chance. "They say, if it hadn't been for his robe, and the number of moldavite stones embedded in it, Sisera would have been unrecognizable. I have to ask…exactly what did you do to him?"

"Dropped him," replied Jocelyn, bluntly. "Although, he was decomposing by the time we did."

"Already?" he asked, his forehead creasing with skepticism. "He hasn't even been dead for what five? Seven hours?"

"Jocelyn told you…The Sevens aren't like us."

"Is that being disputed?" Eran asked, quietly alarmed.

"It's a little hard for them to swallow," I explained.

He didn't respond with anything more than a deliberate nod, which made it look like he was concerned for their wellbeing if they didn't get onboard with the concept quickly.

I then recounted how Sisera's life was ended. They listened intently, occasionally glancing at Eran and Maggie, their interest in them morphing into respect and revelation. The parents in the room appeared upset, but it was directed at Jocelyn and me for returning to the Ministry at all.

I reasoned with their silent opposition by summing up our plan. "We needed to leave Sisera's body in a location that would allow us to send two messages - to The Sevens and to everyone else. We needed to tell them that The Sevens are not invincible, that they have reason to fear for their lives, and that we aren't waiting for them to come to us...we're going after them." Without waiting for their reaction, and to avoid anyone interested in opposing the idea, I continued without breaking my pace. "And, again, you can thank Eran and Maggie for it because I get the impression," I added with a quick glance in their direction, "that they know how to take care of the rest."

Several eyebrows rose at this assumption.

"We do," Eran confirmed and then grinned proudly at Maggie. "Love, would you like to take this one?"

"Absolutely." She took a second to stare into his eyes and then came back to us, launching into her assertions without any easing whatsoever. "There were others like The Sevens."

An almost unified inhale resonated throughout the room, which seemed to surprise her. To alleviate their tension, she went on to explain, "They got the same treatment as Sisera. We thought they were gone, eradicated, but when I sensed Sartorius in Jackson Square a few months ago we knew that wasn't exactly the case. Seven of them, your Sevens, have been in hiding in your world. But from the looks of their headquarters, the place you all call the Ministry, they're about ready to make their entrance. So we need to get to them before they can hurt anyone else. The challenge we're facing is-"

Nolan, a Weatherford known for a deficit of manners, broke in to finish her sentence. "That they can shift abilities between each of them whenever they want so they become indestructible as a whole."

He seemed overconfident about his interjection, yawning as if Maggie was wasting his time, at least until she responded, bluntly.

"That is a farce. They've made you all believe it for the same reason they've created their army of Vires, and hung innocent people in their Ministry courtyard, and established rules for you all to follow. Fear. It's a strong device when you're trying to control something naturally unruly, which would be humankind. So they have convinced you that they are more powerful than you. They aren't. They simply have unique defenses."

"So you are saying that they can't shift abilities between each of them, taking whichever one suits them best at the time?" my mother inquired, not skeptically but thoughtfully.

"No, they cannot," Eran stated.

"And how do you know this?"

"Because we hunt them," Maggie said, divulging their situation in a way that sent a shockwave through the audience.

"What?" Nolan countered in blatant disbelief. "You're just a girl at school who talks to the dead. And you're just her boyfriend who follows her around."

While Jocelyn seemed offended by this, it appeared she was the only one. Maggie and Eran showed no reaction aside from Eran flatly pointing out, "We're also the ones who killed Sisera."

That shut Nolan up.

"And that's the reason why we know how to kill the rest, permanently," Eran added.

"But first," Maggie continued, "as I was saying before...the challenge we face is that they don't all die the same. They each have their own special defenses. It is these defenses that made them look impervious, that they manipulated to look like they come from your world."

My mind drifted back to the few minutes before Jocelyn was abducted and taken to the Ministry, when I had slit Peregrine's throat. "Peregrine's skin regenerates."

"Good to know," Eran said with an appreciative nod.

"And Sartorius can manipulate fire," Maggie asserted. "Which tells me that he can't be burned."

Jocelyn's jaw dropped open on hearing Maggie's statement.

"Are you all right?" I asked.

"Yes," she replied, and addressed Maggie. "That's...that's how he burned you every time you defied him in the prison?"

"Sartorius burned you?" Eran interjected, his expression darkening instantly from contained rage.

Maggie brushed it off as if it were nothing important. "Jocelyn healed me," she replied offhandedly. "And it was worth it to see Sartorius' frustration."

Still, Eran's hands balled into fists, looking torn between wrapping his arms around Maggie or heading out the door to exact his revenge. She sensed this and refused to allow either one to happen by changing the subject.

"We've been researching them, identifying their vulnerabilities through their behavior. But there's something that's been eluding us. We can't figure out a way of determining where The Sevens will be at any specific point in time."

"What about Sisera?" asked Vinnia, whose natural insight into the behavior of others made her the most likely candidate to help them solve the problem.

Unfortunately, it didn't seem like it would be that easy, after Maggie explained.

"Sisera was pure luck. As it turns out, the DeVilles left themselves wide open. The Sevens knew they weren't hiding. All the Vires had to do was watch them for any behavior out of the ordinary, and they'd know it was time to move in."

"What was it they did that was out of the ordinary?" asked Vinnia.

"Well, call me crazy, but throwing out one of those stones you all wear doesn't seem to be a good idea. At least not when it's a moldavite stone, the kind your Vires wear."

I lifted my hand to my collar, found the stone missing, and groaned. Jocelyn observed me doing this, so I leaned down and whispered, "She must have removed it while we slept."

"So therein lies the problem," Eran said, getting us back on subject. "We can't kill them if we don't know where to find them."

It was obvious he was appealing for suggestions, but with heads turned and eyes downcast it didn't look like anyone had anything to offer. And then Isabella spoke up.

"I have one ally inside the Ministry walls," she stated quietly, hesitantly. "He has a lot to lose, we all do, if his identity is exposed, because he's gotten closer to The Sevens than anyone ever has before."

"How close?" I asked.

"He's Sartorius' confidante."

I grew excited over Isabella's declaration. "Will he help us?"

"If we ask him, he will."

"I don't think we have any other option," Eran surmised.

Isabella agreed with a nod. "I'll reach out to him," she said, already starting for the door.

Before she got there, it occurred to me to ask, "Isabella, what's his name?"

She stopped and slowly turned around, an indication that she knew his identity would stir something in us. "Stalwart."

And she was correct. Jocelyn, Eran, and Maggie launched into loud opposition of the idea.

Jocelyn was the last to speak, by insisting, "He can't be trusted."

Isabella held back a smirk and it became clear to me that she knew all along how we escaped the Ministry and Lacinda's house. She had gotten the inside story on it.

"Stalwart didn't turn on you," Isabella stated with unwavering certainty. "He convinced Lacinda he wasn't a threat by siding with her so he could return to the Ministry."

Jocelyn countered, "But he didn't defect. If he was truly on our side, he would have."

"He did, he just never left." I said, and Jocelyn turned to me, stunned.

Sensing support, Isabella appealed directly to me then. "Wouldn't you, Jameson, in all your strategic forethought ever consider leaving someone on the inside to relay information back to us?" She paused, waiting for my answer.

"Yes, I would."

Jocelyn's expression sank further while the glimmer of a proud smile lifted Isabella's. It crushed me to see that.

"Correct," Isabella declared. She then confirmed what I already knew, what had come to me in the DeVille's storefront while trying to keep Sisera from killing Jocelyn. "You, Jameson, would have asked him to position himself around Sartorius to ensure he was chosen when the time came for Sartorius to implement his plan. When he did, Stalwart safely escorted you from the Ministry, ensured that Jocelyn was freed, and did it all without giving up his cover."

I took a quick look at Isabella. She met my eyes and I knew she was thinking the same thing as me.

"What?" Jocelyn asked, having seen the glance between me and her mother.

"You figured it out, didn't you?" Isabella asked.

I nodded and the stark, painful feeling of betraying Jocelyn settled over me.

"You figured what out?" Jocelyn demanded. "I'm not following you two at all!"

"Neither am I," added Maggie, as Eran crossed his arms preparing to wait for an explanation.

I condensed it as best I could, starting from the beginning. "Sartorius brought Jocelyn and me together in the theater because it was time to put his plan into action."

"What plan?" Jocelyn pressed.

"The plan designed to allow you two to escape."

"Escape?" Maggie demanded, glancing at Jocelyn, who was just as baffled.

"Yes…escape. That's why he sent Stalwart, a Vire whose position it is to transport prisoners. In this instance it was Jocelyn and Maggie who he was transporting. And it's why we met no resistance leaving the Ministry."

"But why? Why would he let us all go?" Jocelyn asked, shaking her head as if it made no sense. But it did.

"Sartorius is always several steps ahead. He knows that once The Sevens start dying off, they'll see you, Jocelyn, as too great a threat to keep alive. Your life would have been ended by the second Seven's death."

"And why would he think The Sevens were going to start dying off?" Spencer, the intellectual of the Weatherford siblings, asked.

"Well, that's where Maggie comes in," Eran commented, piecing it together. "He let her go so that she could kill the rest of them."

Maggie sighed, deep in thought. "So Sartorius has figured out that I'm the only one who knows how...."

"All he had to do," I summarized, "was make us touch, and he knew I'd find where you were hidden, setting his plan into action."

Maggie shook her head doubtfully. "Wait...wait. He could have just released us. Why the charade?"

"And that's where I come in," I explained, and then chuckled at the grace of his plan. "He had to make it look real. He needed a scapegoat, someone to take the blame for the escape, and that was me. It's the only reason he allowed me to stay at the Ministry in the first place. He knew I was looking for you. Isabella knew this," I said tilting my head in her direction. "It's the only reason Isabella didn't invade the Ministry to get you. Having lived with Sartorius, analyzing his manners, his strategies for nearly twenty years, she knew he'd take this tack." She had been quietly observing the realizations transpire, but now gradually raised her lips in a shrewd smile. "If we had gone in chaotic, tumultuous, you would have died before we reached you. Isabella knew it, I knew it, Sartorius knew it."

"So you're saying...," Nolan ventured, "Sartorius helped us."

"The Sevens don't help anyone but themselves," Maggie muttered.

"He's saying," Charlotte chimed in with her typically snide tone, "Sartorius wants the rest of The Sevens dead so his oligarchy would become a dictatorship." Her eyes landed back on me and she demanded, "What are you gonna do about that?"

"Well..." I observed the room for their reactions as I made my next statement. "We're going to take advantage of the opportunity he's given us and bring down the others, once we know when and where to find them."

On her cue, Isabella left without acknowledging us again. She was a woman of few words, but diligent in the execution of her duties, and I knew she'd bring back news of The Sevens future whereabouts one way or another.

When the door closed no one spoke, the gravity of our situation weighing on each of us.

Charlotte, whose innate character welcomes conflict and allows her to overcome it quicker than most, put our situation into terms I wouldn't have initially thought of. But she was correct.

"So…we're partnering with Sartorius," she concluded, and after some thought I nodded.

"Yes, Charlotte. Yes, we are."

10. REFUGE

I hadn't eaten or slept in more than twenty four hours but when the discussion came up about where Jocelyn and I would sleep, it left me more than just a little aroused. We hadn't been in a bedroom together since the DeVilles, so after the question came up, I had trouble keeping my eyes off her. The smoothness of her skin, the curl of her hair down her back, the attentiveness in her concentration, the simple nearness of her, teased me without mercy. She didn't seem fazed by it at all, though, as she listened intently to the conversation.

"We live at the only purple and pink Victorian two-story house on Magazine Street," Eran informed the room as we prepared to leave. "If you're looking for us, you can't miss it."

Since it would take Isabella time to establish contact with Stalwart, we didn't expect her back for a few days, and we couldn't stay in the village. So Maggie and Eran were generous enough to give up a room in their house.

"Purple," Estelle murmured, her jealousy visible to anyone who knew her penchant for the color.

"And pink," Maggie corrected. "It's a purple and pink house."

I knew what Estelle was thinking. She would love to stay with Maggie and Eran. As it was, without the DeVille store available to Jocelyn and me, we needed a new safe house far more than her. No, she'd have to find a way to survive in the plush, newly-redecorated 1,100 square foot room beneath the Fielding's staircase. Still, she watched with envy as we headed for Miss Mabelle's boat.

The woman insisted on escorting us, so she would know where to find us, but I had a hunch it was because she wanted to be around if we ran across a Vire. I didn't bother reminding her that she was frail enough to need a cane and that she wouldn't be much help if we encountered a Vire. But I figured my silence saved me from a hit to the head from that cane.

There was only one person I had any interest in upsetting. I stopped directly in front of her on my way out the door.

She tilted her chin up at me, jutting out her jaw like she did when she was five and stole my toys. The only difference now was that her eyes narrowed at me because she knew there was a reason to be fearful.

"Charlotte, you will recant your cast tonight," I instructed, keeping my voice low because if anyone on the Weatherford side overheard our conversation it wouldn't end well for anyone.

Confirming Charlotte knew I was referring to her preventing Jocelyn from having any contact with me, she smirked arrogantly in response. "So she can hurt you?"

I ground my teeth together to keep from shouting. "Recant or you'll experience the cast yourself."

"I don't need to touch anyone," she declared boldly.

Damn, she's rebellious.

"No, she's loyal," Jocelyn's voice came through my head, correcting me. "Let it go, Jameson. You're already fighting The Sevens, Lacinda, the perception of our world against you. I don't want you fighting your-"

She got that far before the cast set in. The second it did she bowed forward in anguish, crying out a muffled whimper, grabbing her stomach and heaving for a breath through the pain.

I bent forward with her, keeping her from collapsing. Once I had a hold of her, I shot a look at Charlotte that made her step back, out of range.

"End it! Now!" I shouted.

She denied me. "No!"

I was so angry my sight blurred, but despite what Jocelyn was going through, she was able to wave off the Weatherfords as they ran for her. And I knew why. While their touch wouldn't hurt her, she might cling to them by mistake.

"You're doing this to her?" I heard someone say over Jocelyn's whimpering.

It was Vinnia, the more judicious of the Weatherford girls, but a protective one. This was not good.

Sure enough, a disturbance followed, but I was too focused on Jocelyn to look up.

"Get her out of here!" I heard my father shout and knew he was referring to Charlotte.

"They're starting…," Jocelyn channeled to me between groans, "to feud…again…."

That was when it hit me. She's channeling. Which meant I could channel, too. And from that moment, I drew into me everything she was feeling, every throb radiating from her stomach, every cramping ache through her arms, every muscle twitch.

I felt brain dead for not having figured this out earlier.

Stupid as-

That was when the full measure of what Jocelyn was feeling took hold of me and I was blinded by it. There was no longer any shack, no floor where I was standing, no presence of other living souls around me. There was only the pain.

Jocelyn was stronger than me. By a lot. She had the ability to control herself, to speak, to notice what was going on around her, despite this incomprehensible pain. And that was when it occurred to me...what she had started to do once she acquired her ability to channel. She could deal with this cast better than me, far better, because she had built up a tolerance. Every time I'd watched her take hold of a patient, she'd been absorbing their injuries, diseases and illnesses all along. And if I hadn't been in so much damn pain, I would've been in complete awe of her.

By the time Jocelyn had pulled away, and the cast had run its course, we were both on the ground. Both of our families were gone, Kalisha included, probably escorted in a rush, out the door and back to their safe houses by Miss Celia and Miss Mabelle.

Only Eran and Maggie were still with us.

"Are you two okay?" Eran asked, somewhat indifferent to the answer we might give.

"Fine," I said, waving them off, picking myself off the floor while giving Jocelyn a hand.

"I've seen a lot of action in my time," he went on to say, "but nothing like that."

"Yeah," Maggie nodded, eyebrows raised in shock. "When I heard about your families feuding I thought it was just a rumor, something for the gossips to talk about at school. But no...they were right about the intensity between you all."

Jocelyn gave me a weak smile, which I returned. "Are you all right?"

"Yes," she said, as the color returned to her cheeks.

"Did anyone else get hurt?" I asked Eran.

"No...." He shook his head slowly in his customarily apathetic manner. "Just you two."

"Good," I stated, taking Jocelyn's hand and leading her toward the door. There was the briefest hesitation as our skin met, but then I realized I was making the overture and we were safe. "We're okay to travel now. Let's go."

The sun had set already, which gave us the cover of darkness and allowed us to get back to New Orleans without being seen. Jocelyn levitated us directly into the city, dropping us rapidly from a decent enough height that we weren't seen coming in or landing.

On the ground, I did a cursory check of the surroundings looking for Vires, or anything out of place, but found nothing. A shed was built in the back corner, but the door was secured with a massive steel combination padlock.

It prompted me to ask, "What do you keep in there?"

Eran smiled knowingly. "Magdalene's motorcycle. Not sure why she bothers locking it, though. If anyone touches it, she'll track them down and then...," he chuckled, "God rest their soul."

The trees gave the house good coverage, and the rest of the yard posed no risks. A small garden was planted at the end, and a set of juice jars were lined up on the small patio outside the back door. In all, the place had the appearance of a traditional southern home.

In fact, the only oddity came from the interior of the house. I was about to step up to the back door, behind Jocelyn and Maggie, when a screech came from inside.

I tensed, and Eran noticed. "Don't worry. He's harmless."

When the door opened, I understood what he meant. A guy, thinner than a yardstick, was running around the kitchen with hands wagging in the air and a big grin on his face. He had a purple glob in his bright orange hair and a smear of it mashed down his apron.

"Eggplant mousse!" he screamed before he saw us. "Absolutely divine!"

He was kissing an older man on the cheek by the time I stepped into the kitchen. Then his screeching seemed to be directed at us.

"You brought dinner guests!"

He had his wiry arms around Jocelyn and me before we even had time to respond.

"Actually, they'll be staying a little longer than dinner," Maggie informed him, dropping into a chair at the circular dinner table squeezed into the tiny kitchen. "If that's all right with you."

Neither of the men seemed too concerned, which I took as a good sign.

"Oh, pray tell!"

Eran laughed in a way that made it clear he was familiar with this guy's antics. "Felix, this is Jameson and Jocelyn. And this," he said to us, "is Felix Pluck."

I noticed that as our names were mentioned, their expressions morphed from curiosity to understanding.

Without hesitating, Eran motioned to the expressive orange-haired man and said, "This is Felix, our resident cook."

Felix seemed to appreciate that title as he tilted his head and cupped his hands to his cheeks. I wondered if he knew he was coming across like an adoring little girl, or even cared. *Probably not,* I decided.

"And this is Mr. Tanner, Maggie's father."

Mr. Tanner approached us with an observant, but sincere, gaze and shook Jocelyn's hand first. He then took mine before confirming what I already knew. "We've heard a lot about you."

I was about to respond when three more people came through the door.

"And this is Ezra Wood," Eran went on to say, tipping his head at the first to enter, a stout, dark-skinned woman with colorfully-beaded dreadlocks. She gave me a knowing look and headed for the counter where she poured herself a cup of coffee.

"And Rufus O'Malley," Eran continued as a man the size of a tank trailed Ezra. He was tattooed with various symbols and names, and he was frowning. If anyone was going to give us trouble, I figured it would be him. But then he opened his mouth and directed his vehemence at Felix.

"Ya got rubbish in yer hair," he grumbled in a thick Irish brogue. "It's purple." He then said something unintelligible under his breath as Felix attempted to bat it out.

The rest of the room tried not to laugh, but most of us were unsuccessful, and we ended up getting a hearty glare from Felix.

The last person to enter the room was Mrs. Tanner, Maggie's mother, a woman the same age as her husband and with a maternal look about her. I had no doubt she and my mother would form an easy friendship if they met.

"You all live here?" Jocelyn asked, and without waiting for an answer, added, "Are you sure there's room for Jameson and me?"

Ezra laughed to herself and replied, "There's always room here for those in need."

"Well, thank you for that," I said and she gave me a warm smile from behind her mug.

"So you're the ones who are working with Eran and Maggie against the Fallen Ones," she said, inquisitively.

"The what?" Jocelyn and I replied in unison.

Maggie grinned. "That's what we call them." To Ezra, she remarked, "They call them The Sevens."

"Ah," Felix said, still wiping the purple from his hair. "Because there are seven of them left."

"Six now," Eran pointed out, and an elated pause in the conversation followed.

"Well," Ezra sighed. "Thank you for your help."

I felt my eyebrows go up. "I thought it was the other way around, but in any case I'm glad we're working together."

"Some of us are working together," Ezra informed us with open displeasure before glowering at Eran. "But not all. Eran refuses to allow us in on the effort."

Eran sighed. "I'm sorry, Ezra, but you are aware of what happened the last time we attacked." To me, he explained, "We've considered another outright assault, but I'm not willing to risk losing Magdalene again."

Maggie's hand crept across to Eran's, where their fingers curled together. My hand was already in Jocelyn's, but seeing this gave me the impulse to squeeze it.

Eran and I didn't know how long either of us had with the woman we love, and we wanted to make the most of every second.

"Sounds to me like you have an uphill battle, Jameson," Ezra said, leaning on the counter. "The Sevens want you and Jocelyn dead and the rest of your world isn't sure if they can trust you."

"You heard about that?" I asked, amazed at her insight.

"I take a special interest in whatever situations Maggie and Eran get themselves involved in. Yours is of particular interest to me because of the Fallen Ones." She closed her eyes and smiled widely when she reopened them. "The Sevens," she corrected herself. "I understand you'll be taking them out one by one?"

"Yes."

"And if that doesn't work?"

"We'll need to attack in force."

"If you can't get those in your world to trust you, how will you rebuild your army in order to do so?"

"I've been thinking about that," I admitted.

"And?" she pressed.

"Still thinking."

She assessed me for a long minute, and then nodded her head as if she'd made her mind up about something. Whatever it was, it seemed to be positive.

"You're just in time for dinner," she announced, taking a plate from the mismatched stack next to a pot with purple...something...bubbling from it. "We're having eggplant mousse, is that correct, Felix?"

"Yes, it is, my dear Ezra," he said with a dramatic bow.

She bowed back, thanked him and scooped a good-sized portion onto her plate.

While it didn't sound appetizing, Felix's purple dish was just what we needed. Jocelyn and I finished ours and went for second helpings, which I got the impression gained us the status of lifelong friends in Felix's eyes. It could have been because we hadn't eaten anything in more than twenty four hours, but when I finally put down my fork I was beyond the point of feeling full.

Dinner conversation was fluid and light. No one brought up The Sevens again, but it never left my mind that these people were risking their lives if any Vires tracked us here. And I deeply appreciated it.

At the end, Jocelyn, Maggie, Eran, and I washed and dried the dishes as the rest left for their rooms. Ezra and Mrs. Tanner, however, stopped at the doorway. Simultaneously, they turned back to face me.

"If you're staying here, you'll need to follow the rules," Ezra mentioned.

"Rules?" I repeated.

"Eran will fill you in."

When she was gone and the girls were busy putting the dishes away, Eran whispered, "Separate bedrooms," and my stomach sank.

Then I saw the way Eran's mouth turned down in a suspicious smile and it made me think he got around that rule somehow.

"They're not adamant about it."

That was literally the best news I'd gotten in days.

The four of us headed upstairs afterwards and down a hallway that spanned the length of the house. The girls had their own rooms and I'd be sharing with Eran, just as Ezra had warned. Jocelyn's room was on the right, next to Maggies, and Eran's was directly across the hall. His was sparse, but I didn't need much. My body was accustomed to sleeping conditions that would challenge most others. So when he threw me a blanket and a pillow, I laid them on the floor and settled in.

I was severely sleep deprived, and with food in my stomach, dozing should have come easy. But my mind and body were in synch and neither one wanted to shut down. After showering, I lay there listening to Jocelyn moving around her room. And a sort of peace came over me. She'd finally be able to sleep in a real bed. While that thought didn't quench the arousal of knowing she was in bed, it made me feel like something considerable had been accomplished today. And in our situation, that meant a great deal.

When the house grew quiet, other than someone's snoring rumbling through the walls, I heard Eran whisper my name.

"It's clear," he said. "Go to her."

It felt like I was liberated, freed from a pair of chains.

By the second part of that sentence I was on my feet. By the time he'd finished it, I was at the door. I slipped through it and down the hall, hoping to God that her door didn't squeak when I opened it. But as I put my hand on the knob, the snoring stopped, and I froze.

What am I doing? I thought. *I'm in someone else's house, sneaking into my girlfriend's room, who is also a guest here. What a total lack of self-restraint...*

But I couldn't stop myself. I'd been given food, and that part of me was fulfilled. The greater part of me, the part that needed Jocelyn remained empty. That part hungered for her, yearned for her, ached for her.

"Jameson." Her voice came through the dark, and the door opened to her silhouette, and I completely abandoned every sense of respect, every notion of civility, every manner I'd ever been taught.

I took her face in my hands and pulled her to me. And I kissed her deeply, taking her in, all of her...her taste, her scent. I was consumed by her. We stumbled back into her room, and I swung the door closed with my foot, a perfect force that allowed it to simply lock in place with a soft click. I was two steps in before realizing she wasn't responding.

She couldn't, not unless I absorbed her-

Jocelyn yanked her lips from mine. "No," she declared in a firm whisper.

"Were you listening to my thoughts?"

"Yes," she said without a hint of guilt. "And I won't let you do that again."

I frowned, although she couldn't see it.

Restraining my thoughts, because my hands were still holding her and I didn't want her to read them again, I said, "I have another idea."

She didn't move, and I figured this was because she was attempting to do what I didn't want her to.

"You can stop. I'm not going to think it again. You've missed your chance."

She snickered, although it sounded light-hearted.

"Where's your bed?" I asked.

Her voice broke when she answered, and I knew she was nervous...excited but nervous. "Ov-ver there...."

"Can you lead me?"

She nodded, and I slid my hand down her arm, noting that it felt like silk against my skin, and then entwined my fingers with hers.

Once there, I whispered, "Lay down, Jocelyn," and she did.

I settled into the exact same position I'd been in the last time we were in bed together, our bodies pressed together, my front to her side. But when I laid my hand on her stomach, this time, her heart fluttered. She knew what was coming, or so she thought; she anticipated it, wanted it. And knowing that was extremely rewarding.

So I did to her what I had done the last time we lay in bed together. Except this time, I used my lips. She quivered and moaned and sighed and each sound was a roadmap, leading me, showing me how to satisfy her. And when her back arched and she released, forgetting in the moment what that contact with me would do, I drew in her pain so that she could feel complete.

"Jameson?" Her voice came to me fuzzy, hollow, from down a long tunnel. "Are you all right?"

"Give…," I grunted, "me a minute."

The pain was just as intense as it had been the first time. There was no diminishing the potency of it even though I knew it was coming.

She sighed and reached out to comfort me, stopping just in time.

I'd recovered sufficiently to warn her. "Let me…get through this."

She sat back and waited, and when I looked up, in the faint light drifting in from the window, I found there were tears in her eyes.

"No," I sighed. *This was the last thing I wanted.*

I took her in my arms and pressed her next to me, wanting to absorb this new sense of pain. When she recognized what I was doing, she wiped the wetness from her cheeks and insisted, "I'm fine."

"You're sure?"

"Yes, I just-" Her hand came up, pausing in midair on its way to my cheek. "I just want to touch you, Jameson, before..."

And I knew what she meant.

She wanted to feel me once more, just once, without any pain, before she took my life.

"You will," I said resolutely. "I'll make sure that happens, Jocelyn." She had lowered her eyes and was shifting her head slowly back and forth. "Do you believe me?"

When they rose again, there were fresh tears, but she nodded. And when she whispered her response, it summed up her entire life in one sentence. "Jameson...you're the only one I believe in."

THIS IS NOT FAIR! my mind screamed. And as vengeance swelled in me, I pulled her back to my chest. I then pressed her head against me and tucked her hands around my waist because I knew she couldn't.

"Are you comfortable?" I asked.

"Mmmm," she murmured.

And that alone dissipated the anger I felt and made me smile. If it hadn't been for her response, I'm not sure sleep would have been possible for me.

But it came with her head resting on me, the rise and fall of her breathing lifting my arms rhythmically as they lay wrapped around her. It was a solid shuteye, undisturbed by dreams, uninterrupted by what was happening halfway around the world, because we hadn't been told yet.

The next thing I knew Jocelyn's mother's voice stirred the house. But it wasn't her arrival, or even the urgency in her tone that brought me fully awake. It was the message.

"The Seven's are launching their first attack."

11. FLAVIAN

My feet hit the wood floors hard, but I only slightly registered it. There were so many thoughts going through my head that pain didn't make it onto my list of priorities.

Where was the attack being launched?

How many Sevens were on the ground there?

How many Vires were being used?

When did they strike?

Lastly, and most importantly, *how do I keep Jocelyn from insisting on going?* Because I knew she would.

Every one of my questions, with the exception of the one concerning Jocelyn, were answered after I pulled on the black Vire uniform and met up with Isabella downstairs. Jocelyn came up behind me, breathless and wide-eyed, and again my concern over her wanting to go flared. And she had dressed for it, having borrowed black, tight-fitting clothes from Maggie. Needless to say, she was a distraction.

"Flavian began launching waves of Vires across western Africa less than an hour ago, and they're taking down everyone, not just those in our world."

"Just one Seven?" I asked, stunned.

"Yes. The rest are positioning their Vire forces in each of their provinces, but they haven't moved yet."

"Which means they are using Flavian as a test...," I deduced.

"That's likely," Eran said, coming down the stairs. Maggie followed him, nodding in agreement. I didn't notice this so much as what she was wearing...a black leather suit, the same one she wore to Sisera's execution. *Different*, I thought, *realizing that singular description applied to so many characteristics about her.*

By this time, the rest of the house was flooding into the small parlor room just inside the front door.

Maggie agreed with us. "That sounds like the Fallen-umm-The Sevens' method. If all goes well, the rest of them will strike."

"Not if we don't give them the chance," I mumbled, as a plan formed in my mind. It was hazy, moving itself like puzzle pieces fitting together until the picture as a whole transpired. When the image settled, it was lucid and had a high probability of success.

"What's on your mind?" Eran asked. Evidently, he detected what I was doing.

"I think this Vire uniform might come in handy. But we'll need you and Maggie there, too."

"Good, let's go," Maggie stated.

"We're wasting time," Jocelyn added as the two of them headed for the door.

I almost groaned, knowing where this was headed. "My plan doesn't involve you, Jocelyn."

She stopped a foot from the door and turned back to face me with her mouth agape. Maggie paused too, glancing curiously at Eran.

I took a quick look at Isabella and found that I was on my own. Judging by her frown, she knew she lost authority over her daughter a long time ago. If she pushed, Jocelyn would pull. And vice versa. The expression she gave me confirmed it was up to me now. It was saying: Good luck.

"You need me there," Jocelyn declared, with fire in her eyes. She wasn't going to back down.

Ezra had been standing by the kitchen doorway with a mug in her hand observing. "Huh, looks like Maggie and Jocelyn are cut from the same cloth."

I didn't know what that meant, but it really didn't matter. I was more focused on talking some sense into Jocelyn, although I didn't have much hope of accomplishing it.

I appreciated when Ezra suggested that they all give us some privacy.

Jocelyn didn't wait for them to leave, marching back to me, determination etched into her face. "I'm not going to stay here. I won't be able to heal you from here." She said this with genuine fear.

"I won't need to be healed."

"You don't know that. The Sevens want you dead just as much as they want me."

"They won't even notice I'm there."

"What?" she demanded. "How can you say-"

"I have a plan, Jocelyn. It doesn't include you."

"You're going to have to modify it then."

"I can't risk you being captured again. I can't," I said, stressing my point through the resolve in my voice. "If you come, I will be focused on you, not on Flavian."

"And I can't risk you not coming back," she said, trembling, her voice almost a shout.

A clearing of the throat suddenly halted our debate. "Is your issue resolved?" Ezra asked, peering from around the corner of the kitchen hallway.

"No," I said, frustration unmistakable in my tone.

"Well, you need to hurry it up because there is a mob forming on my front porch." She tipped her head toward the large window overlooking the front of the house. Sure

140

enough, my family and the Weatherfords gathered, their heads silhouetted against the streetlight outside.

I sighed and shook my head. "They're harmless," I stated before second guessing the truthfulness to that statement. The fact they were lining up on opposite sides of the porch didn't look comforting.

"This isn't over," Jocelyn stated as I opened the door, and I felt my mouth sink into a frown.

"Well, it's good to see you too," my mother said as she entered, and my frown deepened until I realized that they weren't alone.

"Theleo?" I muttered, surprised.

"Jameson," he greeted stiffly. "You didn't come for me." He stepped up to the welcome mat once the last of the Weatherfords had filtered inside.

"Why would I?"

He stared at me, making me think I had asked a ridiculous question. "You killed a Seven," he said remaining expressionless.

It made me realize then that he still wanted to be a part of what we had started, to help in our undertaking. I had turned them all away, every Dissident, every Defector, and given them a safe location to ride out this war between The Sevens, Jocelyn, and me. And they had left, as I asked, and the rumor had started convincing them that I was working for The Sevens, so it never occurred to me that any of them would ever want to be involved again.

I felt an urge to slap myself upside the head, because I now realized that of course they would leave. They were taught to follow commands. They did as I told them. But Theleo had always thought for himself, and was now proving once again he didn't follow pack mentality.

"I can be of service," he claimed, as if reading my thoughts.

And that's when it came to me.

"Yes," I agreed. "Yes, you can."

Stepping aside so he could enter, my gaze drifted to Jocelyn, who greeted Theleo with an embrace. Awkwardly, he leaned in but didn't raise his arms. Vires weren't taught to hug.

"What are you doing here?" Jocelyn asked, just as amazed as I had been.

Before Theleo could answer, I cut in. "He'll be escorting you to Africa."

They both gave me a stunned look. Jocelyn's was especially inquisitive.

To Theleo, I said, "Keep her at a distance, hidden. She is not to move, period, unless I give you a signal."

"I understand."

"Is that resolved enough for you?" I asked Jocelyn.

"Yes," she replied bluntly.

I was angry with myself for giving in. But what choice did I have? There was no doubt in me that she would ignore my wishes and show up on the battlefield where she would be truly endangering herself.

My lips tight in resistance, I nodded to her and turned back to the room. Again, both families had been split down the middle and were parked on opposite sides of the parlor. They were torn between looking at me and keeping an eye on their adversaries across from them. "The rest of you came because you heard what's happening in western Africa, am I correct?"

Various nods and grumbles gave me my answer.

"Well, you've come for nothing," I said plainly. "You can't help. Not yet. It's best if you return to your safe houses."

"We'll stay," my mother replied adamantly.

"We'll wait," Isabella announced.

My gut told me that wasn't a smart idea, but every second we waited discussing it would mean more lives lost to Flavian's forces. *I'll have to deal with whatever happens between them when I get back,* I reasoned. *If I get back.*

"Eran? Maggie?" I called to them as they collected in the hallway leading to the kitchen.

"We're ready," Eran confirmed.

After Jocelyn and I weaved our way through to the back door, I stopped next to Ezra in the kitchen. She knew what I was asking and gave me a nod of consent.

"Thank you," I said. "If they are any trouble, kick them out."

She flashed a huge grin. "I will."

Her uninhibited reassurance gave me some relief.

Regardless, as the door was closing behind me, I called out in a final attempt to get them to strongly reflect on their actions before committing to them. "Behave!"

Unfortunately, the scowl beginning to creep across Charlotte's face didn't leave me with the sense that I got through.

Theleo levitated us through the treetops to just above the more common flight paths taken by the airlines before pointing us toward Africa. Once on our way, Eran yelled out, "All right, Jameson, going to enlighten us on this plan of yours?"

"Well," I began, knowing I'd face some resistance. "We're going to find Flavian's command center and walk right in."

Anyone not already looking quickly turned in my direction. Eran's only reaction was to hold back a laugh.

"We can't defeat his forces head on, so we'll come in from behind." I paused and then summed it up the best way I could. "Take out the leader, leave the forces in chaos."

After a few seconds of silence, Eran spoke as he nodded approvingly. "Right, cut the head off the dragon before the tail knows what's going on."

"Okay, but how do we even get close to the dragon?" Maggie asked with a puzzled shrug.

"I'm going to deliver you," I said. "You'll act as my prisoners, and we'll walk right in. Flavian won't know what hit him until it's too late.

"Camouflage," Eran repeated. "I like it, Caldwell."

I do too, I thought, *so long as it works.*

Theleo brought us in from the side, not too far back from the front line. It was mid-morning here, which made it easy for us to realize we had reached our destination. While our speed hindered us from catching sight of all that was happening on the ground, it didn't obstruct everything. And what I saw made me want to tell him to land right then so I could beat the cra-.

"They're fighting back," Maggie said with an optimistic edge to her voice.

That jolted me. I expected a complete annihilation.

"Looks like they've learned some things while fending off this area's rebels," Theleo surmised.

A steadier look told me that they were correct. In between makeshift huts and along the dry, barren landscape, people were running, most being chased by black uniforms. But directly at the feet of some of those pursuers flashes of flames and sparks of ice hit the ground. Some landed with better aim, on the chests of those in black, and either ignited them or encased them in ice. Not all were using their feet to outpace their attackers, either. Some were taking great leaps, higher and farther than was possible by any common man, only to be tackled in midair by levitating Vires. From there, they fought, suspended, each trying to force their opponent back to the ground.

Not everyone was retaliating though, and I figured it was because they couldn't. Those running weren't only from our world, which meant they were being made privy to our abilities, which had been kept hidden for centuries. Although, I doubted they were paying much attention while running for their lives.

I felt my hands squeeze into fists while watching, and I knew this was a reaction to literally wanting to rip the heads off the Vires pursuing the innocents below.

"Can you pick up the speed, Theleo?" I asked, on edge.

He did and no less than a few seconds later, we came across a large tent. With Vires encircling it, forming a solid band around the outside, we were pretty sure we'd arrived at our destination.

Theleo dropped us swiftly behind a line of tall brush before we could be seen, and we huddled there for a second, listening.

Screams of terror and loud bursts vibrated back to us, penetrating the silence. There was a metallic smell to the air, as if the energy here was highly charged. The sun that scorched this countryside until only sand and dried bushes could exist, immediately began to bake us.

"Okay," I whispered, keeping my eyes on the edge of the bush, ready for anything or anyone to circle around it. "Jocelyn and Theleo will stay here. Do not move unless I give you an okay." I said this to Theleo, knowing Jocelyn wouldn't give her consent. "Eran and Maggie, you'll walk in front of me with your wrists connected behind your back. Keep your heads up. We want you to be the focus of attention."

Together, we stood, preparing to move, but I stopped.

"There's just one more thing…," I muttered, took Jocelyn's face in my hands, and guided her lips to me. The kiss was deep, giving me one last taste of her, an enticing one. In it, I tried to channel hope, faith, and the confidence that I'll always be with her, in body or spirit. I wasn't sure I got through to her, though. The fact that she held on to my hips, with her fingers wrapped through my belt loops, was telling. I understood. It was a struggle for me to pull away, too. But I did, and she gave me a weak smile as I let her go entirely.

Maggie and Eran had the same idea, parting just as I stepped back from Jocelyn.

"We're ready," Maggie declared with conviction, and they positioned their hands as I had coached.

Our walk to the tent was gradual, allowing us to observe the area. It was easy to discern why they chose this location to test their efficiencies. Any mass murders would be pinned on the local rebels, while allowing Flavian and his forces anonymity inside such a desolate area. The rolling hills aided in their cover, the open territory allowed them to see any defensive enemies approaching. Of course, they were looking for a group larger than three people, which made our size become our strength.

As we approached, Maggie's head twitched, and I asked if she was all right.

"He's inside," she muttered, almost entranced, as if she were detecting him.

"Is he alone?"

"I don't know," she said, making me wonder how she knew his whereabouts without knowing about the presence of others.

"Did you see him?" I asked, inferring this was the reason.

"Not exactly," she said rolling her shoulders up and tilting her head back to rub her neck along them.

"It'll be over soon," Eran comforted her, visibly unsettled by Maggie's pain.

And he was correct. A hundred yards later, we reached the tent's opening. The Vires there saw us approach, and just as I'd hoped, their eyes were pinned on Maggie and Eran instead of the Vire behind them.

"Move aside," I said, intentionally giving my voice a gruff edge. I then dipped my head and sneered, obscuring my face. "I am delivering prisoners to Flavian."

Either there was no protocol for this kind of delivery, or they recognized my "prisoners", the later more likely being the case, because the Vires blocking the entrance shifted to the side. Then the flap of the tent wall folded up, and I rationalized this as one of them levitating the fabric in an indication for us to enter.

My eyes rapidly surveyed what I could see of the room, noting that furniture, heavy wood pieces, had been hauled out to the site. Fabric with various scenes hung down the walls and the floor was covered in plush rugs. The lavishly decorated tent stretched several yards back to the left where an ornamented desk and a massive throne were set. I wondered who Flavian was trying to impress.

The second the tent flap fell behind us, Maggie and Eran's hands relaxed and they strode farther into the room.

Dressed in slacks and a scholarly pair of suspenders beaded with moldavite stones, Flavian stood behind the desk with his pale, lucent hands spread flat across the top, a sword tucked beneath them. His head was hung as we entered and remained that way until Maggie and Eran moved toward him. Then it lifted and a gleam in his eyes told me that he was expecting us.

"Magdalene," he said, his voice deep and tinged with an accent that I couldn't place. "At last we meet."

"I only wish it had been sooner," she replied.

He sighed and his eyes dipped. "So you could end my life that much quicker?"

"So we could have saved the innocents you hurt."

"And what of saving me?" he asked, standing to his full height, leaving him towering over us. "Why discriminate so? Do I not have the right to be here? Who claims that right?" Without pause, he went on with his bizarre soliloquy. "Is it determined by choice? The will to return? Why condemn me because I have been given no choice at all? The innocents you speak of have been given theirs. They *can* return."

"Only to face you again," she muttered, continuing her steady approach with Eran directly to her left. I fell in on her right.

Flavian's head slumped as he laughed to himself. When it rose again, his eyes darkened. "You do understand that I have been left no choice. In the absence of choice, I am limited to no other alternative but to kill you. It would be in self-defense, I hope you know. Only you, Magdalene, can unlock another path. And so it is, I wonder, would you be so balanced and fair in your pursuit of what is right, what is just, to allow *me* to live?"

"And what would you do then, Flavian? Donate your time to charities?" I countered. "Repay your debt to humankind?"

Staring at me blankly, he replied, dumbfounded, "No, I would not deviate from the course I have chosen."

He was a Seven to the core, unable to see beyond his all-consuming greed.

"Well then," I replied, "Neither will we."

Flavian's lips turned up in a grin of mock sympathy. He was already assuming I'd fail. "Jameson, there isn't much I don't know about you, having studied you well before you were born. So, I have no illusion over your inability to cast. You can't hurt me."

Ironically, he was correct. Using a cast, an incantation wouldn't work well. But what he didn't know about me, what he couldn't know about me, because I'd never told anyone before, was that casting didn't appeal to me. What I'd dreamed of, had always anticipated, was to get my hands on him. That was where my strengths lay. In channeling.

My hand tightened into a fist and slammed into his face before he knew what was happening. But I didn't end it there. On contact, I sent with it all the feelings I'd endured while witnessing Jocelyn, our families, and all the innocents of our world be condemned to subjugation.

Flavian fell back, across the tent wall, clutching his face, heaving for air. The sword he was holding became a prop to hold himself up or he risked collapsing.

Unable to stop myself from enjoying the result, I bent toward him. "Did *that* hurt...Flavian?"

Eran's head jerked back and he glanced at me, perplexed. "What did you do to him?"

"Gave him a little taste of what we've endured all these years."

Eran laughed under his breath, but I didn't pay much attention to it. I was already going in for another strike, another dose of channeling. This one landed on the opposite side of his face, sending his head and body into the wall again.

He let out a whimper.

And then I let myself loose, giving way to the craving that had been squatting inside me whenever a Vire threw a fist in my face or brought fear to Jocelyn's eyes. These were the images that surfaced as I pummeled Flavian one blow after another.

Somehow, a grunt broke through my crazed fixation on Flavian and I swiveled my head around to find Maggie and Eran fighting Vires behind me. They were coming to rescue Flavian, but they wouldn't get that chance. I was going to finish him off.

But that brief moment gave Flavian the time he needed to collect his thoughts. The sword he still had in his hand rose. I shoved his wrist into the wall, bending the blade back. That motion sliced the tent and a Vire's hand came through from the other side, slipping around Flavian's chest, and pulling him out. His body widened the opening, where I could see Flavian's being hauled to safety. I had one foot through the opening when something wobbled behind me. I turned back to find Maggie beginning to crouch.

When she sprang, it was with amazing agility, onto the desk, where she made a fluid, and precisely placed, kick to Flavian's chest before he was out of range. He fell back into the Vire carrying him, his fingers repositioning his hand around the sword, his lips curved down in vengeance, his eyes narrowed to me.

Eran and I pursued him, tearing through the opening together and meeting Maggie on the other side.

Having shed the Vire trying to assist him, Flavian now stood, sword in hand, crossed over his body, ready for us. The Vires who had been surrounding Flavian advanced on us but he called them off.

"No! This is my kill."

Flavian wielded his weapon expertly, taking a nick from Eran and causing Maggie to jerk from his lunge. I saw my chance then, his ribs exposed, I sent a fist directly into them, and felt the corresponding crunch of bones. His sword fell and he doubled over, clutching his torso.

Maggie picked up the sword and sent it directly through Flavian's chest.

The Vires surrounding us released an almost synchronized gasp.

But Flavian didn't fall. He stood, taller than before, if that was possible, and slowly dragged the blade from his body. Once freed, I noticed there was no blood. None on the sword, none on his shirt.

And then he grinned.

Drawing in a deep breath, he tossed the sword at Maggie's feet, goading her, and ripped the shirt wider at the cut left by his sword to expose a wound healing itself.

"You may now try again," he remarked, fear entirely absent.

Maggie dug in her pocket and pulled out a lighter.

This seemed odd to me until she flicked it, generating a flame, and stooped to ignite the shallow dead grass below our feet. Immediately, Eran, Maggie, and I moved back, but Flavian didn't shift from where he stood, even as the flames engulfed him.

Still grinning, his head ducked so that he stared at her from beneath his eyebrows, he mocked, "Try again."

Remembering that she and Eran had warned that none of them die the same way, I looked around in search of some hint, a tip as to what Flavian feared. It definitely wasn't the sword or fire.

"Maggie," I said. "We're in an arid climate, and I don't see any barrels of drinking water."

It was a long shot, but after a quick survey of the area she seemed open to the idea.

Flavian's smile faded, and I knew we'd hit on his vulnerability. What I didn't expect was to witness his strength.

A second after my suggestion was voiced, his shoulders rolled forward and his back arched. A ripping sound came from behind him, and then something emerged, something that seemed to grow directly from his back. It extended upward in a single line, split in two, and spread, sending a single grey feather into the flames still flickering at his feet. It caught fire, bursting into an intense flare, before shriveling into oblivion.

Wings.

Flavian had just grown wings.

Even his Vires, the men and women trained to protect him, stepped back.

He stared Maggie down, and she stared back.

Then, without any warning at all, she and Eran charged him, slamming into his body with a force that made Flavian stumble.

His wings caught, producing a powerful draft as he lifted the three of them off the ground to carry them up and over the hill behind him.

The Vires dedicated to preserving Flavian's life seemed to forget I was there, their eyes pinned on the horizon as they debated over whether to follow.

I had no option. I didn't have the benefit of flight. So when my feet swept out from under me and I was carried over their heads in the direction Flavian had disappeared, I didn't expect it. Not until I realized Jocelyn and Thelco were directly behind me, rapidly catching up. By the time they did, we found ourselves encircled by levitating Vires, their focus narrowed strictly to the horizon where Flavian had dropped out of sight. None of them seemed to notice we were flying in the middle of them.

When we breached the hill, they came to a sudden stop because what they saw must have been terrifying for them. It must have made them question their perception, because they couldn't have ever seen anything like it before. These men and women had been taught from childhood what to believe and the core of that belief structure was that The Sevens were indestructible. So when we met up with Maggie and Eran hauling Flavian's slumped body up the back of the hillside, the Vires didn't know what to think, what to do, or who to believe. They didn't seem to understand, or particularly care, that Flavian's body was being dragged or that he was soaked and the dirt was collecting in brown clumps on the edges of his slacks.

I'd bet they were concentrating on something else entirely.

His skin.

It had started to decompose like Sisera's had done, turning grey and shriveling like a raisin in the hot sun. As it deflated two things happened. First, his suspenders decorated with moldavite stones slipped from his shoulders to catch in the weeds. Second, it exposed the wings that had grown from Flavian's back. The feathered attachments that caused the Vires to step back in shock a few minutes earlier, scuffed the ground, leaving streaks in the earth behind him.

When Maggie and Eran noticed us collecting at the hill's peak, they unceremoniously dropped Flavian in the mud and continued their ascent.

But that wasn't good enough. Not for Flavian. Here was someone who...No, here was a *thing* that had pursued Jocelyn, our families, me, and countless others. It was his deceit, his laws, his punishments that kept us living in fear, chased us from our homes, made us conscious of ever step, every action. Yes, it was rewarding to see him dead, but it wasn't enough.

I strolled down the hill, passing Maggie and Eran, intending to make damn sure we left an impression with the Vires watching.

I paused at Flavian's body, took hold of his wings and, one after the other, broke them off. The crunch of their dislocation seemed to echo in the stunned silence. I threw them aside, where they landed and crumbled to dust, and then yanked the suspenders off Flavian's body. I then proceeded up the hill as the Vires remained motionless, too dazed to move.

"For proof...," I said, holding the suspenders up, "for those questioning their resilience."

Eran nodded just as the hint of a grin emerged.

I turned to Jocelyn and said, "I think it's time we leave now."

And we did, without a single Vire in pursuit.

In fact, when Jocelyn insisted on landing sporadically on the way back, to heal those needing her help, the Vires appeared to be vanishing, until there were none left in sight.

Our plan to take off the head to incapacitate the body worked.

By the time we returned to New Orleans a storm had stalled over the city, but that didn't dampen our spirits. We considered this a good omen, of sorts. Cloud coverage, the density of the downpour, and the slim chance anyone would look up allowed us to come in for a concealed landing. And this was especially important because I was carrying Flavian's suspenders, an object that would invoke respect from some and a death warrant from others.

We entered Maggie and Eran's house through the back door, with Maggie muttering something about why the lights were on in the parlor, which could be seen through the kitchen door window.

The scraping of what seemed to be glass screeched through the house as we opened the door, and my muscles tensed, making me freeze.

"What?" Eran and Maggie asked in unison, their eyebrows crossing in nervous confusion.

Jocelyn and I exchanged a hesitant glance.

"That's not a good sound," I said under my breath, stepping fully into the kitchen, and laying the suspenders on the table.

With a direct view of the parlor down the hall, I groaned and felt my shoulders sag as a deep pang of shame riddled me. The destruction was obvious; pieces of glass and porcelain were strewn across the floor and trailing into the kitchen.

The sighs and gasps coming from the door behind told me that they had seen it, too. Only Theleo, whose emotion was limited, seemed unmoved. He'd seen worse. We all had, but this time it was my family who had caused the damage.

It took a lot of effort for my feet to move in Ezra's direction. She was on her knees with a dustpan in one hand and a hand broom in the other. Ezra lifted her head to see who had entered as Jocelyn moaned, "Ezra, I'm so sorry."

Remorse hadn't hit me yet. Anger ruled my emotions.

Maggie moved by us demanding, "What happened here?"

Cringing, I waited for it...

"Well," Ezra sighed, "we had a little battle of our own. Nice to see you all back."

That was altruistic of her. Here she is, cleaning up after our families, and she's welcoming us back. Our families could take a lesson from her.

Felix, however, wasn't so understanding. "Little?" he said as his head appeared from around the corner. "I wouldn't call this little."

As we reached them, Rufus didn't say a word, remaining expressionless as he picked up a picture frame and brushed the shattered glass from the photo with his bare hand.

"Who started-," I said and cut myself off. "No, I don't want to know."

"Where are they?" Jocelyn asked, and I knew she was wondering if she was going to need to heal anyone.

"I split them up and kicked them out," Ezra stated matter-of-factly, as if it were just another day in their household. "They're fairly impressive, your families. They speak a few Latin phrases and things start flying."

"Evidently," Jocelyn said, stooping to collect a broken candle vase at her feet.

But I stopped her. "Where can I find another broom?"

Ezra directed me, and the next few minutes were spent scooping, sweeping, and dusting fragments of porcelain and glass from nearly every surface in the parlor room.

"Any challenges with Flavian?" Ezra asked, as she held a bag open for Jocelyn's trash.

"Not really," Maggie replied flatly, while Eran focused on brushing pieces out from beneath the couch.

It seemed like what they had done to Flavian they had done to others countless times before.

I stopped collecting pieces of glass from the mantel and stared at them.

"He was impaled and burned, and recovered from each one," I pointed out. If that wasn't a challenge, I didn't know what was.

My gaze drifted out the window to the rain pouring from eaves over the porch. "Water was his weakness...just water."

"What's your point?" Eran asked.

"When you and Maggie stopped coming to school last winter," I ventured, wondering if he'd actually tell me the truth. "Was this what you were doing? Taking down Sevens, or those like him?"

"Yes."

"Did you happen to learn the rest of The Sevens' vulnerabilities?"

"They're all different," Maggie said, plainly. "Every one of them."

Jocelyn figured out where I was heading with my questions, and asked, "Then how do we know how to execute the rest?"

Maggie began explaining that she and Eran determined their weaknesses while in the middle of the conflict, which made it clear why she didn't see a problem with how Flavian died. That didn't work for me. I was going to need something more solid.

That's when the pieces came together.

"There are others who have dealt with The Sevens before," I declared.

Theleo's focus shifted to me instantly, because he knew what I was referring to.

Felix, however, was stumped. "Who?"

"They stay on the periphery of our world, aware of its existence, but never entering unless absolutely necessary."

"So they haven't actually met The Sevens?" Felix countered.

"Let the lad speak," Rufus grumbled, and Felix rolled his eyes dramatically but remained quiet.

"They watch The Sevens," I clarified, "and they've been doing it for centuries. If anyone has learned about their weaknesses, it would be them."

"You're thinking of Miss Mabelle and Miss Celia," Jocelyn speculated.

I smiled. She knew me better than anyone else, but she didn't know this.

"There's one in particular, a woman who plenty of people know about but not many have met. She's someone you go to when you're sick or hurt, if you can find her."

"Is she a healer?" Jocelyn asked, intrigued.

"The opposite, she assesses what makes you weak."

"And you think," Eran contemplated, "that she can tell us what makes The Sevens weak."

"She did it for me, when she identified me as the Nobilis."

"She was the one who...," Jocelyn let her voice diminish as the shock of what I said took over. She recovered and said, "She saw your faults?"

"Really, Jocelyn? You notice faults in me?" I asked, teasing.

She smiled at me through a glare. "I'd like to meet her."

Foreseeing the problems that would create, I said, "I'm not sure that's a good idea."

"Why?" she countered.

"Because you won't like what she has to say."

"I'm a tough girl," she said with a smug sideways grin. "I think I can handle it."

When my lips pinched closed in protest, she ignored my reaction. "I'm going," she announced with enough resolve I knew she wouldn't yield.

While every part of me wanted to keep her here, where she wouldn't learn the truth about what made me weak, where she wouldn't be hurt by it, the intrigue was too great for her. And I knew that I would only be throwing fuel on the fire by opposing her.

Ignoring the tension I felt, I did a sweeping evaluation of the room, finding that it was almost entirely clean of broken pieces and debris.

"It's all right," Ezra said, noticing. "Go, the cleanup is done."

"Go where?" Felix asked, with a shrug, as if he'd missed the entire conversation.

Jocelyn had already started down the hallway, as determined as ever. Maggie, Eran, and Theleo followed. I hesitated, watching Jocelyn's black hair disappear out the back door.

"Go where?" Felix pressed.

Sighing, I held back the urge to berate myself. I should have handled the situation better. I should have foreseen her interest in meeting the woman.

"GO WHERE?" Felix nearly shouted, obviously frustrated over being ignored.

It was loud enough to jar me out of my thoughts. "Sorry, Felix…we're going to visit a voodoo priestess."

12. VOODOO

The downpour outside was both a blessing and a curse.

It gave us cover from the ground but it also inhibited our view of it. I contemplated this after giving Jocelyn directions to a remote part of the bayou, untouched for decades and overgrown with kudzu. It was a place seemingly uninhabitable for its lack of contact with civilization, without any roads or manmade paths to it. In short, it was hard to find, and designed to be that way.

When I thought we might be close, I mentioned, "I was only here once and it wasn't from the air, so it might take me a few minutes."

"How did you come before?" she asked, studying me, and I knew that it was just the start of many questions, including the one I wanted to avoid.

"By boat."

"Like that one?" she asked, pointing at something pink between the trees.

"Exactly like that one."

Taking my hint, she lowered us through the scraggly tree branches of a living cypress grove. In the middle of it, jammed between the trunks, was an old, beaten up fishing boat, dented on both sides from passing storms and with paint peeling from the beams.

The deck where we landed was no better. Water rot had eaten away the wood, leaving gaping holes in some places. Dirt that had never been washed off found its way beneath the corroding pink wood, collecting there as if it were propping up the peeling paint.

Theleo, Eran and Maggie immediately surveyed the area.

"It's safe," I reassured them.

Proof came when the only sounds that could be heard were the flat pings of raindrops across the water.

"Someone lives all the way out here?" Jocelyn asked, mesmerized, not intending to be patronizing at all.

Unfortunately, that's how it was interpreted.

"Yes," snapped a scratchy voice from a doorway leading inside. "Someone lives here."

Jocelyn's eyes widened at me. I took her hand, paused to enjoy the feel of it, and channeled, "Don't worry. Her bark is worse than her bite." Out loud, I greeted our host. "Mrs. LeClaire, your French accent has weakened."

"There is nothing weak about me, Jameson Caldwell," she said furtively before turning and walking inside.

She looked just like I remembered. Her head was wrapped in a scarf, placed far enough back that it exposed some of the wiry black hair she kept underneath. Despite living on a boat, she chose to wear a dress that covered her from chin to ankles. Countless pockets were poorly stitched into it, which she teased me with when I was younger, threatening to pull out a snake or a spider if I misbehaved. Her eyes were cat-like, always watching, and her lips remained permanently turned up at the ends as if she were making you aware that she knew what you didn't want her to know.

Recalling that Mrs. LeClaire's disappearance through the darkened doorway was her form of an invitation, I trailed her, hoping Jocelyn wouldn't follow. Of course, she did. Eran and Maggie did the same, alert by instinct even if they didn't need to be.

"Theleo?" I called out, already knowing he'd decline.

"I'll remain at my post," he replied, firmly.

Once a soldier, always a soldier.

Inside, I found that Mrs. LeClaire's residence hadn't changed, either. It was surreal, like being transported back in time. In the dim candlelight, everything still had a red tinge. The walls remained cluttered with shelves of various herbs, bowls, and the bones of long dead animals. The sparse furnishings were piled with pillows and colorful blankets. There wasn't a speck of dust anywhere, but there was plenty of disorder. The only difference between when I saw it last and now was that this time she had guests.

Seated around Mrs. LeClaire's cramped table, was a collection of the most powerful coven in our world: Ms. Veilleux, Ms. Boudreaux, Ms. Roquette and Mrs. DeVille. Mr. DeVille was sitting to his wife's right, appearing humbled in their presence. They wore the black cloaks so common in our world, and seemed out of place on a voodoo priestess's boat.

I was the only one not surprised, having been the person who sent them here when they went into hiding.

Ignoring the pleasantries, Ms. Veilleux declared, "You've been busy. Two Sevens dead...."

"You heard?" I asked, wondering how, given their distance to town.

"We read," Ms. Veilleux clarified, with a gleam in her eye.

"Being teachers at Ms. Veilleux's school," said Ms. Boudreaux, motioning to herself and Ms. Roquette, "we tend to read every now and again."

She was being snide, but I was used to it. As a teacher to the younger, newer students, I learned at an early age to avoid her as much as possible. That didn't seem possible right now, unfortunately.

"I imagine you've come to speak with Mrs. LeClaire?" she asked, and for dramatic flair adjusted her pointy black hat and ended up tapping Mrs. DeVille in the forehead. In response, Mrs. DeVille quietly grumbled, "Always…always, you must wear that hat."

Ms. Boudreaux ignored her.

"You've come to see Mrs. LeClaire?" she repeated, undeterred.

"Yes," I said, glancing in the woman's direction. She was currently sifting through the jars on one of her shelves.

"Believe she can tell you The Seven's weaknesses, hmmm?" Ms. Boudreaux asserted.

Ms. Veilleux shot a look full of warning in her direction, as if she had said too much.

"Yes," I uttered, suspiciously. "How did you know?"

"Oh, hmmm, yes, well…," she replied, flustered, and settled on a vague answer. "Good guess."

Jocelyn gave me a curious look, because we both believed Ms. Boudreaux knew more than she was admitting. I figured Maggie and Eran were doing the same.

I didn't get a chance to press her on it, because Mrs. LeClaire had ended her search and was now approaching us. She paused, drew in a slow, deep breath and circled us, and I got the feeling we were being inspected.

"The Relicuum?" she murmured. And a few seconds passed before adding, "Yes, yes…Isadora was correct. They have found the one." She hummed quietly to herself, finishing her rotation and coming to a stop in front of Jocelyn. "You fear the future. You fear what you believe will come to pass. You fear you cannot exist beyond it. That is your weakness, child. It burdens you, weighs on you. It degrades you. It is the source of what holds you back. But there is strength in you, even if it has been

162

wasted." She nearly spat out this last word in disgust and my instinct to protect Jocelyn ignited. Sensing this, Mrs. LeClaire turned on me. "Stop! This is her fight. She alone must learn to apply her power against the forces that corrupt." Returning to Jocelyn, her voice softened, and that was the lone reason I allowed her to continue. "Love, Relicuum, love...."

"I love Jameson," she declared, and my chest swelled.

Mrs. LeClaire appeared not to be impressed. Turning from Jocelyn, she replied indifferently, "And that is what will save you."

Jocelyn appeared to be thrown by this vague reference to our love being the resolution she'd been seeking, but in typical Jocelyn fashion, she moved on to the more practical reasons for our visit. "Can you tell us how to defeat The Sevens?"

I waited for an "or not" to be added, and given her tone I thought it might. But she stopped herself and that was perceptive of her. I remembered Mrs. LeClaire not appreciating poor behavior, and wondered at one point when my mother brought me here what had happened to Mr. LeClaire.

She didn't get her answer, in words anyways. Mrs. LeClaire collected the bowls, herbs, and bones she had been searching for earlier and gestured for us to move back.

Carefully, she lined the bowls up, all seven of them, in a single row, and then poured a mixture of herbs from several bags tucked underneath her armpit. Stowing the herbs on a shelf, she then took the bones and aligned them, each one positioned in front of a bowl, so that there was a bone pointing at each bowl.

We watched then as she began to shake, lifting each leg so that her knees came up to her chest. When she began to walk around the bowls this way, I peeked at Jocelyn, who was enthralled, and Maggie and Eran, who seemed inquisitive. Those sentiments only grew more intense when Mrs. LeClaire started to chant:

Papa Legba ouvre baye pou mwen, Ago eh!

Papa Legba Ouvre baye pou mwen,

Ouvre baye pou mwen, Papa

Pou mwen passe, Le'm tounnen map remesi Lwa yo!

She repeated these phrases three times, continuing her bizarre dance until the last word. Her body froze and she threw her hands out at the bowls as if she was tossing energy from her fingers. An unseen force caused the bones to slide wildly, scraping along the wooden floor and landing in front of their respective bowl Some were slammed hard enough that the bowls now sat askew from one another.

Mrs. LeClaire remained stationary, bent at the waist with her hands projected at the bowls for several seconds. Then she picked up the hem of her dress and shuffled forward for inspection. She murmured something to herself, apparently satisfied with the results, and stepped away as the rest of us leaned in and took her place.

The herbs had disappeared and each bowl now contained something different: a pool of water, shrapnel, shards of glass, a burnt surface, a splinter of bone, a small piece of ice, and then nothing at all.

"The last one," Maggie remarked. "It's empty."

"Nothing is ever empty," Mrs. LeClaire corrected in her strangely vague way. She leaned back and clasped her hands in front of her, conveying that we would need to decipher what her ceremony had told us on our own.

I stooped down for a closer look, the Vire pants still drenched from the rain stiffening my movement. I figure that's what led me to understand the bowl of water.

"I get it. There are seven bowls, each one representing a specific Seven's vulnerability. This is Flavian," I noted, pointing to the bowl containing the puddle.

"Ahh," Jocelyn murmured. "He was affected by water."

"Then this must be Sisera," Maggie added, gesturing to the shrapnel. "Because he was killed by my blade."

"Right," I agreed and appraised the remaining bowls. "So the others are susceptible to glass, fire, blunt force, cold, and…." I got stuck at the last one.

"I think we'll need to figure that one out as we go along," Eran suggested.

I acknowledged him with a nod.

"How do we know which bowl represents which Seven?" Maggie asked with a shrug. "Anyone have any ideas?" She tilted her head to the women at the table. "Any at all?" she pressed, insinuating that a little help would be appreciated.

When they dropped their eyes to the table, it was clear they wouldn't be helping us, either.

"Okay then…," she muttered.

A few seconds of silence passed and someone shifted, prompting the rest of us to stand. Jocelyn drew in a deep breath, weighted with nervous tension, and thanked Mrs. LeClaire. I took her hand and channeled the feeling of peace to her until she looked at me and smiled.

As an unspoken acknowledgement that our visit was ending, Maggie, Eran, Jocelyn, and I said goodbye to the women and headed for the door, but Jocelyn slowed as a question drifted through her mind. Listening to it was an invasion of privacy on my part, but an unintentional one.

The truth was, I knew it was coming. It was the reason she had come with me in the first place, and it hadn't been fulfilled yet. So when she turned back to the women, I tried to stop her. "Jocelyn, you don't want to ask that question."

"Yes, I do," she replied, her focus pinned on Mrs. LeClaire. And before I could warn her again, she addressed the priestess. "You discovered Jameson's weakness when he was younger. Is that accurate?"

Mrs. LeClaire assessed Jocelyn before responding, probably determining how Jocelyn would handle her answer. I took advantage of that pause.

"She doesn't need to know, Mrs. LeClaire."

Turning suddenly to face me, Jocelyn gawked at me, clearly appalled. Undeterred she repeated, "Is that correct, Mrs. LeClaire?"

"It is," she replied quietly, and I felt myself grimace.

Damn it, was now the only thought making its way through my mind.

Jocelyn relaxed, thinking she had won this argument, without any notion that no one would come out a winner.

"Mrs. LeClaire, will you tell me what Jameson's weakness is?"

The woman hesitated, continuing her assessment.

Urging her for an answer, Jocelyn explained, "If I know what it is, I can help him avoid it."

"That would be a challenge."

"Why?"

"Because," she said, a hint of sadness in her eyes. "*You* are his weakness."

13. REBELLION

"So our love will save me but hurt you?"

This notion had been festering in her since we left the bayou, forced down Felix's strange kidney and porcupine pie, and waited for the rest of the house to fall asleep so I could sneak into her room. She hadn't engaged with anyone since Mrs. LeClaire led her to believe it, not a single glance in anyone's direction and not a word at dinner. And this was exactly why I didn't want her to know.

"Don't take it seriously," I replied, coming into her room. Although, I knew that she would.

"You're obviously not, or you wouldn't be here with me." She sighed in the darkness.

Proving her point, I moved toward her voice. "Where are you?"

She ignored my question in favor of the far more pressing topic, making me want to kiss her just to shut her up. "How many people need to tell you that I'm a danger to you before you'll believe it?"

"Jocelyn, I know you better than anyone. The only danger you put me in is when you put yourself in jeopardy, because I have to risk my life to save yours."

She sighed again, a sound that was seductive even if it wasn't meant to be. "This isn't a game, Jameson. You take everything so lightly."

"And you," I said, finding her and pulling her to me, "are taking this far too seriously." I slipped my arms around her waist and held her against me. When I spoke again it was quieter, more sincere. "All right, I did believe it once. When I was younger, and had never met you. If I had any idea who you were, other than a Weatherford, I would have stayed clear of you." Hearing this statement leave my lips caused me to stop and assess the accuracy behind it. When I continued, my head shook with my confession. "No, no, that's actually not true."

She sighed in frustration.

"The truth is," I said, with a shrug, "that by the time I found out that you were the Relicuum, it was too late. I'd already fallen in love with you, Jocelyn. There was no turning back after that, or in this case, there was no turning away. There was nothing anyone could do, not you, not your family, not mine, and definitely not me. You are my weakness, because I can't say goodbye. And I'm willing to accept that if it means being with you for only a few more days, a few more hours, a few more minutes. Whether the prophecy is correct or not doesn't matter to me. What does is making the most of the time we have on this earth. I'm going to take it, regardless of the risks that might come attached with it."

With my eyes adjusted to the dark now, I saw her frown.

"You look…torn…."

"I am," she admitted. "Part of me wants to kiss you, part of me wants to push you away. You are impossible to argue with, do you know that?"

168

"Yes, I've been told," I said, unsuccessfully trying to hold back a grin. "And Jocelyn?"

"Hmm?"

"You should choose the kiss."

The hint of a smile lifted her cheeks and I tightened my hold around her waist.

She leaned in and before either one of us remembered Charlotte's curse, our lips touched.

Jocelyn let out a moan, making me think it was in passion. Not until she swayed to the side in an effort to put space between us did I understand. I held her up, steadying her, and drew in the pain to relieve her of it.

"Stop," she whispered. "Jameson, stop."

I shook my head, because that was all I could manage, and continued to draw the hurt from her. Then she withdrew from me and moved away, in an attempt to save me.

We healed, slowly, both of us panting and with our hands on our knees, propping us up. Only when we looked up to check on each other did I know the effects of the curse were dissipating.

I reached out and took her arm, straightening her to a full standing position. "Are you all right?"

"I'm going to be...when Charlotte recants this curse," she muttered, somewhat joking. She glanced at the bed, and in the moonlight I saw the craving on her face. "Think you can hold me tonight?"

I was surprised she even asked. "Yes," I said and watched her considering what to do next.

"Jocelyn," I said, although it came out a question.

Her head spun back to me. "Hmm?"

"Are you...Have you...been with anyone before?"

Her face went still before she answered. "Never."

She strolled to me, leaned in and kissed me softly on the lips. "You'll be my first," she said, her sweet breath brushing my face. "And my only."

Oh my go-, I thought as my body responded to her. It was so potent, my reaction, that I had to close my eyes against it. But when I opened them she did something I couldn't have guessed was coming.

She stepped back, smiled lightly, and locked eyes with me as her fingers pinched the waist of pajama bottoms she wore. My heart leapt, stalled, and started beating double-time as she slipped them down and off her legs.

"Do you know how badly you're teasing me right now?" I asked.

Still watching me with that trivial grin, she took the hem of her pajama top and started to lift it.

Unable to stop myself, I strode to her, slipped my hands around her waist and kissed her. She didn't move, not her arms, her body, or her lips. Because she couldn't. When I was done, I pulled my lips away but not my head, instead resting my forehead on hers. I was afraid if I looked up, I'd fail at what I was about to do.

With more control than I'd ever used in my life, I kept my hands where they were and warned her, "If you continue, there's no stopping me. And this isn't the way I want our first time to be." When she didn't respond, I forced the next words out of my mouth, because they were an incredible struggle to utter. "I can't believe I'm asking this...." I stopped to draw in a shaky breath. "But would you mind keeping your shirt on?"

That was so hard for me to say that I had to exhale deeply at the end.

"I thought you'd like it." She wasn't hurt as much as confused.

"I do," I said hastily before summing up the situation with complete honesty. "I just can't physically take knowing that you're naked beside me without acting on it."

"I'm sorry, I-"

"Don't be," I said and laughed. "If you could respond to me...if we were alone and I could make sure your first time would be perfect, there would be no way we would be having this conversation right now. We'd be...well, we wouldn't be standing any longer."

That must have struck her as funny because she laughed, which was an incredible sound after feeling the suffocating tension that had been filling the room.

I took her hand and walked her to the bed. She laid down on it and again I sent out a silent curse to Charlotte, hoping she'd come down with the stomach flu just so she could endure a little taste of her own medicine.

When I laid my body next to Jocelyn, and she lifted her head to my chest, it was still a struggle to keep my arms wrapped around her torso and my hands on my forearms.

My heart was beating so damn hard I was surprised it didn't keep her awake. But when she closed her eyes a few seconds later, she whispered, "Jameson?"

"Yes?"

"The pain was worth it to feel your lips again."

And I realized that Jocelyn was teased just as much as me by our hesitant contact. As my heartbeat slowed, I began to doze, thinking about that touch, and smiling.

It was a good, solid sleep, and when the pounding on the door the next morning woke us, we found ourselves in the same position.

The knock came again, more rapidly, rattling the door with its force. Rufus called out from the other side, urgent and demanding. "Yu'll wanna get up fer this 'un. Yer people 'er fightin' back."

Your people are fighting back? I thought, and shot out of Jocelyn's bed.

She was up just as fast. "I'll meet you downstairs," she said, sweeping her eyes down my body.

I nodded and headed into Eran's room for my clothes while Jocelyn dressed in one of the various outfits that had mysteriously appeared in her room. I credited Miss

Mabelle for them, just like I knew Miss Celia had left fresh ones for me on Eran's dresser.

Thinking that a Vire uniform wouldn't be the best idea when our own people are rebelling, I slipped on jeans and a white t-shirt, grabbed Flavian's suspenders, and headed down.

When I got to the foot of the stairs, Jocelyn noticed and seem to appreciate the change. I, however, was paying attention to the fact that both doors, the front and the back, were wide open. From my vantage point, I saw my family collected on the porch and the Weatherfords in the back yard. Each of them appeared to be suffering from some type of injury.

Apparently, neither family recanted their casts after the earlier battle.

Besides those who resided here, there was only one other person standing in the parlor. Isabella - the only one with the courage to enter the house after what had been done to it the last time both families congregated - ran her hands through her now grey hair, remnants of one of my family member's casts. She sighed heavily and then made her announcement, "After hearing about Sisera's death, and now Flavian's, preemptive strikes are being made against Vires."

"Where?" I asked.

"The fifth and seventh provinces. And the others will follow." Isabella was guarded, yet optimistic. This was something that I'd never seen in her before, which told me these weren't random rebellions and they weren't insignificant in size.

"Can you take me?" I asked.

"Us," Alison called through the front door. "Can you take all of us?"

Isabella deserved a good dose of praise for setting aside our family feud in favor of the larger issue. It couldn't have been easy. So when she nodded in approval and my family began streaming into the house, I leaned in and quietly thanked her.

She acknowledged me with a stubborn, "Mmhmm," and trailed my family as they moved toward the back door.

Jocelyn did the same, which made me nervous.

"Jocelyn," I said cautiously because she wasn't going to like the point I was about to make, but at least she paused to hear me out. "With Sisera and Flavian dead, the rest of The Sevens will have merged their forces. They'll be looking for us, so it isn't a good idea for you to-"

"Again Jameson?" she asked, appalled.

"Yes, again, I don't want you to go."

"I am," she replied flatly, starting for the back door. "Someone might need a healer."

Eran, who overheard us, stepped up next to me as I watched her leave. "You really love her, don't you?"

Without shifting my stare from Jocelyn, I admitted, "I'd give my life for her."

"Well," he said, clapping me on the back, "let's make sure that doesn't happen."

"Just keep an eye on her for me?"

"Already planned on it."

"Thanks."

Once outside, we found that the storm had reduced itself to a drizzle overnight, which allowed us the obscurity we needed to travel by levitation. Isabella thought it would be better to visit the fifth province first. This encompassed Eastern Europe, which meant there were uprisings in Norway, Germany, and Poland. We stopped in Norway first, a place I'd never been, and therefore was at the mercy of Isabella and her navigational abilities. We passed over Oslo, unseen at our height, and she deposited us at the base of a mountain range.

It was daylight and the sky was clear and blue here, which meant a rapid descent. Luckily, she was just as good as Jocelyn at catching us before we hit the ground at full speed. Once stationary, we got a good look around.

The field in front of us was littered with bodies, some in Vire uniforms, some in plain clothes. They were bloodied, frozen, or burnt. Not a single one was unscathed.

"We're too late," someone muttered from behind me.

Jocelyn shook her head in disgust and immediately went to work, checking the bodies for any sign of life. Maggie did the same, seeming to pay closer attention to their backs, for some unexplainable reason. The rest of us followed, keeping an eye out for any movement that would indicate life.

Midway through the field, I overheard someone ask, "Are you going to be okay?"

Turning, I found Estelle cautiously watching Charlotte, which was gratifying considering Estelle was a Weatherford.

"You look…greenish-grey," Estelle pointed out.

There was no possible way that Charlotte was sickened by the sight of the bodies. If anyone could be as unmoved by it, it was her. But she did have a different skin tone, which I hadn't noticed before. "You feeling bad?" I asked, with some amount of pleasure.

She waved us both off. "Stomach flu. Nothing that'll keep me down."

I noted that she was slightly bowed forward as she said this, a sign that she wasn't being entirely honest.

"The stomach flu?" I repeated, remembering my inclination last night to see her suffer with it.

"Yes," she said warily. "Why?"

Stifling a grin, I walked by her, muttering, "You'll be healed if you recant your curse against Jocelyn."

"Did she do this to me?" she demanded, appalled.

"No," I replied, continuing to check the bodies. But I did pause to look up at her before answering, giving her the benefit of seeing the sincerity in my expression. "I did, Charlotte."

She grunted, I looked away, and we didn't speak again for the duration of our walk down the field.

When we reached the end, I turned to find someone leaping through the air, their legs bent and ready for a landing. He was wearing suspenders, a single alexandrite family stone on each side, to hold up his trousers over a round midsection. Below his balding head, his plump face was glistening and firmly fixed with apprehension.

"You shouldn't be here," he said with a thick Norwegian accent before his feet even reached the earth.

His warning caused the rest of our group to turn around.

"Why are you here?" the man pressed. "It isn't safe."

Jocelyn laughed disdainfully under her breath. With her usual sarcasm returning, she replied, "We can see that."

He pressed his lips together at her.

"Who are you?" I asked. "Do you live here?"

"We need to leave," he said, checking the sky. "The cleanup squad will be here any minute."

"He's correct," Lester said, stepping over a body as he approached us. "We should depart."

Considering that Lester had worked at the Ministry handling that very task, I believed him.

"Isabella?" I called out, but we were already being lifted into the air.

"Come with me," the man shouted back, elevating us across the field. "You won't make it overhead without them seeing you."

We darted across the ground, in a method I'd never seen used before because it left us easily visible. We reached a barn on the outskirts of the field but weren't released until we'd all landed inside. Although I didn't appreciate the man's control over us, it turned out to be a good idea because the second we landed a group of black uniforms dropped out of the sky. The door was closed quickly behind us, and my instinct was to step between it and Jocelyn.

The barn had weathered over time, shriveling the boards that made up its walls until slim gaps were formed. Through them, we could see the Vires commencing their work. As fifteen or so walked the field, just like we had done minutes earlier, the bodies before them disintegrated, one by one.

"They're casting," Estelle determined, and was shushed by the man who had urged us off the field. His curtness kept her quiet for the rest of the Vires' work.

Once finished, they levitated into the air, leaving as rapidly as they had descended.

The man waited several seconds and then turned sharply to address us. "What were you thinking? Don't you know what happened here? Are you sightseers?"

The threat seemed to have shifted now, so I moved to come between him and Jocelyn.

"Sightseers?" Burke muttered in disgust under his breath.

The man angled his head toward him. "Yes, idiots who show up after the uprising has ended for a look at the dead." To the rest of us, he repeated, "Are you sightseers?"

"No, sir," my father said, stepping forward. "We came to help."

"You're a little late," he ridiculed.

"We can see that," Jocelyn said.

He didn't appear to like her trivial remark, and with the Vires gone, he didn't seem opposed to shouting. "Are you in the habit of insulting those who work to claim your freedom?"

Without waiting for an answer, he strode rapidly in her direction. His head was bowed as he charged her, his cheeks blowing out with each huff, and his short legs carried him quick enough that no one had time to consider him a threat until it was almost too late. No one, that is, but me.

With one hand, I took hold of Jocelyn's wrist. With the other, I pointed my palm at him. He was one step away by then, but I had already used Jocelyn's ability to levitate and channeled it into a hard burst toward the man. He flew off his feet, backward, into the barn wall on the opposite end, legs and arms flailing from the push. When he hit, the barn shook, sending pieces of loose boards and pockets of dust down on us.

A few screams rang out, everyone ducked, but the man didn't move.

Then everyone was staring at me.

"Sorry for that," I chuckled, heading for the man. I might have been too aggressive with my approach but he was blindly coming at Jocelyn, which is a bad idea if I'm around.

I was wrong about their reaction, though.

Nolan, who rivaled Charlotte at being callous, clapped me on the shoulder and snickered. "Doesn't look that way to me. You got him, just the way you wanted him. He is down and out...."

Eran came up beside us, laughing to himself. "You'll need to show me that trick some time."

Jocelyn, however, was focused on her attacker. She trailed us until we reached him and then squatted to place her hand on his to begin healing him.

Spencer stepped up to watch. He'd always reminded me of a professor in a younger body, so when he started rubbing his chin and appearing pensive and reflective it didn't surprise me.

"He just asked are you in the habit of insulting those who work to claim your freedom," he reiterated. "*Who work to claim your freedom*...Is he a Dissident?"

The man's eyelids fluttered but didn't open fully until he mumbled, "That I am, Sightseer." Then he was staring up at us, frowning. "That was a good hit."

"Thank you," I replied.

"Now help me up," he grumbled.

Once on his feet, he gave Jocelyn an intrigued stare. "You're a healer," he stated, as if he'd just come to that conclusion.

She nodded.

"Aren't many of you left. The Sevens have done a good job of erasing you. How did you manage to go unnoticed?"

"I haven't," she replied flatly.

"What's your name?" he asked.

His eyebrows furrowed then and I wondered if he was beginning to recognize her.

"Jocelyn."

"Weatherford?" he asked, sharply.

"Yes."

"You're Jocelyn Weatherford?"

"Yes."

"The Jocelyn Weatherford?" he asked again, and then drove home his point. "The Relicuum?"

"Yes."

His mouth fell open and he took her hand, kissing the back of it. I cleared my throat. He pulled away, but his hands didn't release her fingers.

"So you aren't sightseers," he concluded, glancing at the rest of us.

"No. What's your name?" I asked, moving the conversation along. "And you can release her now," I added, prompting a knowing smile from Jocelyn.

He did, reluctantly.

"Hans."

"What do you know about this uprising, Hans?"

He blinked, and it looked like he was shocked. "What do I know? My friends and I saw the Vires land. We saw what they were up to. And we weren't about to sit back and let it happen, like the rest of the world. So we caught them off guard and annihilated them. *That's* what I know. And it wasn't the first time."

There was an uncomfortable pause until Jocelyn murmured, "Excuse me?"

"Oh, no. Excuse me, my lady. I only meant this wasn't the only instance when we hurt the Vires."

She shifted her gaze in my direction, insinuating that she might take over the conversation, and I tipped my head to her.

"What do you mean," she inquired, "by 'the first time'?"

His lips tilted to the side in a sneaky grin. Leaning in as if he wanted only Jocelyn to hear, he whispered, "We've been doing it in secret."

"For how long?" Isabella interjected, unable to hold back her question.

Hans remained fixated on Jocelyn as he answered, continuing his hideous leer. "Since Sisera."

Our eyes widened almost in unison.

"It told us they weren't undefeatable," Hans finished. "They're not, you know."

"Really?" Jocelyn said, to keep the conversation going, and I fought to contain my smile.

It was amusing watching her spin her web of stupor around Hans.

"No, no they're not," he claimed, earnestly. "You've heard of Flavian's death too, haven't you? He has fallen as well. Yes, he has. We know because his Vires…hear this…they watched as he lost his life. And," he held up a finger signaling us to wait for his announcement, "he died even though he had…wings…"

He paused for her reaction, which she passed off as genuine surprise, slapping a hand over her mouth and widening her eyes.

"Yes, wings! I always knew there was something strange about them, didn't you?"

She nodded vigorously, still covering her mouth. It took everything I had not to laugh at her excellent acting performance.

"And his murderers," Hans went on dramatically, "tore the wings off him."

Jocelyn gasped. "No!"

"Yes! Did it to take his suspenders as a trophy."

"Flavian wore suspenders?"

Hans reeled forward in astonishment. "Every day! And they were beautiful! Not like these," he said, snapping his own suspenders. "They were…were…" He stopped and an odd expression contorted his face. He quietly tilted his head and blinked.

Nolan, who was still standing next to me, hit the suspenders that were tucked inside my waist. "Covered with moldavite stones? Like these?"

Hans blinked again and lifted his eyes to mine. "Where did you get those?"

I answered simply with a smug grin.

He gawked at me for a long couple of seconds and then, almost inaudibly, he uttered, "What is your name?"

"Jameson Caldwell," I replied, and he inhaled sharply.

"You-you became a Vire," he blurted in bewilderment, and then he lunged for me. Before I knew it, his hands were around my throat. "You traitor! You were to unify us! And what you did was desert us! You turned down a truce that could have saved us from war only to…to build your own personal army!"

Either because I was familiar with my life being threatened or because of the training in my earlier years, I didn't pay as much attention to the squeezing of his fingers as I did to the realization that he was incredibly well-informed. I wanted to ask him how he'd learned of the truce The Sevens had falsely perpetuated to make their case against me or how he knew about the army of Dissidents rising up against Sartorius in the bayou.

But Hans was bent on revenge. "And now you...! You...! You will die for it!"

He didn't get too far with that death threat. My family pulled him off me, dragging him aside where he huffed wildly with crazed, glassy eyes.

I stepped up to him, where Burke put a meaty hand on my chest, restraining me. But I didn't have any plans to hurt the man.

"You're right," I said. "I did become a Vire. I was supposed to unify you. I did desert you. I did turn down a truce. And I did build my own personal army. Everything you said was correct, Hans."

"What? No!" Jocelyn shouted, always my loyal supporter.

"That's not correct," my mother insisted vehemently. "He did none of those things."

"It's all right," I replied, never taking my eyes off Hans, whose rationale was returning. "I did everything you mentioned. Everything. But I did them with the best of intentions...and I failed."

Failed, the word ran through my head again, and I had to hold back a scowl. It was an accurate word, but not one that I had ever applied to myself. It meant defeat, to lose, to walk away in shame.

And that wasn't me.

I drew in a deep breath, clearing my thoughts, and coming back to the point at hand. Pulling out and holding up Flavian's suspenders for everyone to see, I stated, "Flavian is dead. Sisera is dead."

Hans's nodded once, acknowledging his understanding.

"And the others...," I said, meeting his stare. "I give you my word, Hans. We'll get to them, too."

Turning, I tucked the suspenders back in at my waist and made my way through the throng behind me to the barn door, the surge of adrenaline and pride bringing my back erect and my head high.

Because nothing…nothing would stop me this time.

14. CALIGULA

The hours that followed couldn't pass fast enough.

I sent Isabella back to the Ministry for a meeting with Stalwart, which would give us information on the whereabouts and future plans of The Sevens. I sent the rest back to their safe houses. But my plans didn't end there. Before Estelle separated from us, I asked if she could design Vire uniforms and gave her loose measurements for the intended wearers. Being our resident seamstress and fashion-forward counselor, she asked a bit too eagerly if they could be in purple. I said no. They needed to be black, which she griped about but ultimately conceded to. She seemed to be more willing after I handed her Flavian's suspenders and asked her to use the stones for the collars. She nodded, in awe of the gift, and said she'd do her best. The rest gave me questioning stares, which I answered vaguely, saying they might be of some use. The truth was we were going to need them to get close to the next Seven.

Afterwards, there was nothing we could do but wait. That was the worst part. I knew The Sevens wouldn't be waiting, and the Vires who did their bidding were already positioning themselves around the world. I heard the clock inside me ticking, the rotors making their clacking sound with each passing minute. Jocelyn could sense my urgency and addressed it as soon as she could.

We'd just finished dinner, another curious meal by Felix, this one cured opossum over mossy grits, which made me crave Miss Celia's fried chicken and mashed potatoes. While the rest of the household played a loud board game at the kitchen table, Jocelyn and I offered to do the dishes, giving us a few precious minutes together.

Midway through the pile Felix left us on the counter, she leaned toward me. "I've considered taking a peek at your thoughts, but figured that would be an invasion of your privacy." The hint embedded in her message made me grin.

"Everyone seems to be in their own world today," I muttered.

"Oh…so that's what you're thinking about…the Dissidents rising up."

Releasing a heavy sigh, I admitted to her as much as to myself, "If I don't get to The Sevens, there won't be any Dissidents left."

"We," she corrected softly. "If we don't get to them. You forget that you're not in this alone."

"I don't want you to be in it, Jocelyn. I don't want you anywhere near it."

For once, she didn't argue with me. "I know. I feel the same way about you."

That made me want to kiss her, until my next thought surfaced.

"They'll do it again. The Dissidents will attack the Vires, putting themselves in danger in the worst possible way. They'll do it alone, without forethought, without skill." I laughed through my nose at myself. "And with all my training, all my strategic planning, I can't help them. Because they don't trust me." I had to stop and release the tension in my hand before I broke the glass I was gripping.

"They will," she insisted, full of optimism I didn't feel. "Give them time."

"Time, unfortunately, is something we don't have."

She didn't respond, focusing instead on the dishes.

"So your thoughts are consumed by the Dissidents...not me?" She seemed amused.

I let my hands fall into the soapy water before pausing to answer. "I'm always thinking about you. When we're separate, I wonder how you're doing, what you're thinking, if you're happy. When you're with me, I notice the way your hair falls down your back, the shine in your eye like you have right now, whether you're laughing or content."

"My eyes are shining?" she murmured, and I wondered if she'd heard the rest of what I'd said.

"They're beautiful, mesmerizing."

Stunning, remarkable, intoxicating...

She stared at me with those eyes, drawing me in until it took all of my strength not to kiss her. "You're teasing me."

"Yes," she admitted smugly, just before her expression shifted to genuine sincerity. "I love you."

Her words made my heart skip.

She lowered her head back to the sink. "And I am content," she whispered, before a smile gradually lifted her lips.

Watching her made that pulse inside me increase its tempo.

We returned to the dishes, finishing them in silence throughout sporadic bursts of activity coming from the table behind us. These were caused by either unexpected twists in the game or Rufus objecting to Felix's interpretation of the rules, and it was always entertaining. But that excitement was nothing in comparison to what I felt standing next to Jocelyn. We had our own game. There was an ebb and flow to our movement, almost brushing against one another, coming close but never enough to touch. It created an electric vibe so intense I wondered how the rest of those in the room didn't pick up on it. Our families would have, and we'd have been called out on it. Instead, the shift in our stances, the slide of our arms outward, the near brush of our fingers in handing over the next plate were left just for us to enjoy. These silent exchanges were followed by glances at the reflection in the window in front of us, tempting us, teasing us.

"You two want to play the next round?" Eran asked, breaking the gaze Jocelyn and I were sharing at the moment.

I waited for her to respond and when she didn't I clued in that she was doing the same. "I think we're going to pass," I replied.

"Suit yourself," he said with a shrug.

When the last dish was dried, we turned and found them engrossed in their game.

"I think we'll head upstairs," I announced.

"Yeah," Jocelyn said, yawning. Whether real or bogus, it was convincing.

Rufus and Felix gave us perceptive glances while the rest kept their focus on the board. We made it to the base of the stairs before Ezra realized she'd forgotten something.

"Keep the door open," she warned. "You know the rules."

"Yes, we do."

Of course, I didn't mention we'd been breaking them nightly.

Already knowing what I was going to do to Jocelyn once we were alone, a tightening of expectation took hold of my stomach. On the first step up the stairs, I had already started yearning for the ability to levitate, to whip Jocelyn off her feet and up to the second floor before Ezra had bowed her head to the game board again.

Of course that was wishful thinking. I knew this when the back door opened and Ezra called out to us again, "Jameson? Jocelyn?"

And it made me drop my head and groan. "No...," I muttered.

Jocelyn giggled behind me and I looked back. "You heard that?"

She smiled and nodded.

By that point, the visitor was at the end of the hallway. It was Isabella, who didn't bother with a greeting to anyone in the kitchen, so I knew her news was urgent.

Only then did my disappointment at her interruption fade.

"They're doing it again," she said, coming to a halt, her face pinched with tension. "The Dissidents are attacking the Vires."

"You were right," Jocelyn muttered, gazing at me.

"Where?" I said, turning full circle.

"Sixth Province. Eastern China. The Pinggu District. It seems they've set their sights on Beijing."

Heading for the kitchen, I called out, "Eran? Maggie?"

"You're going to need more than two in your group," Isabella cautioned.

"Why?" I asked, pausing in the hallway.

"Because they've combined their forces."

My body was suddenly immobile, feeling like I'd ran into a brick wall. Numbingly, I began processing this information.

Sartorius was getting his wish. The Sevens were following his plan perfectly. As we eliminated his associates, the fighting force - the one he would claim when he remained the sole Seven alive - grew larger with each death. Kalisha had been correct. Forces were uniting as The Sevens fell, and it was unnerving to watch it unfold. This meant they would know to expect us, which made Estelle's uniforms all that more important.

I nodded to Isabella to show my understanding. "Let's hope Estelle has those uniforms finished," I muttered. "We're going to need them."

"Behold!" Estelle spun into the kitchen, melodically singing her own praises. "At your request, sir, the most beautiful renderings of a Vire uniform in history!"

I was under the impression that Isabella had come alone, so I was surprised to see her, and in such a giddy mood. My first thought was to remind her that people were dying, but somehow I don't think that would have put much of a dent in her reality.

She pinned the uniform to her shoulders by the tips of her fingers as she swept around the room. It flew off her torso like a wave of black until her rotations came to a stop in the center of the room, to promote her achievement. She was in luck. No one in the room missed her entrance.

"Thank you, Estelle," I said, strolling into the kitchen and taking the canvas bag next to the door where she'd left it.

I noticed the rest of our families clogging the doorway outside and ushered them in.

"There are three, just as you asked," Estelle announced.

"And which three will be wearing them?" Jocelyn inquired on behalf of everyone filtering into the small kitchen.

I gave her a look that told her I was weary of her insistence in participating, but she only folded her arms in opposition.

"Maggie," I said, attracting her attention. "You'll need to forgo your black suit this time."

She stared back at me, hesitantly. "Because?"

"Because you'll be wearing a Vire uniform instead," I explained, passing Estelle's handiwork to her.

Her lip curled up in disgust.

"Trust me," I told her, "I know exactly how you feel."

"Why this?"

"Again…you'll need to trust me."

"I'm fighting on the good side," she reminded me.

"Which is precisely why we need to be wearing this if we're going to reach Caligula."

"Caligula?" Eran asked.

"The sovereign leader of that province. I'm assuming he'll be there this time."

"What makes you think so?" asked Spencer, the more cerebral of the Weatherfords, as he leaned against the kitchen counter.

"It's a hunch, but I imagine if they have a large force on the ground, they're protecting someone or something." I turned back to Maggie and handed the uniform to her.

Clearly opposing the idea, but seeing no other way around it, she snatched it from my hands and marched upstairs.

Eran leaned toward me, while keeping his eyes on the stairs, to whisper, "Magdalene doesn't like uniforms very much."

I chuckled, and replied, "I got that impression. Hope you don't have the same issue."

He lifted one shoulder in a shrug and smirked. "I'll go naked if it'll do the job." Ignoring the chuckles that followed, he headed upstairs with his uniform in hand.

"And the third?" Jocelyn pressed, lifting her eyebrows at me.

I took the remaining uniform and strode to her. Feeling victorious, her eyes lit up, but calmed when I didn't release my grip on the clothes.

"I'm hesitant to allow this, Jocelyn. You entered the conflict last time when I told you not to, not without my signal. And that signal never came. Did it?

She sighed and rolled her eyes.

"I'm serious, Jocelyn. I love you. The very core of me wants to keep you here. But you bring up a valid point. Your healing ability is needed on the field. And with the

Dissidents rebelling there will be injuries. That said, you will remain behind with Theleo until we have secured the area and I personally tell you it is safe to enter. Let me repeat that...I personally will tell you when it is safe to enter."

In a paramount gesture of acceptance, Jocelyn whispered, "Yes, Nobilis."

My eyebrows shot up in surprise.

And then her lips turned up in a sideways grin. "I will allow you this one wish, oh Great One."

With that, she tore the clothes from my hands and waltzed upstairs.

Snickering broke out around the room, and when I faced them, they were cowering behind hands clapped over their mouths.

"Nice to see you all finding common ground," I pointed out, which prompted several dirty looks across to the opposing family.

"Common ground?" said Charlotte sarcastically, always instigating. Although she still looked flushed from the stomach flu, it didn't seem to impede her taste for conflict.

"What's with your attitude, Charlotte," Nolan demanded, his notoriously brute side showing.

My mother opened her mouth, and appeared interested in quelling the growing argument, but she never got a chance.

"What's with your attitude?" Dillon countered. "You have no class, Nolan."

"Class?" Nolan laughed. "Who needs class when they're dealing with a Caldwell?"

From there, the small kitchen became a battleground. Dishes spun and shattered, fireballs singed the curtains, icicles slammed into several heads. Ezra and Rufus were on their feet, either protecting themselves from the damage or screaming to be heard. Felix had slipped from the room after the first assault.

"ENOUGH!" I shouted over the anarchy. "ENOUGH!" And when they still didn't listen, I took hold of Charlotte's arm, channeled her ability, and sent every one of them up against the wall. That quieted them down.

With their attention now on me, and my hand still on Charlotte while she remained pinned to the refrigerator, I carefully explained, "Your fighting is becoming a nuisance, and worse, a distraction. There are people, friends...family members, out there who need our help. Right now, our allies, people with less training than you, are defending themselves against Vires. And you're here, bickering, as The Sevens stride into history as the rulers over our world, the innocent world beyond it, and every world that comes after ours has been obliterated and forgotten. We need to focus and rely on each others' strengths. I have seen you cast the most amazing spells – but at each other. You need to ask yourselves who you should really be casting at. Focus. This is exactly what the Sevens want. To tear us apart from within. What are we really trying to do here? We all have incredible abilities – but imagine what we can do together. Together we have the power but only if we use it together. That is exactly what the Sevens fear the most – all of us uniting – an uprising, and for good reason. If we can come together we can be a great and powerful force. Understand, those of you pinned to the wall at this moment, that you are being neither great nor powerful. Because those two forms of leadership traits are hidden beneath layers of anger and criticism. But it is up to you to overcome it...because there is far more at stake than this feud, than your indifferences, or the preservation of my life." I drew in a deep breath, letting this message sink in. "Now, because you have proven yourselves to be lacking restraint, I will release the Weatherfords first. And I warn you all, if you so much as give the opposing family a sideways glance, you will find yourself back where you are now. Only this time, I'll leave you there…indefinitely."

No one spoke as I slid them to the ground, not even when the back door was opened and they sifted through it.

Behind me, Jocelyn, Maggie, and Eran stood at the opening to the hallway leading into the house, watching them leave, leery about what might flare up again. But only my mother paused at the door.

"You've become stronger, Jameson," she said.

I blinked in confusion and she explained, "Your ability to cast us against the wall was telling, but I'm not talking about that. I'm talking about your wisdom. You see with clear eyes, while ours are clouded with emotion."

"It's Jocelyn," I replied instinctively, not sure how she'd accept that news. "The longer I'm with her, the stronger I am."

She considered this for a moment and gave me a hesitant smile, before taking a speculative look at Jocelyn, and left. As she cleared the doorway, I was met with Charlotte's grim face.

"She makes you strong, huh?"

"Yes."

"Strong enough to defend yourself against her?"

I knew where she was headed with her question. "I'll never retaliate against Jocelyn. You should know that by now."

"But you could if you needed to?" she pressed. "Because you're channeling her strength, her ability to heal, correct?"

She's hinting at something, I thought.

And that's when it came to me.

Charlotte had cast against Jocelyn knowing that I would do everything in my power to ease her pain. I'd find some way to reduce it, and Charlotte knew eventually that solution would lead to channeling. And if I could absorb her pain, if I could absorb Charlotte's ability to levitate, then I could absorb Jocelyn's capacity for healing.

Charlotte, in her twisted way, had shown her wisdom.

Slowly, and in a barely audible whisper, I answered, "Yes, Charlotte, I can."

With the hint of a smile and a reserved tip of her head, she said, "Good luck in China."

As her feet swung off the ground and up behind her and she levitated into the darkness, I found myself torn. I was grateful for her guidance, and yet angry at her for using Jocelyn to steer me toward it.

"Ready?" Jocelyn asked.

Turning, I finally took in Estelle's uniforms, and admitted to myself how startling the three of them looked. They were the faces of those who I trusted yet they wore the uniform of those who I'd unsympathetically kill on a second's notice. Had I considered the implications then, I might have been able to avoid what happened later. As it was, I found it ironic that Jocelyn's hand swept up and from it hung my Vire uniform. "I figured you'd need one too," she said with a shrewd smile.

After changing, we headed for China. On the way there, I kept an eye out for yawns and eye rubs. Drowsiness led to lethargy, which led to errors, which ultimately led to death. Although I'd been trained to perform well when sleep deprived, I wasn't sure the others could, so it was a relief when they showed no signs of fatigue. Still, to keep them alert, I filled them in on what I knew about Caligula.

"This one has the most military experience out of all The Sevens, and unlike most leaders he doesn't hide behind his forces. Caligula loves the battle. Some say he thrives at the sight of blood. This is probably why he oversees executions at the Ministry. I've never seen or heard of him being sick, injured, or weakened in any way, so we can deduce he is extraordinarily resilient. There are stories about him, which Theleo can support, about him fending off Elementals, Levitators, and Channelers who have attacked him at the time of their executions. Not a single one was successful. If he has a vulnerable spot, no one knows it."

"I'll find it," Maggie said resolutely.

I liked her nerve, but she needed to know that she wasn't in this alone. "We'll be there too, Maggie."

She gave me a sincere nod and redirected her gaze forward.

From then on, our time in the air was spent quiet, each of us doing our own assessment of what to expect on the ground.

Once there, we hovered over Pinggu, using the dense, dirtied air as cover. The Sevens were here all right, and the Dissidents were retaliating. Even from this height, and despite the thick foliage of the mountainous region, we could see movement, sparks of light.

"Jocelyn," I asked, and she turned her eyes to me. "Wait for my sign this time."

"I will," she conceded, grasping the seriousness of the situation now that we were looking down on it.

"There are a lot of black uniforms down there," Maggie noted. "It'll be easy to blend in."

"Let's hope so," I commented and gave Jocelyn a nod.

We descended and Jocelyn placed us at the rear of the assault, where Caligula was most likely to be. There were no tents this time, only native structures that served as homes and municipal offices.

"Easy to see why Caligula chose this location to strike," I muttered.

Eran nodded. "Because there are no main roads leading here."

"And the mountains offer protection," Maggie added.

And once again I felt like we had the right allies with us.

"Caligula must be in one of these," Eran said, slapping the corner of a white-washed building as we landed.

"Yes, he will have made himself an office here," I agreed. And then it dawned on me where. "The most ostentatious one..."

"What?" Eran asked, keeping his eyes on the alleyway leading to the main street.

There were Vires down there, lots of them.

"We need to find the most lavish building. That's where Caligula will be set up."

They nodded in agreement and we headed for the street.

Blend in, my mind was telling me. And I was sure that's what Maggie and Eran were telling themselves.

We did a fairly good job of it, passing unnoticed, even unrecognized while moving next to the buildings. The Vires didn't shift their eyes from whatever target they had locked on, allowing us to pass by as ghosts. For once, their robotic programming worked to our benefit. It was a refreshing change of pace.

There was a calm, almost routine, mechanical feeling to the city, a tempo that said, "We're here. We're going to stay, let's get on with it". Clearly, it was now occupied by The Sevens, our world and the one ours was embedded in merged here, becoming one. There were no more witches and those who didn't believe we existed, just subjects and The Sevens. The veil to our world was lifted, the innocence the other world lived in was now wiped away. If they hadn't believed in witchcraft, they would now or soon enough. The elders might call us Wu, or shaman, and the younger generation might reason our ability to levitate, channel, and manipulate the elements to be technological advancements. Either way, denying it would be a futile exercise.

When Maggie cleared her throat, my eyes immediately darted in search of what she was referring to. Finding it, I instinctively started in that direction, my intuition telling me that we'd arrived.

The monastery was traditional, constructed of stone and brick. It was balanced in design with each element being a separate and equal counterpart so that if the building were split in half each would be mirror images of the other. The roof swept upward, after the Buddhists' belief that it would ward off evil. Unfortunately, it didn't seem to work this time.

Surprisingly, the front hall we entered through the main door was vacant, absent of people and furnishings. There was, however, an enormous Buddhist statue.

An almost inaudible snort came from Maggie, a sound that I interpreted as her being insulted somehow.

"A monastery?" she whispered harshly. "A place of worship? Can you believe the shamelessness of it?"

I was starting to wonder if her anger could be contained when Eran warned, "Focus, Magdalene. They won't be here long."

That last part got me moving again, heading into the great hall. Overhead, the intricacy of the roof looked like art and lining both sides of this long, narrow room were statues of the Buddhas. They appeared to be observing us, questioning if we would be successful in liberating this building from the man standing at the far end of it.

He was the sole person in sight, facing the mural painted on the back wall as if he were trying to decipher it. His fingers were intertwined behind his back. His arms lay limp against his hips. He appeared relaxed, self-assured, giving the impression that he had all the time in the world.

That was not going to be the case.

We walked directly to him, our Vire uniforms working as intended, permitting us to get close despite the fact that two of his associates had already lost their lives.

In fact, I thought, *I figured he'd have a security detail surrounding him.*

When we were within fifteen feet of him, movement caught our attention, followed by a blur of black shifting in my peripheral vision.

We stopped just as they descended on us, swinging around the backside of the statues with the fluidity of acrobats and dropping to their feet. Surrounding us before we could go any farther, they stood firmly waiting for orders.

Trap, was the word that went through my mind. The next one summed up exactly how they knew to expect us, *prophecy*.

Caligula slowly turned to face us, his large nose and thin, nearly nonexistent, mouth pinched in a tight frown. Astutely, he visually measured us, assessing the threat level as a general might. The ancient Roman battle garb he wore definitely gave him that likeness. The moldavite stone welded to the breast plate helped a bit.

"After I was banished here, I helped build this structure," he reflected, surveying it, inspecting it like he had done with us. He turned his palms up at none of us in particular. "With these hands, I labored, perspired, bled. It was tiring work in which at the end of the day I was given nothing but water, a piece of meat, and an aching body. And then," he said, his tone lightening, "then I learned it would no longer be required. You see, I discovered what I never believed possible. I was different. I had a gift, and it offered me endless opportunities. The world became mine. I took what I desired, effortlessly, aware and carefree of those who opposed me." He leaned forward, the twitch of a sneer momentarily shaking his lips. There was no reason to fear them, because they could not kill me. I, however, I could kill them. Yes, Jameson, Magdalene, and Eran" he whispered with a tip of his finger toward each of us, "you are the victims, and I am one no longer."

By this point Maggie and Eran were growing restless. They settled calmly into a fighting stance as Caligula broke the line and entered the circle of death where we now stood. Boldly, he continued.

"You see, Jameson," he whispered leaning closer. "We all arrived with an exceptional ability, my six friends and me. I found mine when in a fist fight, on the ground, with an attacker's face suspended over me."

He leaned closer still until he was only an inch from me.

"Would you care to guess my ability?" he asked before closing his eyes and drawing in a seemingly bottomless breath. Then he paused, tilted his head up almost in reverie, and smiled.

Instantly, I became woozy, weak, as my vision danced in front of me. Confused, I blinked, attempting to straighten Caligula's image.

Examining me intently now, he grinned. "You feel it don't you?"

And he inhaled again.

As I struggled to draw air, my hands instinctively moved to his throat, but his grin only widened.

"Now you understand, don't you? I cannot be killed because it is I who draw the life out of you."

I grunted and saw Maggie and Eran move toward me, before I stopped them with my hand.

"Life is as fleeting as a single breath."

Those were the words Caligula chose to sum up this brief episode in which he felt powerful, dominant. Of course he did. He had his guards there to protect him. What he didn't know was that they only served to create a false sense of security.

As my hand came around Caligula's neck, his eyebrows fell. He was confused, mystified. And while he struggled to understand exactly what was happening, I did something I'm certain no one had ever done before. During his attempt to absorb my life, I opened my mouth and spoke.

"So is your power."

Then it was his face contorting, his mouth open, his breath rushing from his body.

Detecting that Caligula was in trouble, the guards attacked. Maggie and Eran intervened, but it was too late. I realized this as my body was hurled upward and through the roof.

15. RESURRECTION

The air rushed into my lungs, now free from Caligula's grasp and from my focus on returning the favor. I felt my energy return, my heart beat slow to a steady pace. It was satisfying, renewing.

And then I reached the apex of my flight and began to descend.

My eyes snapped open.

And the pain flooded me.

Looking down I saw two factors to my situation, neither one being very positive. First, my body was rapidly approaching the hole that I left after being shoved through the monastery's roof, and second, I was covered in red liquid.

Blood, I reasoned, *that's why my skin is burning.*

I was so preoccupied by these issues that I didn't notice Jocelyn had, once again, blatantly ignored my orders to stay put. When my body stopped just short of the hole, and I could peer down at the fight raging below, I was disappointed.

My head jerked up, searching for her. My intention was to tell her to release me, but it quickly changed.

"Go back, Jocelyn!" I shouted, as she and Theleo sped toward me.

She slowly shook her head at me.

"Damn it! Go back!"

"No!" she screamed, not bothering to slow her pace.

"Theleo!" I raged. "Get her out of here!"

Because hell is about to break loose.

Instead, Theleo passed through the hole and entered the fight.

"Drop me," I insisted as Jocelyn came to a hover beside me.

"Shhh," she said, hastily taking my arm.

"Did you just shush me?" I asked, amazed. "You shouldn't even be here. Go back, Jocelyn."

Through the course of my rant, she ignored me and finished what she came to do.

"Incantatio sana," she uttered, and then looked up at me. Her jaw stiffened with determination and what wounds I had healed instantly.

"Thank you."

"You're welcome," she said, satisfied. Then she leaned in, planted a kiss on my lips, and pulled away. "Be careful."

She released me and I landed in the belly of the conflict. Bodies were moving in chaos, but I was able to find the one I wanted. Racing to the end of the hall, almost in the exact place where I left him, Caligula stood calmly surveying the action.

He was calm because he was preparing to do something, which I didn't see until I was only a few steps from him.

With his eyes locked on me, large grey wings sprouted from behind him, large enough to meet my face when he flapped them forward. He shot backwards, skirting the ground.

Damn, do all of them have wings? I wondered as my feet continued their race toward him.

He flapped them again and rose toward the ceiling.

Without warning, my view suddenly encompassed only the ground because a Vire had landed on my back.

A roar escaped me as I channeled his ability, and we shot upward together. I wrapped my arm around my back, grabbed the foot planted there, and shoved it off me. But to the Vire's horror, I didn't release my hold, instead allowing him to dangle as we rushed for Caligula.

The Vire kicked, trying to loosen my grip, but it didn't work.

I wasn't about to let this guy drop me.

Caligula floated just below the hole I made earlier, scrutinizing the scene playing out below him. Like most leaders who send their flocks into battle, he remained safely out of reach, or so he thought. It was the second miscalculation he made today in relation to our abilities, and I appreciated it. Being an underdog or one of low expectations has its advantages. It means you can pursue the enemy and he won't flee, and his arrogance results in the downfall of his capture.

But I wasn't interested in capturing him.

With my free hand outstretched and my speed swift, I was prepared for the impact.

It never came.

A flash, a blur of black and white, darted by me and took Caligula up and through the hole.

I channeled harder, fought for any measure of additional speed I could summon from the Vire, and still his velocity felt like dripping molasses.

"Can't you go any faster!" I yelled down to him. "You should be ashamed!"

The Vire didn't respond, other than making another attempt to reach up and grab me. He continued to flail as we made our way through the hole and into daylight.

As my eyes swept the horizon for any sign of Caligula, another object shot past me. This one was the same, a blend of black and white. It didn't seem to be aimed at me, so I continued my search only to find the wrong two people coming at me.

"Jocelyn..." I began, but she soared right by me, grabbing my arm.

"They went this way," she called out, charging toward the middle of the provincial city.

Theleo, who positioned himself beside me, tipped his head at the Vire whose foot I still held. "Are you going to bring him, too?"

Despite the situation, I laughed. Shouting down to the man, I apologized before unwrapping my fingers from his ankle. "I hope you can catch yourself."

He plummeted, screaming shrilly until colliding with a roof below.

I caught Theleo watching and shrugged aimlessly. And for the first time since I'd met him, he actually chuckled. It didn't last long, though. A few seconds later, we found Maggie and Eran in hand-to-hand combat with Caligula in what appeared to be the city commons.

Just as we were set down, Vires flooded the park. Preoccupied with protecting Jocelyn, I lost sight of Maggie and Eran in the disarray. Theleo and I plowed through the Vires, taking them down one, two, sometimes three at a time. And then I turned in time to see Eran shove Caligula against a building and pin him there as Maggie took his head and slammed it into the building. Caligula went limp and his body slid to the ground as Eran stepped back.

I let out a sigh and Jocelyn gave me a questioning stare.

"Maggie," I said by way of an explanation. "She has got to stop doing that..."

Knowing me well enough, Jocelyn understood and I heard her giggle behind me as we made our way across the commons. By the time we reached them, all that was left of Caligula was the metal armor he'd been dressed in.

"Blunt force," Maggie said, breathing heavily from her exertion. "This one was susceptible to blunt force."

Recalling the voodoo priestess's guidance, I realized she was mentally checking off the list of each Seven's vulnerability.

"Makes sense," I agreed. "His armor was designed to protect him from it."

Eran laughed heartily. "Should have known to use something stronger when going up against Maggie."

Jocelyn and I quietly agreed with a nod, observing the results of the execution.

"All right," I mumbled, articulating my thoughts out loud. "That leaves glass, fire, ice, and...an empty bowl."

But before we could get to the rest of the Sevens, we needed to deal with the ones defending them.

"Should we be expecting the Vires from the monastery?" I asked, searching the alleyways and sky for any sign of them.

"Not any time soon," Eran replied, smirking.

He was feeling confident, which was good, so long as it didn't turn into arrogance. Because I found that we weren't alone after all.

Above the roof tops and on the streets next over from the commons, bodies could be seen flying. But these weren't Vires coming for us to condemn Jocelyn to death or kill all of us on the spot. They were too busy, preoccupied by a wave of unexpected reinforcements.

"Stay with me," I instructed Jocelyn and she nodded.

Then we were running, down the alleyways, into the maelstrom, unprepared for the force that met us. I was slammed into at the same time Jocelyn's body dropped to the ground. Over my attacker's shoulder I saw her go down and it made me furious.

My assailant continued his shove until I was bent over a fence, my back arching, making it difficult to raise my fist. Sweeping the legs of my attacker from under him, he began to collapse, but I held him up, swinging him around. He landed on the corner of the building next to us.

And then I noticed something was off.

He wasn't wearing a Vire uniform. A quick look around told me that none of these people were dressed in Vire uniforms. The two who had Jocelyn pinned to the brick sidewalk were in overalls. Maggie and Eran were fending off boys in jeans and t-shirts. The rest, coming to these peoples' aid, were in black cloaks and street clothes.

This meant one thing: They were Dissidents.

Unfortunately, my fist was already in motion with the force of my body behind it, urging it on. There was no stopping it now, but I could divert it from its intended path. The flat of my fingers hit just to the left of his head and in those brief seconds, when his eyes opened and his contorted face fell in surprise at my apparent mistake, he stared back at me in shock.

"We're with you," I growled, disregarding the pain of slamming my fist into an immobile object.

At that same point in time, the man recognized me. "Nobilis?" he mumbled under his breath, his eyes growing wide.

Taking advantage of his surprise, I spun around and went after Jocelyn. After pulling the two kids off her, I stepped in front to prevent them from coming at her again.

"Back off!" I roared, ready with closed fists in case their adrenaline got the best of them.

But they did stop, one blinked and the other tilted his head to the side.

They're recognizing me, I thought.

"Jocelyn, are you hurt?" I asked without turning away.

"No," she muttered. "They hit like girls."

I stifled a chuckle as the older boy evaluated me.

Then he lunged, shoving me back, baring his teeth like a rabid dog. "Deserter!" he snarled.

In the distance I heard someone shouting. "They're retreating!" And a second later, it was restated with a victorious tone. "They're retreating!"

The announcement didn't seem to faze the boy, who wrestled me from the wall, working at getting me in a headlock. He was skilled, but not enough. I slipped from his grip several times until I found the opportunity to push him back.

Jocelyn, with that spark I love so much, kept trying to intercede, but Theleo held her back.

I'd have to thank him for that later.

The boy came at me again, but I slid to the side, free from his angle. He lunged again, and still he missed me. With his lips curled back in fury, his body bowed, and his eyes determined, I thought there was a decent chance he'd try it again, and then I heard Hans.

"You stop that, boy," he shouted with that unmistakable Norwegian accent.

I never would have expected it, but the boy stood, rising up from his crouch.

I did the same, pausing to see if his reaction would last. It did, and I strolled to Hans, who was standing with his fists propped on his hips.

"Hans," I acknowledged.

His glare didn't veer from the boy, but he did extend a hand in greeting.

I shook it and then repositioned myself next to him, folding my arms across my chest.

"Your son?" I asked.

"Mmmhmm," he grumbled.

I nodded.

Hans marched to the boy, grabbed him by the ear, and hauled him back to me. "He's…ambitious."

I held back my laughter, considering his son looked embarrassed enough. "It's a good trait...that can be put to good use."

Hans' frown didn't diminish. "What did you have in mind, Nobilis?"

I looked around, noting that Maggie and Eran now stood with Jocelyn and Theleo. Behind them and down the street, more Dissidents were arriving. But they wouldn't be enough. Not if they intended to fight the growing Vire forces.

"If you're serious about defending yourselves against The Sevens, you'll need to train."

Hans considered my point and nodded.

"And if you want to train, you'll need to do it discreetly."

"Mmmhmm. Ya have an idea?"

"I do," I said, and then I explained how to find the bayou village.

By the time I was finished, we had a solid group of Dissidents listening. This would have been my chance to redeem myself, to appease their fears that I would use them in a personal war and then desert them again. As it turned out, that wasn't necessary. Hans did it instead, applying his gruff, no-nonsense demeanor to explain how I was helping to quietly take out The Sevens, risking my life for theirs, and if that didn't prove my trustworthiness he didn't know what would. He motioned to Caligula's now decomposed body, the wings shriveled and unidentifiable alongside it, as proof. When he was finished, there wasn't a single face in the crowd with a hesitant expression.

I thanked Hans, told him that we'd be expecting him, and turned to Jocelyn.

I wanted to tell her how impressive she had been today, how sexy she looked with her tousled black hair, and how incredibly thankful I am that she is still here with me. I wanted to take her and kiss her and-

My heart stopped, skipped a beat, and restarted again.

And she had done that very thing to me just a few minutes earlier. She had touched me without consequence.

"What?" she asked, seeing my expression change.

My lips lifted in a relieved smile. "I'll show you when we're alone."

Her eyebrows crossed, but she didn't press the issue.

"We'll need to bury the Dissident bodies," I said. Maggie and Eran, who were curved into each other's arms, and Theleo, who was next to them, nodded.

Someone in the crowd called out. "What about the Vires?"

I turned around, searching for the man who asked this question. He was standing in the middle of the crowd that had formed, face bloodied, a cut along his chin that would ultimately become a scar. Here was a man who had just fought Vires to save his life and the lives of his loved ones, and he was asking what kind of burial we should give those people who had done this to him.

It was time for us to stop caring what The Sevens thought of us. It was time for us to end the fear of their repercussions that drove every choice we made. My answer, in part, was based on these beliefs. The other part was because I just didn't give a damn.

"Let The Sevens deal with them."

A gasp stirred the crowd, and I thought it was out of shock or upset over my indifference. But when Jocelyn lifted us into the air, I looked down to see something we hadn't in far too long, something The Sevens never tolerated:

Boldness. The steely-eyed, guts made of concrete kind of boldness.

And this was good, because we were going to need it.

There were only four of The Sevens left now, Jocelyn and I still lived, and that knowledge combined must send a blunt, cold point through their hearts. While this was exactly where we wanted to be, it was also the time when our enemies would up the ante.

Now, we were more at risk than ever before.

16. A R M Y

Traversing the world was rapidly exhausting my sense of reality, blurring the line between day and night. Even with the sun overhead while landing in Maggie and Eran's backyard, it all felt surreal, like a light bulb that was never turned off. Fatigue is the cause, corrupting my sense of what is real and what is not. The only way to overcome it is to rest, but I wasn't in the mood for it.

When Jocelyn and Maggie headed for the stairs, I stopped on the step into the kitchen. Through the door the relieved faces of those living in the house followed the girls. And I knew they had waited up for us.

Still, I turned back, weighed down with heavy thoughts, scanning the backyard without actually seeing any of it.

"Probably better get some sleep," Eran said, coming up behind me, "before we head for the bayou."

I took in a deep breath, enjoying the smell of the wet earth. Its aroma reminded me of renewal, rebirth, a chance to start again. That was a nice change from the death and destruction we'd been experiencing lately.

"I'll wait for you all."

Eran appeared next to me, arms folded across his chest. "Then I'll wait with you." A few seconds passed, before he interrupted the silence. "It's easier to solve a problem when more than one mind is working on the solution."

I shook my head. "The issue is my state of mind."

He laughed once, deeply, and confirmed, "Wondering if you're a lunatic?"

"No, not really."

"Good, I'd need to call Ezra out here. That's more her line of work."

I tipped my head back and chuckled. "I'm fighting pessimism."

He absorbed my message and responded with a grave nod.

"If it was me, alone, walking into the conflict with The Sevens and their Vires, I would welcome the fight, encourage it, even provoke it if there was a chance." I paused. "You're probably thinking now is the time to send Ezra out."

He smiled, although the sincerity of our topic didn't allow for a laugh. "No, Maggie and I have seen what they do, we know what they are, and if I were in your position I'd want the same."

"But Hans, his son, and the few - although growing - number of Dissidents…they don't know."

"How do you know? People can do great things, Jameson."

"I'm not refuting that, and if trained properly they can be a strong, united force. But it won't be enough. We had defenses in place a few weeks ago, when Jocelyn was taken from me, and too many lost their lives in that fight…just…too many. Each time, the number of Vires grows, they are stronger and eventually they'll overcome us. *That* is what Sartorius is counting on."

Again, Eran gave me a well-meaning nod.

"I have some…people," he suggested, drawing my attention, "who I rely on in these types of circumstances."

There was a hesitation in his tone that prompted me to ask, "Nefarious people?"

"No, just…different. Haven't brought them in on what we're doing here because I agree with your primary tactic…infiltration. Works with small groups and when you're outnumbered, but eventually The Sevens will clue in."

And that's when he hit on exactly what had been hanging over me. If the Sevens were paying attention, and I knew they were, this latest execution would lead them to our method.

"So you're suggesting?" I prompted him.

"Magdalene has a phrase she likes to use. Power in numbers."

"Maggie is smart," I said offhandedly.

He laughed to himself, suddenly deep in thought. "You have no idea." Turning on his heel, he stepped back and out of my sight. When I heard him next, no more than a few seconds had passed, but his voice was hollow, as if it came from a distance, and it echoed off the trees. "I'll meet you at the village."

I scanned my surroundings in search of him but he was gone. Gone. There was no movement inside the kitchen, none down the driveway. The only object that seemed out of place was a feather drifting down to land a foot away.

Hallucinations are a common side effect of sleep deprivation, I thought, *get a grip.*

Laughing, I headed inside for some sleep. That was an honest goal. Sleep was required. I felt it in the heaviness of my eyelids and in the sluggishness of my limbs.

And then I saw Jocelyn's door slightly ajar.

I couldn't stop myself from moving toward it. Peering inside, I found her eyes were on me. They were unhurried, calm, at peace. Just as languidly, her hand slipped out from beneath the sheets and beckoned me. I didn't hesitate; my response was instant and reflexive. I wanted to hold her…desperately.

Crossing the room in two strides, I pronounced, hoarsely, "This won't hurt."

Soon I was on my knees at her bed. My hands were cupping her face. Her hair was brushing my fingertips. Her lips were open, anticipating.

She sighed, a stifled release which was wrought with tension. Her fingers came up to my jaw, and she pulled me, gripping me, wanting me.

She needs me too, I realized, so frenzied my next thoughts tumbled together. *To feel her again…to have her respond to me…God, that's all I want.*

Our lips came together, and we kissed…wild, frantic. There was no logical order to our actions, and somehow I found myself lying over her, our bodies pressed together, our hips grinding.

I consumed her, taking in her scent, the taste of her skin, the feel of her, the excitement in her thrusts.

And then we heard the creak, the damn creak right outside the bedroom door.

Both of us froze, our breathing coming to a standstill.

The creaking continued dissipating until the heavy footsteps of Rufus O'Malley faded completely.

It's a good thing he's the quiet one, I thought.

My eyes never left Jocelyn's, unable to tear myself away. She, however, was intently focused on the door, certain it was going to open. If it had, I'm not sure what her plan was, but it probably didn't include my body laying over hers.

"It's gone," I whispered.

"He," she corrected me, appalled. "I think it was Rufus."

I grinned, knowing she wasn't following me. "Charlotte recanted her curse. It's gone. And, yes, that was Rufus."

She giggled, sending her chest seductively into mine.

"How did you know…that it was safe to kiss me?" she whispered.

"When you healed me in China."

She nodded thoughtfully, and I could tell she was holding something back. "You knew earlier, didn't you?"

She shifted her head in modesty. "It was in her expression, when she stood outside the kitchen door. Charlotte is emotional, even though she tries to hide it."

That's ironic, I mused, and a laugh escaped under my breath.

She knows my sister better than me. Must be a girl thing.

Staring down at her, my excitement rose, increasing even more when she sensed it and her inhale brought her chest up to mine again.

"I love you."

And her eyes softened.

"I know," she whispered. Then she kissed me, though it wasn't passionate like before. It was a single connection between our lips. The heat had left the moment, and in its place was kindness.

I added with a voice hoarse from emotion, "So much, Jocelyn."

"I know."

And then she closed her eyes and wrapped her arms around me, shifting her body until we were lying on our sides. Her breathing grew steadier, calmer as she faded to sleep.

I listened to it, my eyes drifting over her serene, beautiful face, outlining the curves of her eyes, her lips. The silence in the room, and throughout the house, felt like a cocoon. But I was unable to resist telling her one last thought. "I would die for you," I channeled.

The pace of her breathing remained consistent, her eyes didn't flutter, and there was no surprise in her reaction. It

214

was as if she knew it all along. The reply that ran through my head confirmed it. Softly, in a sleepy whisper, she channeled, "I know."

Then just before sleep took over, she added something that shook me.

"But I'm not going to allow that to happen."

There was a warning behind it, telling me that she was going to do something reckless to prevent it. And that scared me more than death itself.

Unable to shake the unsettling feeling that followed, I lay awake for hours, and am certain that my lids were closed no longer than fifteen minutes before Maggie was pounding on Jocelyn's door.

"Time to move," she announced, sounding like a drill sergeant.

But when we made it downstairs, we found ourselves alone.

"They're all gone," Jocelyn muttered, spinning around the kitchen as I peered into the parlor and Ezra's study.

"Place is empty," I confirmed, while watching her hand reach for something on the kitchen table. Whatever it was, its magnitude was enough to draw her attention.

"We'll meet up with you," she read. "But Eran should be there by now. Maggie."

How she knew about Eran, or the fact that he was returning to the village, made no sense to me.

Dropping the note, Jocelyn stared at me, perplexed. "Why didn't she wait? She was just here a few minutes ago."

I shrugged, and took her hand, enjoying the feel of it as her fingers responded and laced with mine. "We should get going."

We left, with Jocelyn levitating us like a rocket into the dusky horizon. It was the start of another evening, although I felt this one would be different. Something larger was taking place, a turning point had been reached.

Only after arriving at the village did I understand exactly how true my instinct turned out to be.

We found hundreds of people lounging along the docks, their legs dangling over the edges or sprawled out across the planks. On closer evaluation, as we landed, I noticed that they came from all walks of life. Some spoke Russian, others Italian. Some wore black cloaks and carried brooms, others held swords. Some wore family stones, some did not. Because people tend to gravitate to what and who is familiar, those in our world collected to the north side while the rest gathered to the south. Hans, I assumed, was somewhere on our side of the village.

As they caught sight of us, those who were sitting slowly rose, and followed us with their eyes until we stopped at my parent's shack, which dissected both worlds of people. Whether by accident or design, Maggie, Eran, and their housemates were at the center of these new arrivals, a small group waiting for us by the door. Directly next to them were the Weatherfords, my family, and Kalisha.

The swamp, which typically chirped, squawked, and sloshed, was silent. All ears were attuned to us. Even the insects seemed to be parked and listening.

"These are your people," I assumed, stepping up to Eran.

"They are."

I nodded as a swell of optimism surged through me. "Where did you find them?"

He smirked. "Everywhere."

He turned and faced the men and women he'd brought with him. "This is Jameson Caldwell. You'll be taking commands from him. He has infiltrated our adversary's headquarters, assembled an army of his own people, and has extensive knowledge of our enemies' beliefs, practices, and strategies."

Jocelyn, whose hand hadn't left mine since the house, squeezed in reflex, and I caught a glimpse of an image soaring through her thoughts. It was of me, standing before an army.

By that time, Eran was facing me again, seeming to be waiting for an order.

"We'll need to evaluate their strengths," I commented, intending to segregate and assess them in groups.

Eran had another idea. "Well," he said with a light-hearted chuckle. "We aren't entirely feeble."

Then, as if it was previously synchronized, a ripping sound resonated across the village. Shirts fell away, or fluttered as something pulled at them from behind. Then we watched as feathered appendages extended from behind their bodies, entirely white and spanning three times their arm length. Each shuddered, and then folded behind them, reminding me of a bird coming to a state of rest.

"Holy sh-" Nolan said from behind me, although he was too stunned to carry out the rest.

Others behind me gasped, and the creaking boards told me that some had even stepped back.

"What are they?" Nolan asked, on edge.

Someone behind me replied with thick sarcasm, "Wings."

"No...what are they?" he asked, sweeping his hand in front of those standing before us.

"They," I said firmly, "are our allies."

He did have reason to be upset. We had just witnessed our friends parts protrude from them where there shouldn't be any. Still, somehow, a laugh found its way out of me as I turned to Jocelyn.

"I think we have our army."

"Yes," she muttered with a nod. "I think we do."

Curious now, I asked Maggie and Eran, "So what other talents do you have?"

Maggie's eyebrows shot up. "That's it? That's all you have to say?"

"Well, I had a feeling you two were different."

The side of Maggie's mouth turned up in a smirk. "You're right."

Behind them, a pair of wings shook, causing my eyes to drift back to them. Continuing on, I surveyed the group, and on giving them a closer inspection, I was sidetracked.

"I've seen a feather like that before," I said, staring at Jameson's appendage. "It was picked up from the Ministry's floor on the night it was attacked."

Maggie gave Eran a proud smile, and I knew my assertion was true.

"You're the ones who attacked it, weren't you?"

"It's how we lost Magdalene," Eran confirmed.

"And that's why you ended up in the prison alongside Jocelyn," I added.

Maggie nodded.

"It's why you didn't wait for us at the house on our way here," I continued.

"That's correct," Ezra said.

"And those," I tipped my head at Maggie's wings, "are why you wear the leather suit with the holes in the back."

Her proud smirk was my answer.

"And this is what you meant," I said, motioning to Eran's wings, "when Stalwart noticed you adjusted to levitation easily. You said you didn't have a problem with air transportation. And you wouldn't…because you can fly…."

He smirked in response.

"You said that?" asked Maggie with an admiring chuckle.

"I did."

At that point, only one word came to mind. "Impressive."

"We can be," said Maggie, flatly, without any hint of ego.

"What do you call yourselves?"

Without hesitation, Eran declared proudly. "Alterums."

"Okay," I said with an affirming nod. "What other abilities do your Alterums bring?"

"Right, you asked about other talents. Knowing them would help," said Eran, pausing to assess the shack to this right. "Maggie told you in Lacinda's cavern that I have a way with metal...."

"I remember."

A metal roof near us began to crumple like an invisible hand was crushing a piece of paper. No longer able to reach the walls where it had been propped up, the ball of metal fell inside the shack. Eran casually walked inside, picked it up, and brought it back. Without another word, he used a sharp edge of the ball to cut a deep gash down his arm. As blood poured from the wound, Jocelyn stepped forward, ready to heal him. But by the time she was close enough, the gash had disappeared.

"You're a healer?" she asked, astounded.

"Regeneration abilities," Eran replied. "Limited to my body only."

"And you can manipulate metal as well?" I pointed out.

For another round of proof, he tossed the metal ball in the air, directly over the four walls that had once held it up, and flattened the ball until it was again a roof. It fell back in place with a loud shudder. "Correct. We all have something unique to offer."

"As do we," said my mother, chuckling as she stepped forward. Her second step never hit the dock. She turned and soared over the water in a brilliant display of speed, the force of the air carving the water beneath her body. She returned to the dock with the same velocity, whipping Jocelyn and Maggie's hair and stirring our clothes.

And that's when it began. Everyone wanted their time on the stage that my mother had unintentionally started over the water. Before long, the sides that were initially separated began to merge. Voices intermingled into a constant hum. Those who had wings blended with those who didn't.

Flashes of fire, icicles, and small tornadoes were widespread. Incantations echoed off the trees. Dislodged feathers blanketed the water.

Night crept through the bayou, limiting our sight until we asked the Elementals to show off their ability by lighting the lanterns along the docks. They did this, unified, with one cast. Jocelyn was on hand to heal those who ended up flubbing their demonstrations of power, with singed skin and broken bones being the most common injuries.

During the night, I took Jocelyn by the hand and led her away, carefully weaving a path through the crowd, across the water, and back toward my shack. Along the way, she gave me a questioning look, not bothering to channel, and I gave her a wink. When we got closer to my shack, a smile crept across her face and I knew that she had figured it out.

My shack was located directly across from the activity over the water, which helped to light the inside with flashes of light, like small fireworks being set off now and then without the pop. From that light, I saw Jocelyn standing in the center of the single room, staring at me, her stunning features etched in the shadows as the light flashed across her face. She looked demure, innocent, but that's probably because she was about to be made into a woman.

Without a word, I crossed the room and took her in arms. She met me with the same fervor, leaning into me, wrapping her arms around my shoulders, kissing and shoving her hips toward me.

She was enthralling. Intoxicating.

She moaned, and I knew my lips were doing the same to her. Trailing them down over her jaw, along her neck, she trembled. The collar of the Vire uniform she still wore stopped me there.

Pulling away enough to lay my forehead against hers, I unbuttoned the shirt, listening to her heavy breathing and enjoying the feel of her fingers clutching my hips. When the shirt drifted to the floor and the flash of light fell across her body, I drew in a breath.

"What?" she asked, and I could see the uneasiness stirring her expression.

"My God...," I breathed.

"What?" she demanded, her eyebrows furrowed.

"I am so lucky to have you."

Her mouth closed and then lifted in the start of a relieved smile.

"Thank you," she whispered.

I wanted to chuckle, because she had no notion that it was me who should be thanking her.

"Despite all your strength and untapped power, you still have no idea, do you?" I asked in amazement.

"About what?"

"How much I love you."

Exhaling deeply, trying to keep my head from spinning, I curved one arm around her back and the other beneath her knees before lifting her off the floor. Holding her close, we made it to the bed in one step, a very eager one. Carefully laying her down, I felt her hold on to me, gripping my waist so that I came with her.

Tenderly, I kissed her, and pulled the sheets over us, while wrapping her in my arms. And from there I experienced the most incredible night of my life.

* * *

Later, when her eyes closed and her chest began its even rise and fall with each breath - and I was certain she could only hear me in her dreams - I brushed the hair gently from her ear. "I do love you, Jocelyn. I love you more than life its self."

I then slipped out of bed for the window where, just outside, the display of abilities stretched on. And I knew my premonition from earlier was correct. Something big had happened.

Unity. In more ways than one.

I peered over my shoulder at Jocelyn, who was deep asleep now, still so tempting in her slumber, and back out at the large, strong, indestructible army we had somehow managed to combine.

Yes, something big did happen.

But that was where my intuition of earlier ended. I had no idea that two people, two incredibly important people, hadn't been in the swamp that night. They should have been. One should have been settled over her cane frowning at the entertainment, as was her tradition, and the other should have been right there beside her lifelong friend watching with stoic indifference.

Maybe it was because they didn't come from our world. Maybe my emotions were clouded by elation and hope. Maybe the sight of Jocelyn in my bed dissolved all intellectual thought.

But I didn't foresee The Sevens attack.

And for that I will never forgive myself.

17. TOURNAMENT

The next day started with a smaller repeat of the "games" from the night before. Three men were watching an Elementalist spit into the water where it made the surrounding area of impact boil from its heat. Another group watched a woman levitating several winged men. None of this was strange. In fact, it was good, so I couldn't understand the reason for their perplexed expressions. Then a massive fireball skipped down the water, spraying those on the dock along its path, and I understood.

They were stronger today than last night, than any night before it, I suspected. Their energy was different, more potent and quicker in reaction. That was the cause of suspicious curiosity in their dropped jaws and furrowed eyebrows.

Ah, I get it- I began to think when Jocelyn's hands slid around my waist. I'd heard her stirring behind me and was just about to go to her when the fireball soared passed.

"It's us," Jocelyn stated.

I looked back to find her peering out the window, her cheek cradled against my shoulder. "Us?"

Her voice languid from sleep, she explained, "Remember when you were trying to show me how to cast in Ms. Boudreaux's class? We were trying to heal the rash Estelle gave you?"

I made a sound at the back of my throat that was meant to be an acknowledgement. She understood and continued, after yawning and extending her arms in front of me. My hands found hers and drew her back in place as she spoke. I wasn't ready for her to let me go. "We healed the class," she explained. "And we improved them last night in the same way."

"How?" I asked, intrigued by her insight, a point which hadn't occurred to me.

She put it so simply, I chuckled.

"You channeled my energy in your release."

I thought about it and then nodded. "It was an incredible release," I admitted.

Her cheek moved against my shoulder as she smiled. "I know…"

I laughed from my belly.

"Well, look at them," she said with a tip of her head at the window. "They are living proof how perfect we are together."

I surveyed the growing crowd, who were now engaged in larger, even more powerful casts. "Yes, we are. We definitely are."

A state of absolute comfort washed over me as we stood there, with Jocelyn so close and our forces growing more powerful. There wasn't much more I could ask for, and then…

I stiffened and jutted my head forward, toward the bayou outside. Without realizing it, I muttered, "I don't believe it…"

"What?"

"My cousins are here."

"Really?" She sounded more excited than I felt.

"Really."

"Is that a good thing?" she asked, trying to decipher my tone.

"No," I said before considering it. "And yes."

"Why no?"

I watched as one of them fist bumped a winged man who had come to introduce himself. It was meant to be a gesture of greeting, but with that kind of force... "They're descendants of Celts."

"Which means?"

"They're brutes."

Already, I was heading out the door, preparing to squash any argument Aidan was creating.

"That's a little rude," Jocelyn pointed out.

"It's all right," I reassured her. "To them, it's a compliment."

Shockingly, by the time Jocelyn set us down on the dock opposite my shack, Aidan had made friends with the man who he'd nearly shoved off the dock with his greeting. It was in the middle of a hearty laugh when Aidan happened to catch sight of me. He clapped a hand to the other man's arm, bellowed, "Too true", and began a march in my direction.

"Little cousin," he said, again shouting from his gut, as was typical.

"Not so little anymore," I replied.

"True! I understand you are taking the world by storm, as your destiny calls for."

We embraced as I asked, "What are you doing here?"

He pulled away swiftly, jerking his head back. With a hand sweeping across the rest of my family, he announced, "We heard there was a war going on."

"Took you a while."

"Ah," he nodded. "News travels slow to those on the fringe. We came in last night. Tried to track you down but...," his eyes moved to Jocelyn, "well, now. I can see why you were busy."

His hands fell and he approached her, taking in her disheveled hair and the crystal quartz bracelet she wore on her wrist. If it weren't for the black cloak slung over her shoulders, I had no doubts that he'd be inspecting her curves, too. But either way, she was gorgeous.

"My lady," Aidan whispered, bowing to take each of her hands and kiss their tops. "And I was told Weatherfords were wretched. Not so with you."

She gave me a questioning stare.

"Aidan," I told her. "One of the more brutish of the brutes."

He laughed enthusiastically. "That I am, little cousin."

"And this is Jocelyn, the Rel-"

"She needs no introduction," Aidan declared. "Come, meet my family, Relicuum, now that we all are on good terms."

I grimaced, wondering what she would think, despite resolving our truce - again - but it turned out better than I thought. I should have given her more credit. She walked away from them an hour later with a high opinion. I was amazed.

They, however, weren't the only ones to enter the swamp last night. Some of the most powerful casters to ever exist mingled with the crowd, which never seemed to dissipate along the docks and only grew in size.

I was counting on this but not on the number who showed. It was a testament to our strength and willfulness as Dissidents, but it threw a wrench in my plans to assess every person's capability level. A quick survey of the thriving village confirmed there were far too many of them to do it individually.

My eyes landed on Aidan, who was badgering a man into a contest, and the answer came.

"A tournament."

I looked at Jocelyn who stood beside me and my eyebrows crossed in confusion. It was her voice that gave me the answer, and it had channeled through my head. What threw me was that we weren't touching.

She had seen what I had and read my thoughts, and now I was reading hers.

"Apparently, last night affected us too," she said without moving her lips, other than to lift them in a mischievous smile.

I kissed her, taking my time before pulling away. "I love you."

"Better," she retorted with a sparkle in her eyes.

I went in search of Lester to ask him to separate the forces by ability and to pair the men and women for competition. He did this with amazing speed, and as contestants stood in line, waiting for their turn to prove their prowess, I evaluated our new troops.

We're stronger than before, when the Vires came for Jocelyn and me in the village the night they took her from me, more diverse, with broader intellect. That was apparent as each competitor stepped up to the makeshift line Lester had drawn at the edge of a dock.

Most rounds were interesting, but there were those that stood out as impressive. Theleo was well-paired with a dark-skinned man with white hair and wings to match who went by the name of Campion. Both showed unique skills, keeping the other guessing. In the end, they shook hands, and gave each other the due respect each deserved. Only one woman participated who wasn't from our world and who wasn't able to grow wings. She was human in all respects. But in her black suit laden with weapons, the sai she deftly controlled, and in the maneuvers she made, using the docks, boats, and water as tools rather than obstacles, it was clear she was a force in and of herself. Even her name was memorable, Ms. Beedinwigg. All of Maggie and Eran's roommates performed well. With Ezra

227

using her intelligence to outwit her competitor, Rufus using his size, and Felix using distractions, it was clear they could hold their own. The only one who declined participation was Gershom. I remember seeing him at our high school before he disappeared entirely. He was quiet back then, too. Although, he did mention that his ability would show itself soon enough. I wasn't sure what he meant by that, but I took him for his word.

Everything seemed to be going well, moving along, until Isabella arrived. She was breathless, and I'd never seen her break a sweat before. She landed in the only open spot, between the two current competitors. Her velocity was enough to throw both competitors backwards and off their feet and to leave a gaping crack in the dock's boards.

"Jameson," she demanded, striding directly for me. "We have an issue."

She swung past me and into my parents' shack with barely a glance at the rest of those around her. Jocelyn and I were the next two in the door with our families following. The only one in the room not a Weatherford or a Caldwell was Kalisha. She had a unique ability to find herself in a meeting without attracting too much attention. I imagined this trait was from her old Vire days. There was visible upset from everyone present, except her, when Isabella made her announcement.

"Your housekeepers have been taken. They will be hung at dusk." She said this in her typical no-nonsense manner, but the perspiration on her forehead told of a different reaction underneath.

"How did they get to them?" Alison asked. Being my sister, I was surprised she hadn't figured it out.

"Lacinda," I grumbled before anyone else had the chance.

It appeared the woman wasn't regarding the threat I'd made against her life if she intervened again.

Alison nodded. "Because she's the Surveyor, she would be the one to bring her in."

"It's designed to weed you out," Spencer said from the corner, his voice low and troubled. He was uneasy about the kidnapping, and had every right to be.

It was common enough to take someone from our world, or the other world ignorant to our ways, but voodoos had never been touched. There was a mutual respect between witches and those who practice voodoo. We come to them, ask for help, and then we leave, quietly and without disruption. Other than that, their culture remained separate from ours.

But then...The Sevens weren't either one. This made them immune, or so they thought.

"Lester," I said, turning to him. He read my face and knew what I was thinking.

In his deep brogue, he replied, "They're as ready as they're gonna be."

"Then let's assemble them. We're going to need all the strength we've got."

"What are you planning?" Jocelyn asked.

I was so consumed with determination I almost channeled my answer to her, but the rest of the room needed to hear it, they needed to understand what they were getting themselves in.

"Full, frontward attack."

Aidan let out a whoop from the door, hollered the message to the rest of the crowd, and cheers erupted.

I was relieved they felt so emboldened. Maybe they were more ready than I gave them credit for.

I, on the other hand, had seen the Vires converging. We were heading into battle against a force larger than we wanted, without preparation, without a strategy, and without any time to execute one if we had it. And that, I knew, was exactly what The Sevens were expecting.

It was early morning in New Orleans, which made it just about dusk when we arrived in Italy. Once during the flight, I peered back to find a miscellany of white wings and black cloaks. It stretched for as far back as I could see, and it made me wonder what the radar detectors below us were picking up.

We needed to arrive undetected, but with a force this size, that would be impossible. I knew already that The Sevens, or what was left of them, would see us coming. And they would use it to their advantage.

What I hadn't expected was for them to draw us in so close.

As we approached, a massive number of sentinels waited for us, rows of black uniforms so close together they formed a solid line weaving through the Ministry grounds. But not a single one moved. The orders had been given, and clearly they didn't include an attack.

If anyone was waiting for me to stop and make an assessment, they were sorely disappointed. There would be no stopping; there was no time for it.

"Reminds me of London," Maggie commented to the left of me, her appendages taking up several feet on both sides of her.

Eran, who was on her opposite side, chuckled. "With one contrasting dynamic...this time, we're the ones attacking."

They laughed and I wondered, once again, if they had reached the border between reason and lunacy.

Lunacy would work at this juncture.

"I see them," Jocelyn said, drawing my attention back to the Ministry. My eyes swept across it, as we closed in on it, narrowing to the location where most hangings took place: the courtyard.

We breached the Ministry walls, soaring over the Vires assembled, and still found no resistance. When we landed

230

in the courtyard, with those in our forces with the ability to hover doing so above us, the Vires still did not move.

And then I understood why.

The Sevens wanted us to see what they had done. They wanted to make sure there was no question it had been done by their hands, and not during the battle that was sure to come.

They want us to know their power.

I knew all this for a fact.

My mind, always so focused, stopped then, unable to process any longer. Vaguely, I understood this reaction was for protection, a shutting down of my mind before what I saw could do more harm.

I stood frozen, unable to register my surroundings, unable to move, unable to breath.

Jocelyn, however, screamed shrilly. She ran for the two women dangling at the end of their own respective ropes, who I wouldn't have recognized if I hadn't been told they were here.

In one continuous thought, every memory I ever had of Miss Celia surged back to me. The sight of her snapping beans in the kitchen with her favorite bowl. Leaving for church in her best Sunday hat. Standing inside the house she grew up in while trying to prepare Jocelyn and me for the war we found ourselves in. The pride in her eyes as she educated me about the voodoo culture. The disgruntled frown she retained just for me, whenever she caught me sneaking out to visit Jocelyn. And so many more.

Now, here she hung. The remains of what was once a strong, resourceful, loving woman now destroyed.

In my near-catatonic state, I caught glimpses of the scene in front of me. I couldn't be sure if they were of Miss Celia or Miss Mabelle. Regardless, they both had suffered incredibly before death. The dangling eye. The missing nose. The torn fingernails, a sign they had clawed at something. The patches of perfectly cut skin removed from their thighs, the belly, the left jaw. It all told me that they had suffered. Worse, they had been tortured. No, The Sevens had done this to put them on display just for us. The presence of one woman confirmed it. Lacinda stood on the stairs directly above Miss Mabelle and Miss Celia, the two women who she had unquestionably committed to death.

As my eyes landed on her, narrowed, filled with rage, she did something unexpected. She jerked. She stared back, her expression blank. She was deciphering something.

Decipher this, bitc-

I got that far in my thought before she drew in a breath and looked horror-struck. There was no reason for anything else to cause this reaction in her. Her eyes were still on me. So I understood...

You can hear me, I channeled.

The twitch in her face told me she could.

We're stronger now, I thought. *If I can channel to you across the courtyard, imagine what more we can do.*

Her eyebrows furrowed, telling me that she didn't like that news. And if she didn't enjoy hearing it, she definitely wouldn't care for my next thought.

I smirked and delivered it defiantly. *It must be from making love to Jocelyn.*

And Lacinda's jaw fell. Her eyes swooped to Jocelyn, who was oblivious to her, still trying to heal Miss Mabelle and Miss Celia, and sent sharp imaginary daggers at her.

Something snapped in me then. I understood that Lacinda had not heeded my warning to stay clear of Jocelyn. She never would. I knew that she had used Miss Mabelle and Miss Celia to trap us here. This had all been planned. And for those poorly made choices, Lacinda would die.

I'm going to get through these Vires, I warned, *and then I'm coming for you.*

She spun around, her teal blue silk dress flying out from her force, and then she ran.

This understanding liberated me, removing my mental shackles that kept me bound just where The Sevens wanted me.

Roaring, I ran for the nearest Vire, took hold, and channeled my force into him. His eyes widened before he could even react, my anger swelling inside him until his heart burst. The two on both sides of him, tackled me, but they didn't get far. My energy, potent with rage, eliminated both, rupturing their brains.

A chain reaction followed with the entire courtyard and everyone in it fighting.

In a blind rage, I ran for Jocelyn, who was still trying to resurrect Miss Mabelle and Miss Celia. It was clear to me that she had lost it as much as I had, although she'd gone in the direction of grief.

"Jocelyn," I shouted, sprinting across the courtyard.

I had almost reached her when a woman stepped out from behind Miss Celia's slumped, hanging body. Dressed in a blue batik, a traditional Indonesian dress, she looked out of place surrounded by black uniforms. However, the snide smile and moldavite stone necklace she wore seemed perfectly in place.

"Diomed," I yelled, rattling Jocelyn enough to cause her to look up just as Diomed's face stretched into a victorious smile.

Ice, the word raced through my head, Diomed is susceptible to ice.

As my feet carried me toward Jocelyn, a distance that seemed farther with each step, I searched for something, anything that could be used to freeze water. But Diomed was diligent. She had distanced herself from her weakness, and she had been careful not to reveal her position until the moment that suited her best.

What she hadn't counted on was my momentum.

I didn't hesitate, extending my arms as I reached her and lodged them around her neck. My force slammed her body against the stone wall behind her.

And my channeling instantly caught the images that had been captured in her memory. She had been a prostitute, a maid, a shopkeeper throughout her extended life, taking what she wanted, killing when she could, until meeting Peregrine. They became lovers, but there was no love between them. It had been her idea to seek out the first channelers, to abduct them and use them, and to leave their bodies in the street. It was she who caused Jocelyn to be taken from me weeks ago, having tortured those in her province for information on our whereabouts.

"You're going to die now," I growled, squeezing her neck.

Her eyes dipped to my hands encircling her throat and because her breath was kept from surfacing by my squeezing fingers, her answer was a sideways smirk and a slight shake of her head. But it was the confidence in her glare that frustrated me.

She was relaying the truth, and we both knew it.

Then her body began to slowly peel away from the wall. Something behind her was shoving her forward, but there should only have been stone. It wasn't until I saw the tip of the first appendage did I understand what was happening. By then, it was too late.

She jerked me up, through the conflict above, and into the gathering clouds, as Jocelyn's scream dissipated rapidly from my ears. We came to an abrupt halt several stories over the Ministry, where black uniforms and cloaks blended with white wings.

Up here, the shouted incantations, clanging of swords and explosions by the elements were muted. Only the wind running across my ears and the pounding of my heart were audible.

In the quiet, she observed me briefly, as one might do to an animal they've never seen, and then turned my own words against me. "You're going to die now."

"No, he's not." Jocelyn's voice came up from beneath us, growing louder with each succeeding word. So when her fist plowed into Diomed's face, the woman seemed stunned, unable to understand how Jocelyn had gotten to her so swiftly.

The hit loosened my grip on her, and I plummeted a few feet until Jocelyn caught me.

"Hold on," she called out coming up beside me, her hair catching the wind as she soared by.

My body yanked and suddenly I was moving at her speed, directly alongside her.

"We need ice," I said.

She nodded but didn't turn her focus from what had caught it. Looking ahead, I understood why. Below us, littering the courtyard floor, were jagged balls of ice. Hundreds of them. The Elementalists had good aim. Some were chipped, some broken, but not all. Jocelyn laced us through the maelstrom of fighting bodies and down to Diomed's Achilles' heel.

A glance back told me that Diomed understood our intentions, her cheeks and blue batik flapping from the force of her speed. She was coming for us but wasn't fast enough.

Jocelyn and I reached the courtyard floor, picked up the ice and used the force of our rotations while turning to catapult them into the air directly at Diomed. They hit, one in her chest and another across her ear. But a third ball of ice found its target in her leg and as Diomed's body slid to the ground, face first, skirting over it and bumping until it stopped, I searched for the one person I knew had sent off that last shot.

Maggie.

She paused, long enough to watch Diomed's body begin to decompose. By then someone else was charging her. I recognized him from the throne he sat on next to the rest of The Sevens, and from the murals of his accomplishments in slaughtering innocents while at war before his tenure over our world. Hippocrates' moldavite stone was already covered in blood, and it was clear from his emboldened face that he was determined to shed more of it.

"Maggie!" I shouted, grabbing Jocelyn's hand and bringing her with me.

Noting our speed, Jocelyn lifted and swept us across the ground just before Hippocrates reached Maggie. And then Hippocrates was gone from our sight, his body flying off to the side, in a direction his wings weren't inclined.

Looking quickly, we found Eran slamming Hippocrates into the stone wall that made up the Ministry's staircase and start to pummel him.

Maggie sighed. "He's always doing that," she said, complaining, which surprised me.

A second later, she sprang, her wings pumped once, and she entered their fight. Jocelyn started in her direction, but I held her back with a hand to her wrist.

Shocked, she looked at me. I caught this out of the corner of my eye but didn't have time to explain. Keeping my grip, because I knew she wouldn't listen otherwise, I used my free hand to pick up the bow at my feet. I did let her loose, because she understood, and because I needed my other hand to grab for the flaming arrow a few feet away. In one fluid motion, I seized, aimed, and released it. It shot across the courtyard directly for Hippocrates's chest, where it sunk in, the tip of it becoming completely consumed by his body.

He let out a scream, a chilling, horrified scream that I was sure he'd heard before from his own victims at the moment of their death. But he didn't die. He arched his back and tilted his head away from the flames eating up the wood. No longer noticing the arrow, the battle screaming around him, or Eran and Maggie, his terror was locked on the fire.

"For the murder of innocents, you are condemned to eternal death," Maggie declared, although he didn't seem to hear her. He did see her though, his eyes widening and his nostrils flaring as she placed a finger at the end of the arrow and bowed it toward him.

He struggled, thrashing aggressively to free himself, but Eran kept a good hold, enough that allowed me the time to cross to them and assist.

As my hands came around his stocky shoulders, images of his life swept through my mind, just as Diomed's had done. Hippocrates' existence differed dramatically. He sought conflict, specifically because he took pleasure in his victim's deaths. War was his passion, anguish was his pastime. He was the one who instructed the men to torture the Thibodeauxes, and had been in the room to oversee the effort minutes before I had arrived. Then his life slipped away, along with the clarity of his memory until there was nothing left.

Only then I noticed a change in the conflict. The incantations died away, the fires extinguished, the movement around the courtyard and in the sky above, so rapid and sharp minutes earlier, began to slow. Black uniforms and cloaks lay interlaced, stacked with still chest over still chest, but there were far more uniforms than cloaks on the ground. White feathers scattered across them all. Jocelyn was making her way through the bodies, kneeling to heal those still alive.

I quickly surveyed who was left standing and only relaxed after counting Alterums and Dissidents, the Weatherfords and my family included. Lacinda, however, was nowhere in sight. My promise to her would have to wait.

Aidan bowed backwards to let out a long howl of success, which seemed to signal the end of the battle. Theleo, who stood next to the opposite wall, was breathing heavy from exertion and gave me a nod. Ms. Beedinwigg's sai dripped blood as she discussed the battle with Campion. I felt the general sense of victory while we clapped each other on the backs and smiled broadly. Only Maggie and Gershom sensed something was off. Their lips were pinched with tension as they searched for something overhead.

Then the sky darkened, telling us that what was coming for us had now arrived.

18. SACRIFICE

They came in the same way we had: fast and without hesitation.

The first of them appeared over the roof of the Ministry, from the north, where we couldn't detect them until it was too late. Diving like a flock of birds, the Vires aimed at us in the courtyard. Recognizing it as the perfect ambush point, a curse word slipped from my mouth while sprinting for Jocelyn. Eran ran for Maggie. The rest braced themselves.

As the black uniforms slipped downward like mist over the Ministry roof, my heart began to race again. While it pumped vigorously, harder, shooting blood back into my brain, I could comprehend exactly what was happening.

Witty little Lacinda and slick little Sartorius had figured out a way to eliminate the rest of The Sevens. They were hand delivering them to us. We had been drawn here to save Miss Mabelle and Miss Celia only to be used to eliminate Diomed and Hippocrates' armies, and now they had sent Peregrine, telling the last Seven standing in Sartorius' way where to find us. It was all wrapped up in a neat, concise plan that I was sure Sartorius had devised long ago.

What he hadn't counted on, however, was his prized possession being in the courtyard.

"Jocelyn!" I shouted, my arms falling behind me in a futile effort to block her. "Stay with me!"

By that point, Vires were beginning to land, tackling Dissidents and Alterums across the courtyard, tumbling backwards in a ball of loose limbs. Dissidents flew into the air and against the walls, levitated by an unknown Vire somewhere in the midst of it all. Others slapped their hands to their ears and crouched in pain against the Vire holding them. Alterums lifted into the air - an enormous flock of white wings with readied muscles - and came down on the Vires, attempting to free the Dissidents who needed it.

And from there, a new battle began.

Frantically, I searched for a solution. Vaguely, my mind told me that Peregrine's army, or what he could gather of it on short notice, had stronger fighting skills than any of the others we'd encountered. And they weren't holding back.

Not when their commander was present.

He appeared just as two Vires attempted to tackle me. I slipped beneath the swing of the first, catching him in the gut with my fist. The second, unable to slow himself, kept coming...directly into my leg as I swept it across his ankles. They fell, I stood and found another one coming.

This one was taken out by an Alterum, his wings flapping so close to my face I felt a tip of one brush down my cheek. The Alterum and Vire fell, rolled against the wall they hit, and continued their fight.

The next one to appear before us wasn't a Vire or an Alterum. He was in a class all his own.

"Peregrine," I greeted, as he strode through the conflict with ease.

Theleo, having spotted Peregrine, landed like a rock directly behind me. "I have her," Theleo confirmed, and I knew he meant Jocelyn.

"Get her out of here," I instructed.

"No," she yelled. "I'm staying here."

"Get her out of here!" I shouted.

With equal vehemence, she shouted back. "NO!"

"I've got her," Theleo confirmed, resolute and unwavering.

His insistence was partly reassuring. The other part of me would never believe she was safe until all Sevens had perished.

This one, I thought, *is mine.*

"You won't get to her," I told him.

He chuckled dismissively, and his feathered appendages, already extended, rustled from the effort.

"You have the same look Flavian had." I smirked. "Before I ripped his wings off."

The man's callous gaze didn't waver. He simply kept coming. And this was exactly what I wanted. Draw him in, take him out, end the battle.

There was just one problem. I had no weapon that would help me accomplish it. And I needed glass, which was hard to come by in the middle of a fight surrounded by stone and sand.

I let Peregrine make the first move, an insulting backhand meant to brush me aside. I weaved around it and planted my heel into his knee. The grating snap was exhilarating, but not nearly as much as when he cried out in surprise and pain before falling to the ground.

He pinched his lips closed in displeasure, more perturbed now.

With a sigh, he stretched his leg out and slid it around to the front of his body, his kneecap sliding beneath the skin as he moved. When his leg came to a stop, it was bent again, directly in front of his body, where he used it to lunge upward.

I underestimated his ability to recover, but I wouldn't do it again.

He came at me, aiming for my neck.

Whereas before I was an annoyance, now I was a sincere hindrance in his effort to get to Jocelyn, and he no longer spared exertion to reach me.

Snarling and spitting, his composure gone entirely, he managed to get his hands around my neck. "I can accomplish the same goal with a simple ending of your life, Jameson. And you'll be easier to hurt."

With my airway cut off, I channeled. "Feel free to try it."

As his fingers squeezed tighter, the pressure began to build in my head. Jocelyn's scream behind me sounded muted, as if the world was shutting itself off. Before he got any further, I drew in his anger, his greed, his lust for power, and funneled it back full force.

And then Peregrine blinked. He shook his head, trying to clear it. His eyebrows sank in confusion. His fingers loosened with his distraction but still I explained it to him by channeling.

"Do you feel that, Peregrine?" I mocked. "That's me…torturing you."

He elevated me off my feet, using my neck. I met him with a continuous dose of his own vengeance.

Jocelyn's scream came again. I sensed that she ran for me, but was held back. Fighting her way toward me, she cried out in rage for Theleo to help me.

But he knew better.

Another strong dose of all that made up Peregrine returned to him, and in reaction, his fingers unwrapped my neck. Bending over, heaving from the ache of it, he glared back, knowing it was all he could do.

You might get to me, I channeled to him, *but you won't get through me.*

He jerked back, his eyes widening, and I wondered if anyone had ever been inside his head before. If they had been, he didn't know it. Either way, it was clear he wasn't fond of it.

Overcoming his shock, he stood and, with a great amount of confidence, suggested, "Look around you, Jameson. Your squalid army is deteriorating. I don't need to kill you. You're already mine."

I did take the chance to survey the battle and what I saw sickened me. We had started out small in number, but impressive in strength and ability. And we had conquered two forces already today. Our numbers were even but his forces were fresh, while the Dissidents and Alterums were fatigued, sapped from the previous conflict.

Damn you, Sartorius.

He had synchronized the attacks, ensuring we would weaken with each one. We needed an edge, preferably one made of glass.

Kalisha's voice behind me panted from exertion. "We're...failing," she said emotionless, as was expected of a Vire, even one who hadn't taken on that role in decades.

"Kalisha," Peregrine called out, drawing our attention. "What did you think? You could steal from us, take the records, give the future to your Dissidents, and the prophecy would miraculously be revoked?" He laughed wryly. "It'll take a lot more than a few Defectors to take me down."

With my back to her, I couldn't see the determination she exuded, but I heard it in her voice.

"You are correct, Peregrine...It'll take Jocelyn."

A second later, Jocelyn gasped. Instinctively, I spun to find the source of her fear. But it was Kalisha, drawing a blade across her own neck.

Even Theleo appeared disturbed by the sight.

"NO!" Jocelyn screamed and reached for her, but Kalisha was already collapsing, her eyes rolling skyward.

In a state of absolute confusion, I tried to understand. My initial thought was, *why? Why fight so hard beside us only to take your own life at the end? To avoid facing another depraved incarceration? No, my instinct told me, it's more.*

Jocelyn was on her knees, weeping, repeating her healing incantation while Peregrine observed with mild amusement, as if he were watching ducks frolic at the park. His casual demeanor didn't last long though.

Her eyes red, wet with tears, Jocelyn leaned in as Kalisha used her last breath to convey a message. Then her body went still and silent.

Jocelyn stopped altogether then, and I thought it was a result of her processing Kalisha's death. That was before I saw her expression. She was…startled, dazzled. She was lifting the hand she had on Kalisha's arm in a rush, second guessing herself, hesitating and then placing it back again. It was apparent to me that she wasn't comprehending anything around her.

"Jocelyn," I said, carefully making my way toward her.

She lifted her head, but not in search of me. She was looking for Peregrine. "Kalisha's gift…," she said.

"Is dead," Peregrine interrupted, "along with her."

Jocelyn ignored him, as if he no longer mattered. "Kalisha's gift is the elements," she stated with absolute certainty. "She wouldn't tell me, not until now."

Now? I wondered quietly to myself. There was something strange in that statement…something I couldn't figure out until she pushed herself to a standing position and that look of determination I knew so well washed over her.

When her gaze dropped to the sand at her feet, I knew.

The gift Kalisha had given her, the residue she'd passed on to Jocelyn by taking her own life, was the elements.

Peregrine began moving. I knew this from the crunch of his footsteps. I also knew he wouldn't get far.

Jocelyn's abilities were extraordinary. Peregrine knew what she was capable of but hadn't seen it. Not until now...

The sand at her feet had heated to the point of melting, becoming a gleaming puddle of liquid, which quickly solidified under her focused attention. Before Peregrine could take two steps, Jocelyn bent, picked up the glass she had created, and flung it at him.

He wasn't prepared but was quick enough to dodge it, and it fell to the ground, shattering behind him.

The raging battle surrounding us became a distraction from anything else landing at Peregrine's back, but she came into view by the time he reached me. I had stepped in front of him so I didn't see her until Peregrine's expression contorted from a scowl to a look of subdued confusion. He made no attempt to defend himself against me while I drew back, preparing to strike. Then he fell to his knees and I saw Maggie clinging to his back with one hand on his shoulder to steady her mount and the other still wrapped around the glass plunged deep into his back. His face shuddered, his mouth slackened, and his face planted directly at my feet.

Maggie craned her neck up to look at me. "One left," she said, gleefully oblivious that she had again taken a Seven from me.

I should have been upset. I had trained for these moments she repeatedly stole from me, had given up my childhood, my own goals, my own pursuits. But the frustration I'd felt earlier, with the other Sevens, wasn't there. What mattered was that Jocelyn was safe, and another Seven was dead.

By the time she leapt to her feet, his body was decomposing.

And we weren't the only ones to notice.

The Vires, who were still breathing, slowed to a confounded silence, becoming motionless in their astonishment, as others like them had done when their impervious leader proved to be nothing but a false icon. It was visible in their lack of emotion and in their attention fixed on the body that was now nothing more than dust in the outline of a body.

The next one in charge made a motion, a solitary move in the crowd of still Vires, and they shot into the air, disappearing instantly.

"Collect our family and friends," I instructed quietly, even though the courtyard's calm sent my voice echoing off the walls. I reached back for Jocelyn's hand and breathed a sigh of relief when her fingers settled over mine. "We need to prepare."

A hesitant voice from the crowd asked the question on everyone else's mind. "For-for what?"

I sighed, harboring no illusions on what was headed our way.

"For who," I corrected. "For Sartorius…"

19. LINEAGE

Jocelyn healed the wounded on our return trip to New Orleans. Once there, the mood over the village grew somber. Only intermittent clashes of swords and small explosions as objects burst into flames or cracked under ice broke the silence. The thick cypress trees surrounding us were silent, unmoving, sitting in judgment like elders on a council. It was the quiet before the storm.

While some honed their skills, the rest of us watched the sky. I positioned guards in various locations to signal when our guests had arrived. It wasn't long before one of them dropped to the dock where I was meeting with Theleo, Lester, and Isabella. He didn't bother knocking or cowering from his announcement. That just wasn't like Aidan.

The door to my parent's shack slammed open and he strolled in. "We have company, but it's not who you're expecting."

"Who are they?" Isabella asked on behalf of the rest of us.

He shrugged. "They're wearing skull necklaces and coming by canoe."

That wasn't exactly what we needed from him, so I stood and went to look for myself. By the time I stepped outside, the first of them were appearing around the bend, from the direction of the village's undeclared entrance. True to Aidan's observation, some did wear bone jewelry, including necklaces. Others wore top hats and black suits.

"Voodoos…," Theleo whispered behind me.

I chuckled. "Scared, Theleo?"

He snickered confidently, but I knew the truth. Vires didn't have much experience with voodoo. They were instructed to avoid voodoo practitioners at all costs. The Sevens didn't understand their ways, but they were clear enough about their powers, having taken seven voodoo practitioners against their will centuries ago and forcing them to write the prophecy. None of The Sevens felt powerful enough to defeat them, at least not until now.

They rowed in without a sound, a single line of canoes filled with voodoo priests, priestesses, and practitioners. Their heads were held high and their faces were stern as they passed the crowd of spectators on the docks.

If the village wasn't completely quiet before, it was definitely stunned into silence now. A profound sense of respect was engraved on the faces I saw around the village, and with good reason. The Voodoo remained on the periphery of our world for generations, and therefore they had seemed immune to The Sevens' destruction. There were only two exceptions, the abduction of the first channelers and now Miss Mabelle and Miss Celia.

"Are they here for revenge?" Aidan's gruff voice asked, as he appeared beside me. Another one of my cousins stepped up beside him and then another. They reminded me of their own small army within our large one.

"No," I said. "They don't take revenge. They're too judicious for it."

"But they look ready to fight," he pointed out. "So what are they doing here?"

"I'm thinking it's to make sure what happened to their sisters doesn't happen again."

Mrs. LeClaire, being at the front of the head canoe, reached us first. She climbed to the dock and approached me.

"We are here because the seventh is coming."

Understanding her reference to Sartorius, I remarked, "We could use the help."

"We know," she replied simply.

I tried not to take this as an insult.

"Is Ms. Veilleux and the rest of the coven with you? I didn't notice them come in."

"They're gone," she replied without emotion.

"What do you mean...gone?"

"Gone," she retorted. "Disbanded, took to flight." She wiggled her fingers in the air simulating wings lifting off. "Gone."

"Where?" I asked. Voodoo practitioners arrive to help us and they leave us in our time of need? This made no sense to me.

Apparently, it didn't to Mrs. LeClaire, either. "How should I know?" she snapped.

Aidan raised his eyebrows at me, which I was going to respond to when I saw Gershom on the next dock over.

He was looking at the sky. His mouth drew tight before muttering, "They're coming."

Maggie, who stood next to him, groaned. "Coming? They're already here," she stated with a rub to the back of her neck.

"How do you know?" I called out.

Without taking her eyes from the sky, she explained, "Gershom's gift is the same as my curse. We can feel our enemies."

I needed no more forewarning.

"Jocelyn?"

"I'm with you."

"Good."

"Lester?" I shifted to face him. "Is everyone in place?"

"Yes."

"Excellent."

One last effort needed to be made, but we were running out of time.

I stepped up to the edge of the dock, making myself visible to those lining the village waterway. The sound of the Vires began to be heard now, a persistent, growing drone.

"To all you here…," I bellowed.

Faces, which were initially pointed toward the sky, lowered to me. In them I saw anticipation…and fear.

"I am Jameson Caldwell. I'm also known as the Nobilis. And I see a broad army collected here to stand in defiance against corruption and oppression. Here and now you are free. But will you preserve it? Or will you give it back?

"I am one of you…and I have lived as one of them. And from personal experience, I know our strength far surpasses the power some believe they hold. That power is false! It is manufactured…a product of brainwashing by their leaders. It did not grow in them from birth, as it has with us. It did not lead them here today, as it has with us. And it will not persevere as it will with us! This is your chance, your one chance, to tell our enemies that they do not…they will not…ever…own us…again!"

Howls and whoops sounded out then, vibrating through the trees and across the water. Shouts of resolve and defiance, followed as they turned, just as our enemies crested the tree tops.

The massive black blur in the otherwise blue sky didn't target us immediately. Instead, they circled from above, creating a wide ring around the village. Pausing, they stared down at us, inspecting us as if we were animals in a cage.

To my sides and across the water, our people shifted their stances, readying for the assault.

Everything else around us went motionless, even the glassy bayou perfectly reflected our enemies hovering above.

I wondered if Sartorius might show himself, but I didn't wait to find out. Bending forward, I roared through the bayou. Aidan picked up on my lead, showing his fervor for the fight. Another one of my cousins joined in. From there, the rest of us on the ground, created a rousing, chest-rattling sound that made the Vires stir.

"Elementals!" I shouted, and as we had preplanned, every shack in the village became encased in ice. From them, Levitators broke off long, sharp icicles, their crackling filling the air, as they waited for my command.

I didn't hesitate.

"Launch!"

And the icy arrows were sent directly at the Vires. Some dodged the attack, but most hits were true to their aim, and the bodies of black uniforms plunged to the earth, some tumbling into the dark, murky water.

A second later, the first Vire descended, the rest followed, and the bayou became a battleground.

Trees snapped and were sent hurdling through the crowd. Bodies flew into shacks. Fire engulfed the docks. Incantations screamed through the air. Voodoo chants hummed beneath them.

A group of Vires came directly for Jocelyn and me, but before they could reach us, Aidan and the rest of my cousins intervened. I took advantage of the opportunity and grabbed Jocelyn.

"I'm getting you out of here," I said, sweeping my arm below her knees and lifting her into a cradle.

"No! Jameson, I'm needed here! We talked about this."

"I changed my mind." The uneasy sound in my voice made me angry.

Get a hold of yourself, I said, *Jocelyn will be fine once she's safe.*

"I'm fine now!" she shouted, after reading my thought. "Put me down."

"No!"

We were breaching the treetops by this point, where the conflict was being carried into the air. Vires fought off Dissidents and winged Alterums as I used Jocelyn's ability to levitate her out of harm's way. This sight only increased my desire to get her out of here.

And then something slammed into us, shooting us back to earth. The trees blurred as we passed, the wind whipped in our ears, but it was the arms encircling us that had me more concerned.

We crashed on the muddy embankment just outside the village. My head snapped up in search of our attacker, and I caught a glimpse of the battle raging through the trees.

"You have no idea how to stay out of trouble, do you?" a gruff voice snarled in my ear. His anger fit my expectations, but not his choice of words. He sounded as if he were defending us.

Jerking my head back, I found Stalwart, shoving himself off of us.

"Sartorius is up there, waiting for you," he said with a frown, "and you're headed right to him." He glared at me and then shook his head in annoyance.

Ignoring him, I helped Jocelyn up and then stood myself. "Where can we put Jocelyn so she won't be hurt?"

"I'm not hiding," she seethed. "I'm needed here."

Keeping my attention on Stalwart, he responded with a good answer. "I have a place."

"I'm not hiding!" Jocelyn insisted.

"Where?" I asked.

"Come with me," he said, starting to move around us.

Jocelyn exhaled loudly in disgust, but that wasn't what caught my attention.

If it hadn't been for the shift in Stalwart's stance I would never have seen what was coming. But by then, it was too late. The blindingly fast movement of wings, sweeping downward in an arch along the ground, came to a halt less than a second later, directly behind Stalwart. Before Jocelyn or I could warn him, the dull tip of a cane emerged on our side of his body, directly through his chest.

Jocelyn went for him, but I held her back. He was already gone. His face was slack and his eyes were glossed over by the time he slid forward.

At the end of the cane, holding on to the moldavite stone at the top, was its owner. Sartorius watched us intently as his wings ruffled back into place behind him and the odd translucent skin covering his body slipped across his muscles from their pull.

"Taking my granddaughter away from me?" he asked with mock astonishment. "You should know better, Jameson."

Before I could respond, Jocelyn spat. "You are no family of mine."

"I'm afraid you don't have a choice in the matter," he replied casually.

"It is my choice. We can choose our family."

"That may be, if you consider that cultural hyperbole, but I'm referring to something deeper, something more real."

"There is nothing real about you, Sartorius," she said in loathing.

"My blood is," he replied, "and it runs through you."

He drew the cane back to his side and asked, "Has it ever occurred to you, Jocelyn, why you, of all people, would be gifted as the Relicuum? The person capable of taking on others' residue? Your power comes from me. It is my lineage that gave you life, and the ability to absorb others. And thus…it is mine to use as I wish."

"Absorb?" I said, barely audible. "You absorb others?"

"Like my dead associates, we arrived here with certain talents," confirmed Sartorius. "And that is mine."

I turned to Jocelyn. "The bowl, Mrs. LeClaire's bowl. It was empty, wasn't it?"

Sartorius chuckled. "Oh, I can assure you that I am everything but empty. I am a sponge."

I could see her expression change as she began to understand what I meant. "Empty," she reiterated, "so he could take in whatever came his way."

"You pick up other's abilities," I stated, having already concluded it.

"For short durations, yes. I've needed something to make it last, to make my ability survive. And as I understand it, Jocelyn has now picked up the last residue, control over the elements. Isn't that correct, dear granddaughter?"

She remained silent, in disgust.

Sartorius stared at her with true wickedness in his eyes. "Now, with you at my side," he continued with a sickening grin, "nothing will stop me."

"I'm not at your side," she seethed.

"But you will be shortly," he said with a tip of his head.

And I turned just in time to see the Vires coming up behind us.

20. UNBREAKABLE BOND

I didn't give the advancing Vires a chance to assault us. Stepping forward to meet them head on, I planted a fist in each of their guts while sending a surge of emotions through them. They stumbled back, surprised, giving me enough time to take on the next two coming at us. Unfortunately, one of them was a Levitator so I never got the chance to attack. My feet slipped out from beneath me and I was flung backwards, landing against a tree hard enough to knock the air from my lungs. This didn't stop me. I went back for them until I saw Sartorius' cane pinned to Jocelyn's neck.

Sartorius observed me, pulling the cane tighter against her skin, while shaking his head in wonderment. "Why do you fight?"

"Because I have the choice," I said, working to catch my breath. "That, Sartorius, you will never take from me."

"Hmm," he replied thoughtfully. "I think you'll find yourself questioning that statement in just a few minutes." To the Vires, he instructed, deepening his voice with the command, "Restrain him."

This time I didn't fight, not with Sartorius' weapon at Jocelyn's throat. While it was unlikely he'd use it against her, his delusions might make him think he was powerful enough that his army alone might do the job.

Once I was properly under control, he handed Jocelyn to one of his lackeys, whose own dagger came up to Jocelyn's neck, and led us through the small jut of land behind the shacks toward the waterway.

"You're going to die for this," I said. "Every one of you."

The Vires, having been trained to show no personal reactions, didn't respond. But the quake of Sartorius' shoulders as he laughed under his breath told me that he had heard.

As we drew closer to the village, I noticed with some measure of hope that the fight continued to rage on. Someone resembling Nolan flew by with his feet and arms dangling behind him as if he'd been kicked in the chest. A voodoo practitioner slammed into the corner of my parent's shack, slumped to the ground, and sat unmoving. I watched as his hand came to the bones around his neck. He plucked one off, spoke to it, curled it inside his fist, hauled himself up and ran in the direction he had come. In the background, water spouts and balls of fire flew by. Overhead, cries erupted, both in pain and in triumph.

Jocelyn, however, didn't seem to notice. She had something else on her mind.

"You have everything you want," Jocelyn said, making me wonder about her intentions. "You need me, Sartorius, but you don't need Jameson. Let him go."

Ah, that's what she was thinking...

"Jocelyn," I warned her, but she ignored me.

Sartorius did the same. "Not *everything*, my dear granddaughter."

"You do," she insisted. "You said you wanted the Sevens dead. They are. You said you wanted the army under your command. You have it. You said you wanted me. You got me. You have everything. Let him go."

"Jocelyn," I started again, but Sartorius cut me off.

Coming to a halt, he twisted his head around to face her. "The prophecy," he hissed. "You haven't fulfilled your destiny yet. He must die, so we will live."

And this was what I was trying to keep her from hearing, because I knew one final step must be made for Sartorius to preserve his destiny, and because I knew the reaction she would have when hearing it.

Hopelessness set in as her face went still, the muscles in her body tensed, and her breathing stopped. The only visible movement about her was the tear making its way down her cheek.

The resolve I felt was overpowering then.

You will die, I thought, *every last one of you.*

As our feet met the dock built around the side of my parent's shack, I felt the rumble of the fight in front of us and overhead. The Dissidents and the Alterums were making a valiant effort, but they were heavily outnumbered now. The bodies of their comrades scattered the docks and littered the muddy embankment.

As Sartorius directed us to the edge of the dock, where we were most visible, gradually, the fighting slowed. Strangely, the Vires did not reengage with the Alterums or the Dissidents, which I reasoned came from an earlier command given by Sartorius, which made me realize the delusional idiot had a plan in mind for Jocelyn and me.

Maggie and Eran hovered close, three shacks away, but I was sure the dagger at Jocelyn's throat kept them from launching their attack. The Caldwells saw it too, keeping them ready but at a distance.

Sartorius stood at the edge, back erect, head high. He looked confident, bold, in control…the epitome of a ruler. When he spoke, everyone present watched with apt concentration.

"I am quite certain these two individuals need no introduction. The Nobilis and the Relicuum have been admired, revered, and made notorious for centuries...as the couple in our world in which one lover will take the life of the other."

While there had been heightened apprehension in the audience before, the tension became palpable now. I caught sight of several Caldwells and Weatherfords shifting, preparing for attack.

"This is the historical moment you have read about or have been told would happen all your lives, the one in which the Relicuum ends the life of the Nobilis! And you will all stand witness to this testament that the prophecy is correct! That I am the rightful ruler over this world and the next!" Without hesitation, as his agitation grew, he spun toward me and screamed, "BOW!"

When I didn't move, his eyes floated to Jocelyn, making it clear who would pay the price if I didn't.

Slowly, forcing my muscles into submission, I bent forward.

Once appeased, Sartorius continued, strolling beyond Jocelyn and me, to the inside of the dock. Staring directly, unwaveringly, at the crowd, as if we were nothing more than spectacles, he announced, "The Relicuum will now take the life of the Nobilis."

Within seconds, I found myself surrounded by my family, and Jocelyn surrounded by hers. They encircled each of us, facing each other, leery, on edge, and determined to defend the life of those they were now surrounding. And from that, it became immediately clear that the Vires were no longer the primary risk.

The crowd waited, riveted by the sight of a legendary feud reaching its climax.

There was only one thing left to do now.

I stepped forward, stirring those of my family within eyesight. Rightfully, they were uncomfortable with my movement, because it was in the direction of Jocelyn. I continued my pace, undisturbed, even as I broke through the line my family had formed for my own protection.

"No," my mother breathed, but I glanced at her, and she saw in my expression what she needed.

Resolve.

This was my decision. Not hers.

Still, her effort to get to me unnerved the Vires and they shuffled to subdue her, which caused both families to aggressively shift their stances.

I waited, making certain that she wouldn't be harmed before continuing toward Jocelyn. When I met Isabella and Lester at the line of Caldwells shielding her, I stopped momentarily to redefine the situation for them.

Very slowly, I explained, "I am the one who will be hurt by approaching her."

They blinked, determining for themselves that my statement was true, and stepped aside.

Before I even reached her, tears had soaked her cheeks and her head was drifting slowly back and forth, rejecting any notion of my death.

It was a good thing my beating heart would stop shortly, because I felt the painful rip left in it by the sight of her misery.

"I won't do it," she uttered. "I won't do it."

"Jocelyn," I whispered, taking her face in my hands. "Beautiful, strong, capable, Jocelyn. I love you, you know that, right?"

She swallowed, struggling to speak. In the end, a nod was all she could manage.

"Beyond life itself, I love you."

"And I love you," she said, her voice hoarse from her crying.

This confession brought on another bout of tears, leaving her sobbing, unable to catch her breath. I gave her time, letting her overcome it.

When her heaving slowed and the tears lessened, I kissed her, softly, delicately, on her swollen, wet lips. They were entrancing, causing me to linger there longer than I should have, keeping me from moving away, from getting on with what needed to be done.

Then, very carefully, I pulled away, and took in every fine detail of her. The alternating shades of color in her eyes, the solid darkness of her hair falling over her ears, the curve of her lips, which I wanted to consume right now so incredibly badly.

But right now, words were what we needed, and with select words used to prevent Sartorius from detecting my plan, I began to explain. While I spoke, I realized that my plan might not work, and that these words may very well be the last ones I ever say to her, which left a dark hole of desperation in my chest.

Please, God, make her hear me...

Picking up on my thought, she acknowledged, "I'm listening..."

I smiled softly at her, hoping she would be.

"My life has been so good, so good, Jocelyn. I thought it was fulfilling, too...until you entered it. Then, it became incredible. Every second I spent with you was a miracle. Do you know why? You're strong in ways you don't even know yet. I'm not talking about acquiring all the elements, or that you are more powerful than anyone here. I'm saying that you have endured so much and still managed to find a way to rise above it all."

"Not this," she sobbed. "I can't do this."

"I can channel," I said.

"It's not enough," she sobbed out loud, and I wiped away the tear her outburst had caused. "I want you here, with me."

"What we do transcends time and space. We channel through to others, remember?"

She swallowed and gave me a hard look. She was catching on.

"The night in my shack?" I said tenderly. "That meant something, Jocelyn. It meant you loved me, truly loved me, because you gave yourself to me...entirely. And I did the same. But what I hadn't expected was for it to surpass us. The Relicuum and the Nobilis coming together in a way no one, least of all us, could have expected? It was extraordinary. It was," I paused, searching for the correct word. "It was miraculous. I know this because the next morning we weren't the only ones who had changed. It was everyone around us."

"It was," she said, nodding. "It was."

And I felt a smile break through, because she gave me hope. "I think we can do it again."

And then it was her smile rising up as she processed what I meant. "Yes, we can."

"This ain't right!" A shout suddenly came from the crowd.

"Let them live!" Another called out.

"LET THEM LOVE!"

That spark of opposition inspired unrest, which meant our limited time had come to an end. Any reengagement now would surely kill our dwindling number of fighters, unless Jocelyn and I could do what we planned.

Sartorius, as if sensing this, strode quickly toward us, breaking through the Weatherfords line, and shoving a dagger into Jocelyn's hand. I never let go of her, as he did this, already feeling her strength coming through me.

His abrupt move quieted the audience.

"Take his life or every Dissident and Defector here will die."

When Jocelyn didn't respond, he raged with so much force his breath battered the sides of our faces. "DO IT NOW!"

But another voice, with equal intensity, boomed through the bayou in response. I'd heard it countless times before when it took command over groups of students. I'd never once heard it addressing a Seven or a group of Vires. Regardless, here and now, it held the same amount of poise and austerity.

"We will die, Sartorius, but it will not be today."

Ms. Veilleux appeared through the trees, winding her way between moss-covered trunks, her black dress swaying with her weaving. The rest of her coven followed in the same way with a long stream trailing behind. Some rode brooms, some entered by way of levitation, but all had one element in common. They wore family stones.

So they didn't abandoned us...They left to collect the rest of the provinces to fight alongside us.

Sartorius recognized his defeat before it came and launched into a tirade. "Attack! Attack! Attack!"

Vires swarmed the line as it scattered. Our reinforcements broke apart, swooping in from the sides. And again the sky and docks overflowed.

Jocelyn and I didn't move. That force I was so familiar with, the one that I'd felt that night in my shack, grew steadily, becoming so intense it left me breathless. I released it as rapidly as I accepted it, until I became nothing more than a conduit, expelling it outward, targeting everyone not wearing a Vire uniform.

My hands remained on Jocelyn's face, hers settled on my hips, and our eyes locked together. But as the noise increased around us, I knew they felt our power. There were shouts of excitement and the intensified sounds of those using their newly acquired traits. No one shouted they could now levitate or form a water spout or channel. They were too busy defending and counterattacking their adversaries. But we knew, we all knew, it was happening...Sartorius included.

Understanding the threat level, he raced into the bayou where we'd entered, and a second later, I saw two others with wings, who appeared to be Maggie and Eran, follow him.

When the last black uniform collapsed to the ground, a resounding cry of victory told Jocelyn and me that we had done it. We had won. And still we didn't move. Staring into her eyes, I was in a place I didn't want to leave. And neither did she.

Aidan, however, landed directly next to us, clapping me on the shoulder. "It's over, cousin."

Reluctantly, Jocelyn and I broke eye contact.

Turning to him, I said, "Glad to see you're not hurt."

He bellowed out a laugh. "Not me, but you should see the Vires four huts down."

I did look around then, but it was in search of the rest of my family, as Jocelyn did the same. Neither one of us relaxed until we saw all faces, bloodied but still alive, in the crowd. Ezra, Rufus, and Felix were there, too, alongside Ms. Beedinwigg and the winged man they called Campion.

"Maggie and Eran," Jocelyn remarked, insinuating they had disappeared.

"I know where they went."

Heading in their direction, a few feet in, I found them in a grove of cypress trees flanking Sartorius.

He was sneering back. "What you don't realize…is that you're little ploy backfired," he announced, and for proof he collected a ball of fire in his hand while hovering overhead. "I told you…I absorb the powers of others. And now you've given me all I need."

"And what you haven't realized, dear grandfather," Jocelyn retorted, "Is that it won't last."

No sooner had she said it, did he fall back to earth, the fire in his palm disintegrating to embers down his elegantly crafted suit. Those sparks produced enough heat to ignite the few pieces of dried leaves at their feet, where a small fire caught. Sartorius appeared ready to run but Maggie and Eran pinned him down, over the fire that quickly crept up Sartorius' delicate suit fabric.

"You enjoyed burning Magdalene, I hear," Eran grunted, mockingly, hinting at where his intentions were leading.

Sartorius fought but without success. "No! NO!"

And as Jocelyn and I turned away, the sound of Sartorius' end reached our ears.

"That's it," Jocelyn said, happiness returning to her voice. "We got them, right? No more greedy Seven or wicked Vire wanting to rise up and control us all."

I turned to her, took her in my arms, and saw the hope returning to her eyes. I didn't have the heart to tell her that one more remained. Instead, I kissed her, long and deep, while filling her with the love I felt. And with that gesture, I promised her, without saying the words, that it wouldn't be long before I'd get to that one too.

21. ATONEMENT

Days passed before I could make good on my final promise, before I could do what was necessary to the final Vire. During that time, wounds healed. The bayou returned to normal with the pools of blood seeping into the mud and the water returning to greenish-black. Laughter and the sound of repetitive banging echoed through the trees as the village shacks were steadily rebuilt.

Elsewhere I found signs of recovery, too...quiet ones that you'd miss if you weren't from our world. Olivia and the DeVilles reopened their stores. The Thibodeaux warehouses were auctioned to the highest bidders. Ms. Veilleux launched an extensive search for a new school location. Defectors found a new life, free for the first time to choose a path of their own. It was interesting that some chose art, which the DeVille's held on commission for them.

The abilities each of us absorbed from Jocelyn gradually faded until we were left with what we once had. This was fine with me. After what we'd been through, I was ready for a sense of "normal" to return.

The only change I welcomed was our world's new structure. Since it was left permanently altered, a committee, consisting of Isabella, Theleo, Lester, and a volunteer from each province, was formed to develop a fair and balanced election process. I was given a position but declined. I'd had enough of politics. But they ignored my refusal and said they'd leave the seat open for when I changed my mind.

What I wanted to do, really looked forward to doing, was getting back home, in all senses of the word. It felt like a reward simply to sleep in my own bed again and to wake up to the smell of chicory coffee. And when I signed up for classes again to finally finish out my senior year, it felt like Fate remembered that I still wasn't done being a teenager.

In the course of all that changed, only one wound was left open, and it weighed heavily on me, until I received a message from Theleo. It was delivered by traditional mail and had only three words scrawled on a piece of scrap paper.

I have her

It was exactly the kind of message I expected from him. Short, to the point, and yet nondescript. He wasn't much for elaborate communication, but he always got the job done.

Because this wasn't my wound to heal, I sent my own message to the necessary parties, telling them when and where to meet me. I had planned to harass Charlotte or Vinnia for a lift to the meeting site, but when Jocelyn dropped past my window just before daybreak I knew she was going to insist on being present.

"You were going to leave me behind?" she said, before I even had both feet out the back door. "For this of all things?"

"Muffin?" I offered, holding one out to her.

She took it.

"Jameson," she demanded.

I was already down the steps and in the yard, the dew creeping up the cuff of my jeans, before I stopped and turned. "Jocelyn, I'm not sure what they're going to do to her. I'm trying to spare you the-"

"Well, you can stop," she directed playfully as she loped down the stairs. "I'm coming."

And that was it. She had clearly made up her mind, and proved it by shooting us off the ground and in the direction of France before I had time to respond.

She held on to her contempt for my decision until I reached across and took her hand. Only then did she, begrudgingly, let down that wall. I saw it in her face when her frown subsided, and then in her sigh that expelled the frustration built up in her, and finally in the downward smile she gave after we'd passed the halfway mark. It took that long for her to forgive me. And I realized, once again, that it was a good thing I find her stubbornness appealing.

We made it to the Ministry just before sundown in that part of the world, and landed in the courtyard.

"Huh," Jocelyn muttered, as we stood in the center, surveying the area.

The Ministry was going through changes of its own, with a new administration in place to make it what it should have been all along - a place for our people to assemble.

"They're renovating," I explained. "Removing the stains left by The Sevens."

"In that case, they should consider bulldozing it," she remarked, stirring a laugh from me.

"I was actually thinking of something else, though," she added.

"What's that?"

"That this is the first time we've landed here without having to be conscious of being seen."

She was correct. There was an almost electric vibration running between the people here. They were smiling, laughing, moving with assuredness. There was life here now, and they were using that energy efficiently, tearing down walls, carving out windows. But that wasn't what she meant. She was referring to the fact that the fear The Sevens had lain as a cloak over this place was now lifted. Everyone, including us, was free to come and go as they pleased.

That wasn't the only change made though, and Jocelyn noticed it as soon as we entered the main corridor.

"Everyone's so colorful," she noted. "No one is wearing black."

"Isn't that nice," I muttered, without telling her that it had been my edict that called for cloaks to be worn based on personal preference only.

We took the route that led us to the floor farthest underground. Because Jocelyn had no idea where we were headed, I guided, keeping my eyes open for any sign of those who I had told to be here on this date and time. There was no one, because I found that they had already arrived.

When I opened the door to the very same room where I had found the Thibodeauxes, I realized this would be the last time anyone would enter. After what was about to happen here, this place, and all the remaining dungeons, would be demolished. So, in a way, Jocelyn would get her wish.

The room had been cleared of the bodies, which were then given proper burials. The blood had been scrubbed from the walls, ceiling, and floor. The table used to torture victims was gone. Two metal locks were the only reminders of the violence that had taken place here. They remained drilled into the rock wall at the far end of the room. Inside each of those locks was a wrist, belonging to Lacinda.

When she saw me, the scowl on her face disappeared and desperation took hold. "Nobilissss, you've come for me."

"I have," I confirmed, "but not for the reason you think."

Ignoring me, she exclaimed, "You've always been noble! Always, my lord!"

"Don't call me that," I told her, not bothering to withhold the disgust in my tone.

"You are mine! And I will do anything you wish! Anything to please you!"

"Now that you realize The Sevens are gone and that you are alone in this world?"

She seemed dumbfounded, which wasn't far from typical. "But I'm not...I have you, Nobilis."

I wondered what Jocelyn was thinking about all this until she strolled past me. She stopped at Lacinda, her shoulders back, her head high. "No, Lacinda. You most definitely *do not* have Jameson."

With that, she curled her hand into a fist, drew it back, and swung it directly into Lacinda's jaw. The result was a crack, either from her fist hitting the jaw or from Lacinda's head hitting the wall. Satisfied, Jocelyn spun on her heel and sauntered back to me.

"Nice hit," I said as she passed.

"Thank you."

Now it was my turn to approach Lacinda. Her head wobbled back and to the side before her eyelids fluttered and she understood someone else was facing her. The fear brought her back to us then.

"Lacinda, I gave you a choice. I warned you about jeopardizing Jocelyn's life and you did not listen. You have taken the lives of others. And now, I am going to give you another choice. If you do not give me an answer,

I will make a decision for you. In response to the charges of committing Miss Mabelle and Miss Celia to death, you may face a jury of your peers or you may be delivered to your peers."

Her eyes darkened. "I have no peers."

I felt my mouth twitch into a crooked grin. "I figured you'd say as much. Does that mean you refuse to make a decision?"

She tilted her head back, attempting to snub us, and her silence was good enough for me.

"Then I hereby sentence you to be delivered to your peers."

Her eyelids shot up. "Truly?" she asked, excited. "I won't go before a jury? To die by hanging? In the courtyard? As a spectacle?"

"You mean," I said tightly, "the way your victims were put to death?"

She thought about this for a moment and then said, "On first examination, those hangings might have appeared harsh."

I turned from her, having heard enough. Besides, there were others far more interested than me in interacting with Lacinda.

"Ladies and gentlemen," I called out.

A door opened in a room down the hall and the sound of approaching footsteps followed. When Mrs. LeClaire appeared in the doorway, I watched Lacinda's face turn white. She entered, the first in a long line of women and men who wore bones as jewelry and carried various artifacts.

"These aren't my peers," Lacinda said, the words not able to spout from her mouth fast enough. "These-these are voodoo."

"They dabble in dark arts. They use what tools they have to gain an advantage. They have done inexplicable things to others. In these ways, you are on common

270

ground." To the crowd now assembled inside the door, I announced, "She's all yours."

Jocelyn and I left then, and the door closed behind us with a click that seemed to travel the entire length of the hushed corridor. We made it halfway to the stairs before the silence was broken again, with Lacinda's rattling scream of pain.

22. PROMISE

"Isn't this precious," Charlotte muttered with a smirk.

She was standing in my bedroom doorway, watching me slip my billfold into my back pocket.

"Enough, Charlotte," I said, unhappy with my willingness to play along with her charade.

Her expression gave way to a more genuine one and she replied, "I'm serious, Jameson. You two have been through a lot, more than any teenager should have to. You deserve this date with her."

I paused and then laughed under my breath. There was a bit of an understatement in her message, although I doubt it was intended.

Her eyes lowered to the floor as she pondered out loud, "Who would have thought that a Caldwell would be taking a Weatherford out on a date?"

"The world has changed, Charlotte."

"Yes, it has. For the better."

"Better?" I questioned. "So you now approve of me seeing Jocelyn."

"Well, I still think she has an air about her...," she muttered to herself, but when I sighed loudly it shook her back to reality. "But, yes, there have been improvements. We're back home, the village is thriving again, no one is fighting, there are no more Sevens, no more Vires...no more living in the bayou," she added with a grimace. "Now, if she had ended up killing you, on the other hand...." She stopped and shook her head gravely.

"Let's not go there," I suggested and started for the door.

Charlotte didn't budge. "No black cloak?" she said, and I knew she was teasing.

"Come on, "Charlotte."

"And no Vire uniform?"

"Seriously?" I retorted.

Now, I wondered if she was stalling.

Her hand slid into her pocket as she kept her eyes on me, unwilling to let me pass. She then held out her fist to me, her fingers wrapped around whatever she'd found in her jeans.

My shoulders dropped impatiently. "I have to get going."

Then she revealed what she held and I couldn't stop the smile from surfacing.

"You're a Caldwell," she said with stern sincerity, taking the chain she'd retrieved, holding a single agate stone at the end, and dropping it over my head. "You still need to act like one, even if you're dating a Weatherford."

And, damn it, despite all she had done to keep me and Jocelyn apart, my chest swelled with appreciation.

"Now go," she said, tipping her head toward the stairs. "You don't want to keep the princess waiting."

"Charlotte," I grumbled in warning.

She waved me off, but her face told me that she understood she had crossed a line.

"Thank you," I said before moving by her.

I reached the first floor before she called out to me and what she said was actually comforting. The Weatherfords and my family were back to an easy truce, one that I didn't feel would be broken this time. Charlotte was the only hold out. I'd been working on her over the last two weeks since the occurrence in the bayou, but she hadn't budged much. Her tip meant she considered Jocelyn's point of view and wanted it to be a positive one, and this was good news.

"Don't forget to open her car door," she reminded loudly.

I grinned to myself and shouted back, "Who says we're driving?"

Her snorting laughter floated down to me as I headed out the door.

I took my usual path, cutting between the houses and using tree branches to hurdle gates. It was refreshing, after realizing that I no longer needed to watch the skies or the street corners or the darkest part of the shadows for Vires. I could finally show up on the Weatherford doorstep, ring the doorbell, and not risk my life doing it.

For that reason alone, when I got there and pushed the bell, I relished the sound it made inside the house. The door opened and I half-expected to find Miss Mabelle standing on the opposite side. A pang of sadness ran through me when it wasn't her surly expression greeting me. As unwelcoming as it had been, I knew I'd miss it. Instead, this scowl was worn by Isabella, which suddenly made me feel like I was on display. Even before I was allowed in, she evaluated me closely.

"Nice to see you in street clothes," she remarked stiffly, noting my cotton shirt and jeans.

"Thank you, Isabella, for allowing me to take your daughter on a date."

Her lips pinched closed as she muttered, "Mmmhmm…"

Then there she was, coming down the stairs with her hair flowing behind her, the skirt she wore kicking up to show off her legs, and a smile meant solely for me.

My heart skipped a beat and I wondered if this was how every guy felt on a "first" date.

"Enjoy your evening," she said leaving the room.

"You're not going to ask where I'm taking her?"

With her back to us, just before slipping through the kitchen door, she shrugged and muttered tiredly, "I already know."

I looked back at Jocelyn and said, "Why am I not surprised..."

She giggled, ran for me, and kissed me hard on the lips. I returned the favor and asked, "Ready?"

She nodded, took my hand and I opened the front door to find Maggie and Eran froze with his fist in the air as he prepared to knock.

"Um, hi," I said, confused.

"Sorry," Maggie uttered, although she didn't sound sincere. There was something else of greater importance on her mind. "We don't want to hold up your date-"

"You know about it?" Jocelyn asked, astonished.

"The entire school knows," Maggie replied bluntly.

Eran interjected to smooth over that little shock. "We thought you'd want to know something as soon as possible."

My eyebrows lifted. "What's that?"

"Can we speak in private?" Maggie asked, her eyes darting from side to side, scanning the rooms beyond us.

I looked to Jocelyn, who said "sure" and led us into Lizzy's study. It was lined with books but dimly lit, so I couldn't see how it would do much good for reading. Still, it suited our needs just fine.

Once inside, Eran ensured the door was closed by giving it a suspicious rattle.

"What's this about?" I asked.

Eran gestured to Maggie and she launched into her bizarre explanation. "You've heard the rumor at school about what I can do? The one about carrying messages to and from the afterlife?"

"They say you speak to the dead," I asserted.

"Well, it's true."

Jocelyn immediately supported her. "It is true, Jameson."

"All right."

"And your Miss Mabelle and Miss Celia visited me last night."

That news sent a jolt through me and through Jocelyn; I knew because we were still holding hands.

"They wanted me to give you something." She glanced around the room. "Do you know where Miss Mabelle's cane has gone?"

"Yes," Jocelyn said, curiously, and released my hand to reach behind the desk.

It was hanging from the arch at the edge.

"Can I see it?" Maggie asked, already extending her hands.

Jocelyn gave it to her, Maggie turned it upside down and began unscrewing the rubber tip. When she turned it upright, a sliver of yellow peeked out. She took the edges and delicately wiggled it free.

Holding up the rolled pieces of ancient papyrus, she began to explain. "These are why Miss Mabelle and Miss Celia knew the right time to bring in Ms. Vielleux's coven, so they could give Jocelyn the scar that brought her into your world. It's why the DeVilles didn't leave their store and go into hiding. They were needed there in order to end Sisera's life. These," she stressed, "are why The Sevens failed. There were multiple sets drawn up, the counterfeits and the originals." She then handed the rolls to Jocelyn. As she took them, Maggie added, "They said you will ask why they didn't tell you sooner...why they didn't tell you that your destiny wasn't quite as you were told. Apparently you were supposed to kill Jameson," she paused to give us an uncomfortably grim expression. "And their answer was emotion and believability. They needed you to conjure the amount of emotion required to help end the final conflict. Only if you truly thought we were at the end of our rope would you summon what was needed. And they needed you to act believable so that The Sevens couldn't detect which set of records they had been given, and the true prophecy could then unfold."

Staring at them, trying to piece it all together, I asked almost inaudibly, "And which are these?"

"The original records written by the first channelers."

As Maggie confirmed what we already knew, Jocelyn exhaled entirely. She carried them to Lizzy's desk, adjusted the light and unrolled the papyrus while the rest of us encircled the records.

"She kept them all this time," Jocelyn commented, and then her face stiffened. "She died protecting them. They both did, didn't they?"

I took her hand and her facial expression relaxed some.

Maggie gave her a weak, sympathetic smile, and nodded. "They're happy now," she added in a way that was too genuine to be questioned. And I felt something warm spread through Jocelyn's heart.

In the silence that followed, our focus shifted back to the records for a closer look. They were laid out now, the corners weighted with various items from Lizzy's desk.

"It's in a foreign language," Jocelyn pointed out sadly.

"An ancient language," Eran corrected. "Sweetheart, can you translate?"

Maggie, to my surprise, gave it an honest shot, repositioning herself around the desk so that she faced the records correctly. After a long, hard assessment of them, she began to speak…

"False futures will be recorded; broken parts of the true future will be passed on as the genuine one, leading astray the malevolent ones. Take note, herein lies the only true future of those who will be called The Sevens...

A noble lass of the sixteenth Caldwell generation and a fair maiden of the sixteenth Weatherford generation will find love. That love be the beginning, the heart, and the end of a rebellion against those who will be called The Sevens.

"The maiden will acquire Relicuum, future remains of those dying. She will accept healing from her father. Channeling will be given from a man who sees the dead. To be able to lift from the ground will come in a marsh as she fails to heal a dying man. She will control the elements when a restored enemy gives her life. This will end her cycle of rebirth.

"Under the noble lass, forces will unite. This will be done in the midst of a false truce offered, the trying of innocent lives, a failed revolt and a massive exodus. Those who are trusted the most will turn on them; alliances will shift; allegiances will change. They will give all they have to save each other. Lives will be offered in battle and in solitude; all hope will be lost. And they will rise up against The Sevens, in secret in the beginning but will grow bolder in their attempts. And each of The Seven will meet Death with the lent hand of the noble lass and the maiden. Before the last is to fall, those who are loved the most will be taken. And while love will be the spark to the rebellion, it will be this capture that stokes the flames. And the last of those who will be called the sevens will burn in the fire he created."

Maggie stopped then, apparently finished.

Jocelyn murmured, "That...all of it...is true. Not how I expected when the counterfeit records were relayed back to us, but still true."

I agreed. "Incredibly accurate. I could see in those passages what almost all of the defected Vires told us about the records - the ones they stole thinking they were the originals. Giorgia, Maleko, Kalisha, even Braith, who we never could find again after we brought him back to the village. His part was clear, too. It must have been the one that identified each of us."

"Or a version of that record," Eran suggested, which I nodded to in agreement, now that we knew there were adaptations.

"But there was one part omitted," I mentioned.

Jocelyn nodded, having picked up on it, too. "It doesn't say anything about the Relicuum taking the Nobilis' life."

"That must have been in Isadora's record," I thought out loud.

"Right, the bogus future they recorded for The Sevens," Jocelyn surmised. "Why would they add that in?" she asked with a perplexed shrug.

I knew immediately, because I would have taken the same tack. "Protection. It was an attempt to convince The Sevens we weren't dangerous or important enough to harm. They just didn't have any idea how much The Sevens would fear us."

"And work to erase the sources of that fear," Eran added.

We processed this information for a few quiet seconds. Then I asked, "Is that it? Is there anything else?"

Maggie was still reviewing the pages of papyrus, flipping them cautiously to the side to ensure she hadn't missed anything. Then her hands stopped and she dipped closer to them, squinting.

"There is one last part here," she remarked. "It's written in the bottom corner of the last record." She laughed to herself, in reflection. "And I think you'll agree with it."

As she translated it, two things happened. I realized that she was correct. I did agree with it, having lived the words personally. And then nostalgia washed over me while I thought of the two women, Miss Mabelle and Miss Celia, who collaborated from the very beginning to make sure our true futures were followed and who seemed to hold a special appreciation for the phrase themselves.

"Things," Maggie read. "They aren't always what they seem."

EPILOGUE

15th Century
France
The Ministry

The room was small, with just enough floor space for a bed made of stuffed burlap sacks, a single chair, and a table large enough to fit it. The door was made of heavy wood with a lock that rivaled the sizes of its more traditional counterparts. The walls, floor, and ceiling were made of rock, sharp-edged so that you wouldn't consider leaning against it even if you were weary. There were no windows. Two torches on opposite sides of the room offered the only light. They cast shadows across the walls, eerie motions that brought on nightmares for any occupant.

The sole inhabitant of this room was small enough that if you looked directly inside at eye-level you would miss her altogether. Her height, having been a childhood challenge, convinced her to develop other strengths, alternate skill sets that might serve her well throughout the rest of her life. This path led to convincing her sisters, five more with the same potent gift that all had been granted at birth, to develop theirs. From then on, they spent long hours in a circle, testing, measuring, training each other. And over time, their notoriety for channeling the future grew larger and expanded to the far reaches of the world.

It wasn't long before seven individuals came for them. They had their futures foretold and in them there was darkness. The woman and her sisters refused to finish and the individuals left. And when they did, the sisters left with them, taken from their homes in a single night. But their horrors had just begun. Separated into rooms deep underground, they carried on for the benefit of their sisters who lived on the opposite side of their walls. They did as they were told by the seven individuals for the sake of their sisters. And what they were told was to record the detailed future of each one of the seven who had taken them.

They worked long, hard, sleepless hours, forgoing food at times, ignoring their illnesses, the inflammation in their fingers, the gradual tears in their only set of clothes, and the exhaustion of their minds. So when the seven individuals arrived for their monthly update, as the records were nearing completion, the woman struggled between elation for her sisters' freedom and fear of repercussion for the future the seven faced.

At exactly the same time as all the years prior, her cell door opened and the seven who had taken her and her sisters so long ago filed in. The sight of them had become a part of the constant routine of life now and their entrance stirred nothing other than the fabric of their clothes. She did notice that their moldavite stones were impeccably polished today, and determined this was likely due to the significance of this particular visit.

They each positioned their gaze at the table where several pieces of papyrus and an ink bottle lay.

"I understand you are the last to complete the record," said the one whose traditional dress included leather straps for holding up his clothes. Suspenders, as he had referred to them once.

"I be very close now," the woman asserted.

Another one of them stepped forward, toward the woman, the gold-trimmed robe he wore skirting the ground. "Tell me when," he demanded.

Calmly, she replied, "Nightfall."

That seemed to appease him and his associates.

"Yu'd be releasin' my sista's then, as agreed on?"

The woman stared back, waiting for an answer.

One man stepped forward to place a hand on her shoulder. "As agreed on, Wilda."

But his words did not correlate with the images rushing through her mind. These were the man's thoughts, and they were strong enough that she had inadvertently detected them.

And they caused her to shudder.

He leaned his head toward her in mock sympathy. "Are you all right, Wilda?" His voice was now coaxing, reassuring.

She brought her hands up to rub her arms. "Cool down hea," she responded. "Would like ta see the sun again."

"Of course you would," he said with a smile. "In due time."

She nodded, managed a smile, and watched as he turned to leave the room.

"Nightfall," he repeated in warning.

But when the door closed, Wilda did not return to the table. Instead, she pulled a long piece of string from her dress, recovered the needle she had used to mend tears throughout the years, and quickly began sewing the papyrus on the inside of her skirt. Her fingers moved swiftly and her eyes repeatedly peered at the door, while the images of what she had seen in the man's thoughts haunted her. They were visions, expectations of what was to come, and they drifted through his mind tinged with a dark sense of excitement. As much as she tried, Wilda could not shake the images of her sisters' doing the same as she was now, or of their bodies strewn on the street corners, or of the mobilization of an army designed to dominate the world.

When she finished, and several pieces of blank papyrus still lay on the table, she sat and conjured an entirely new fate of those who would soon be called The Sevens.

They would not know that she had deceived them. They would not prevent the two young lovers from setting their fate in motion. They would not take control over humanity. No, they would not learn their true fate until it was too late.

She set down her ink writing instrument just before the door opened again. And as it did, she waited patiently for them to enter and take possession of the records, a knowing, wicked smile rising slowly to her lips.

The End

ABOUT THE AUTHOR

Laury Falter is the author of the bestselling Guardian Trilogy and other young adult paranormal romance and urban fantasy novels.

Find out more news and information about Laury and her novels at www.lauryfalter.com

8077309R00172

Printed in Great Britain
by Amazon.co.uk, Ltd.,
Marston Gate.